Hand and Glove: The Path

Hand and Glove: The Path

FIRST EDITION

A Boner Book by
The Nazca Plains Corporation
Las Vegas, Nevada
2006

ISBN: 978-1-887895-33-0

Published by,

The Nazca Plains Corporation ®
4640 Paradise Rd, Suite 141
Las Vegas NV 89109-8000

PUBLISHER'S NOTE
Hand and Glove: The Path is a work of fiction created wholly
by the author's imagination. All characters are fictional and
any resemblance to any persons living or deceased is purely
by accident. No portion of this book reflects any real person or
events.

Cover Photo by Sandra vom Stein
Art Direction, Blake Stevens

Dedication

Hand and Glove is an analogy. The Hand represents the dominate, the Glove the submissive each as individuals knows their roles in the realm but when the two combine as equals they becomes something greater than the two individuals. They become the ultimate Ying and Yang, harmony at its best. Being passive does not mean you are weak. Being passive means you have a strength of character that allows you to submit to freely explore variations of sensuality.

Have no friends not equal to yourself.   Confucius

I speak for myself when I say that we each personify the Hand and Glove analogy by how we structure our lives; associate with others and by how intensely we love. I am dedicating this book to my friends. These friends come from every walk of life and social structure. They are creative, brilliant, fun and in their own way extremely Spiritual. We believe in self-empowerment, walking in balance with our inner natures and struggling against the mediocrity of our world today.

To my friends, thank you...Chuck Higgins, Lady Dee, Hal, Lee, Julian & Scott, Kevin Hiza a.k.a. the Pup, Jenna V, Lin F., Lady V., Lawrence F., Timmy Brough, Goddess Lakshimi & Sweet Limey, Peter & Craig, Daddy Brian & boy jeff, dog blu, Papi David, Gene & Master Will, Eric L., Bearman, Richard S., Papabear & Gary, boy jim F., danny T, Grande Mistress Carla, Amy O @ Marvelous Mayhem, the Sabers M.C.C. of Ft. Lauderdale, the Wildcats M.C.C. of Norfolk, SLLAP of Ft. Lauderdale, SPICE of Ft. Lauderdale, and most of all to my Number One...for your friendship, support and love as we walked this road together.

There is only one good, knowledge, and one evil, ignorance.
Socrates

Table of Contents

Hand and Glove: The Path

FIRST EDITION

A Novel by
Bob E. Genz
© Copyright 2006

A Boner Book

Prologue

The Dream Unfolds

In the putrid jungles of the Vietnam conflict, nineteen men were brought together by the hand of destiny to form a perfected union. They formed a shared bond, a vision that went beyond the conflict between nations and their drug-induced hallucinations. It was more than the sexual-fusion and camaraderie of warriors; it was a secret brotherhood. They dreamed of a private, communal-style farm where they could live a life of unity, fulfilled by their love of domination and submission. The dream grew with each passing day as it evolved from a hair-brained idea to a well-laid plan.

As fantasy became a glimmer of realistic hope, they transferred their meager military pay into a commonly shared trust account stateside and directed their wills accordingly. When death claimed a man, the collective would inherit their estate. For the men who held the vision alive in a world gone insane, money and treasures made their way from the orient to the trust fund and, with the aid of a few select stateside friends, the dream began to flourish. There was a time, however, when it appeared as if Lady Luck had turned her back on them and Death had taken her stead, the dream was threatened.

The team was sent into Laos to retrieve a spook. The recon mission itself was a success, as they snatched the spook from underneath the noses of those bamboo clawed torturers just hours before the brutal interrogations would have terminated his life; however, their rescue did not go unnoticed. Gunfire followed them out of the enemy camp, pursued them through the jungle at a breakneck speed as men carrying the spook fled on foot towards their pick up point.

Destructive chaos followed them through the jungle as gunfire and hand grenades cut down more than just the lush foliage. Enemies as well as brothers fell in the mad dash to safety. Those pursuing them faded as they continued their plunge into the ever-darkening jungle. Halting to access the damages, they found two wounded grievously, their radio blown to hell and their hopes of a speedy retreat shattered. While they paused to rest and care for their wounded, they heard in the distance what sounded like trucks approaching. Scouts were sent to check it out and returned with the report of finding three slowly approaching trucks guarded by one truck filled with men and lots of spotters. Carrying their wounded, they made a path to intercept the approaching trucks in hopes of using one to return to base.

An ambush was set, trip wires run across the road that would take out the lead vehicle and shatter the resolve of the others to enter the fray. Gunfire rained from the heavens as both sides took heavy loses; when the smoke cleared, all the enemy were dead or dying. One truck, the center one in the three, was useable for their planned escape. Opening the tarped back they found - to their surprise - a Marine bound in burlap and baling wire and racks of brown-shelled eggs. The Marine was wild eyed and delirious - ranting about being the Easter bunny. Loading their wounded and dying, they made a daring attempt to move towards their lines. Nineteen entered the mission and thirteen returned, they ditched the vehicle and buried their dead in an ancient jungle-reclaimed temple and made their way back by foot. Their only reward for the mission was a few eggs each of the men grabbed as a remembrance of their trip into hell.

Once the documents were completed and the spook given over to custody; tags turned in along with the Marine the men withdrew to mourn their lost brothers in arms. One couple and three lovers had died in that conflict, and the men needed time to heal. Alcohol, pot, fresh meat and the bounty of fresh eggs would help. Wreathed by smoke from a greasy skillet, the bone weary men gathered with their tins in hand to dine on a rare commodity, real eggs. They cracked the first and poured its contents into the hot frying pan.

"Clank!"

A ball about the size of an egg yolk, made of pure gold, rolled across the pan. Hunger gave way to joy and riotous laughter once the men began examining the other eggs. All had carefully sealed holes in the shells and all contained egg yolk sized lumps of pure gold. They were rich!

They returned many times to that ancient temple till the entire contents of the truck were shipped stateside. Their dream no longer just a pipe dream came into reality. CASTLE Enterprises was born.

Allow me to introduce myself

"Ladies and gentlemen, please take your seats - our tour is about to begin. Thank you! If you will be so kind as to open the portfolios, we will begin while awaiting our final members to join this tour. Within the left side of the folder, you shall find the list of offered slaves for this Spring Auction, a list of their talents, and for what they have been trained. Also note: for an additional fee all of them can be programmed to be of more help to their new owners. Please notice the list of programs offered should you desire a unit that will work more efficiently in its owner's behalf. On the right side you will find our most recent stats on our profit sharing programs and why it is better for you, as new owners, to join one of the local Shields. The Deus has ordered that any owner who wishes to return their old slaves for reprogramming, can do so free of charge, as long as the owners are members within a Shield.

"Please take a moment before the auction begins to read over the contents of the portfolio as it will help you to understand the symbols used while the slave is on the block. Once the bidding starts they will not stop to answer any questions. It's just good form to be prepared before you enter the buying arena.

"Allow me to introduce myself. To my Sir, the Deus, Retired Major Bruce Hunter, this slave is known as His Number One, my slave number 9-745, and his personal property. This slave has had the honor of being with my Lord since before Sir was awarded the title of the Deus. My Master has the liberty as the Deus of owning three slaves at present. As his Number One, this one is trained as a mule, my sperm is valuable to the sperm bank, and specialty programs have been implanted allowing this one to be more pleasing to my Master.

"Our house, Buena Vista, was the first house established within the United States and was established soon after the Vietnam Conflict drew to a close. Soon after other great houses followed: Canada, Germany, Columbia, Laos, and England. Each house is economically self-sufficient, has its own coat of arms and one Manor Lord or Lady who is one of the Founders of CASTLE Enterprises. The CASTLE is ruled by one Deus with absolute power who is governed by a board of trustees. That person is elected for eight years from the remaining Founders. We are into our third Deus, Retired Major Bruce Hunter, as our Lady Beatrice had to step down due to an accident as her term drew to its close.

"Our civilization is not unlike a medieval society except that it is buried within the corporate world and our society is very lucrative for those like yourselves that have been invited to join. Lucrative in ways the outside world has yet been able to define. Our cash crops differ. With each household, however, one thing is our common product. It is sold by all Houses; sperm, alive and very active. Yes, it is genetically altered but 99% of the women who purchase our sperm produce healthy babies. Plus, we offer our mothers superb prenatal care and post-care few in the field can duplicate. This way we can monitor our birthing lines and guarantee limited defects in the gene pool.

"Yes Sir, question?"

"Sir Thomas has asked the going cost of sperm?"

"Forgive this one's ignorance as it is not privy to that information, but this one can offer a guess. If properly collected and stored this one believes its sperm brings in about $1200 per pint but this one may be wrong. When we arrive at the main house, please direct your question to one of the doctors who will be meeting the bus. Thank you, Sir. This one is happy to have been of service, Sir.

"A HOUSE is referred to as a SHIELD and each house has its own Shield Mates. These are men and women, who, not unlike yourselves, own human property. Some are dominate others submissive. All swear allegiance to their Shields, abide by the rules of the Castle and follow without question the directions of the Manor Lord. The allegiance between the Shield and its Mates is an extraordinarily strong and mutually beneficial association as they all reap the benefits from owning a slave or two. All the Shield Mates live in outlying cities, except for a few who are being trained for elevation. Rumor has it that a New House is coming into existence and every Shield is sending representatives to attend.

"Don't you think the fundamentalists would shit their pants full if they knew that our capitol of Castle Enterprises is here within this beautiful setting of the Appalachian Mountains? The 150-plus acre farm is perched on the Blue Ridge, overlooking the big beautiful ever-changing Shenandoah Valley. It's mostly forest, but we are making great progress logging and reclaiming a few fields as are needed for the new crops. That was not the reason for acquiring this land. The land contains a massive subsystem that connects to the Luray Caverns; we now own the whole subsystem of those well-known caverns, they stretch far across Virginia and West Virginia. A recent excavation gave us access to the great Mammoth cave subsystem in Kentucky and with luck we can extend our corporation into wider territories. Buena Vista straddles the entrance of the subsystem. Not unlike an iceberg, Buena Vista harbors little to be seen up top but has a lot of secrets and rooms beneath the ground.

"Our Manor House is a huge cedar log hunting lodge, two and a half stories, a porch running completely around the house, twelve dormers, one for each guest room. If you look out over the porch you can see one of the richest tranquil landscapes that can be seen in the valley. Cords of wood are stacked beneath the porch, drying for winter. The house is set in a bank of lush forest foliage, mountain laurel, and hemlocks scent the cool mountain air. Take a moment while on the porch; pause and listen, there are hidden brooks and streams literally everywhere trickling in the distance. Besides the guest rooms, the Manor House contains a huge great room with two fireplaces large enough to hold a half a tree each, a commercial kitchen, communications room, billiard-recreations room, bathrooms a plenty and our much needed state-of-the-art exercise room. One third of the second floor houses my Master's private suite, which is inaccessible by guests as it's cut off from the balance of the house. So don't even try to have an impromptu audience with him. This year we will finish the above ground great hall, which will be complete before the Manor Motorcycle Gathering in October. On the surface, life within the house gives no hint of anything unusual, except for three, collared and harnessed house slaves. The secret of Buena Vista lies beneath its surface, deep within the caverns.

"Again, Buena Vista is like an iceberg, with more happening below the surface than seen above. The hunting lodge above the surface is only an illusion, as it's set in pastoral surroundings quietly nestled in a forest deep in the Blue Ridge Mountains. The sights of men working in the fields, naked save for collars, heavy leather harnesses and leg irons belies the activity below in the caverns. The cavern beneath the Manor house lends itself well to the Master Plan. If you must know, Buena Vista is held aloft by literally thousands of human slaves who have worked hard to cut limestone from the chambers below the surface.

"The cavern is a series of rooms that has been opened without much effort. The first opened was a great doomed room that presently houses the slave kitchen, feeding stations and opts for one of the public correctional facilities. Off that are three central corridors, which lead deeper into the mountains and stretch further than the 150+ acre farm above. We own all the mining rights in this valley; few know what we mine is not mineral as much as is physical. Please good people, once down inside the community do not wander around aimlessly trying to site see, you will get lost and will end up in a slave pen. Please at all times remain with the slave or slaves that are taking you to your appointed location; elsewise, there is no means of finding you. We are like a little city underground, so many corridors look alike and only if you can read the symbols placed within the walls can you make your way around the complex. We have areas dedicated to dry storage, wet storage, we have our own underground lake that supplies topsiders with some of the best bottled water. We even have the place that breaks even the strongest minds, the pit. The pit is just what it sounds like - a dark dank smelly hole in the ground where an unruly slave is locked away and forgotten until it gets with the program. This slave foolishly had to endure the pit and this one prays daily that it never displeases its owner again - or give him reason to send it back into that hellacious pit.

"One reason you do not wish to get lost downside is that - with the new security system - you will literally be cut off from the topsider world. Each slave has ways that they are marked. If you will look at me I can show you on myself. Here above my right nipple, I wear the brand of my Lord and Master Hunter; this marks me for his personal property. On the underside of my right wrist is a barcode that allows me passage beyond almost all doors in the complex, even the number one slave of Master Hunter must have a security officer to leave the underground and come topside. Each slave that comes to these grounds for training has installed within their body a small microchip that allows security to keep tabs on all slaves. When a slave is bought, that tracking bug is assigned the owner's number. This allows another security team to keep tabs on those off base and tracks any attempts at running away. Also, note that on the right backside of my ear, you will see a duplicate barcode that earmarks my programming and statistics. All slaves here wear the steel collar that encircles our necks but only a few wear the right ankle shackle. Here, that denotes house slave, property of the Deus.

"The first time you visit our Manor, you will not be aware of anything unusual, it looks like any ordinary farm in this area. True, the main house is nineteen miles off the beaten path, so not just anyone can stumble upon it. Still, when driving in, you must first go through security at the gate before the tire spikes are lowered, or else you will not get far with all your tires shredded. Those who were foolish enough to attempt other means of entrance have usually found our land extremely hostile to outward force. We seek only be left alone as we have been for the past years. You may be lucky enough to see field slaves working on the road as we are driving in, tilling fields or chopping wood for the winter. You may see the glint of steel that encircles each slave's neck or the long chains that have them working as a team, or their very secure body harnesses. Or the presence of a very stern, clothed whip-welding foreman on horseback. Nevertheless, they are all there. What you are made aware of is the serenity of the forest, how well the areas look manicured, how quiet the forest and tranquil the setting.

"Ah, here come our last recruits, finally! Please be seated. Here are your portfolios; on the left hand is a brief of the slaves on tomorrows block and on the right a brief of our profit margins from our past year. Please read it before the auction tomorrow. Once you are settled this one will finish its briefing and we will begin our journey. Thank you, Madame.

"While traveling the road up the mountain, the road will clear. The bus will stop and allow all of you that wish to take pictures; this is the best view of the Manor House. From that perspective it will seem to be a modest log cabin but only due to the distance, we all know different, don't we? After crossing the bridge, look up to your left and you may catch a glimpse of one of the five cottages hidden throughout the estate. One is occupied by the chief of security, a handsome African-American known to us as Eric Wilson and his slave, which just happens to be Master Hunter's second in command and Buena Vista's Number One slave. Confusing, yes, but there is a difference, this one 9-745 is owned by Master Hunter, the other is owned by Buena Vista, we both serve our Lord but in different capacities. The second house is used by the doctor when he is given time on topside, the doctor, J.D., was himself a slave who bought his freedom doing years of service and was Master Hunter's slave prior to being elevated. The third house, the one with the flags flying on the porch, now belongs to the Lady Beatrice who has retired to our compound after ruling CASTLE Enterprises for over seven years. The fourth house is set aside for the new chef when he returns from his culinary training in Europe, another slave of Master Hunter's who was elevated, and the fifth house will be occupied once it is completed by someone who serves with their life Buena Vista and CASTLE Enterprises.

"Buena Vista is self sufficient in many ways. Our crops are grown organically, having enough organic matter just within the slave compound alone to keep most plants extremely happy for years. We grow our own grains, mushrooms, herbs and even a patch or two of ginseng, which is traded, overseas, to our Laos Manor House. We generate electricity three major ways here on the compound; excess is sold to the utility companies. We have turbo engines within each stream in the area without destroying their beauty for the tourists downstream. We have solar panels and wind turbines which fill batteries deep within the bowels of the earth. Then we have the slave driven turbines deep within the earth for those days that Master Hunter is not in a good mood. You will not believe how much extra credit we get just from his mood swings.

"As you know, honored guests, having just undergone one of the strictest medical exams you have more than likely ever had in your life that we within our Community and within CASTLE Enterprises observe strict health codes. We maintain files worldwide on all shield mates, slaves and owners. Each of us who are sexually active receives mandatory testing every six months. Yes, it is true, we do have an almost religious fanaticism when it comes to our bodies and health; but our bodies are our greatest source of pleasure. Thus we maintain them accordingly. It is a manner of honor here within CASTLE Enterprises that we follow our Deus mandate. The first Deus was a doctor in Vietnam. He saw first hand the deadly affects that man-made diseases had on humanity, how black VD destroyed more than just the men, but whole generations of talented creative people. He set in motion the first wave of testing on those of his team who returned to the states, and they began the medical data banks that house the records on millions of our people.

"Our doctors are responsible for testing all new slaves, old slaves, mates and even the Founders for any sexually transmitted diseases, as well as being responsible for taking control samples of sperm for the sperm banks reservoir. Our untainted sperm bank has become one of our greatest leverages the CASTLE has in outsider society. Strict enforcement, strict religious adherence to the disciplines by the Castle's partners give those that can afford the price of an excellent and well monitored gene-pool from which many a new healthy human baby can be created. Our doctors can splice genes; modify DNA to give the happy parents a perfect intelligent or higher baby without defects or blemishes if that is what the parents wish. With the addition of hospitals on the outside, we have begun to offer to outsiders the best possible pre and post-natal care. Outsiders have told us that those who think they can provide our level of care are copying doctors with the steel band of enslavement. If you know of any fakers please step forward, there is a handsome reward for the information and credits guaranteed for their destruction.

"It was a shame that our society had to come this route, but it has saved our butts more times than failed. When the powertrippers began to play God by releasing their germ warfare and manufactured diseases in an attempt to eradicate us from the face of the earth, they failed utterly. The CASTLE'S mandate about testing had already been implemented in the late sixties and our disciplines were second nature to our people. Their attempt to kill us failed horribly, they killed instead millions of hetero-sexuals when their gene leapt from homosexual to the other side of the fence. It was a shame that they couldn't see the ramifications of their handiwork till it hit them full face. By then, their own doom was upon them and we were safe. We have become the pure race that Hitler dreamed with one major exception; we are gay. We have no color barrier and we have no desire to conquer the world, only live quietly with our fellow human race and help when we can or hinder as a million focused votes can change the way people think.

"Unlike the outsider society we do not share their antiquated views concern-ing euthanasia. Yes, on occasion someone will test positive for a terminal disease. When that happens, many standard operating procedures, also known as SOPs, kicks into gear. We care for our own with love, honor and with the grace that each person deserves while they are dying. They work if they choose till they feel they are unable. Here all their needs are met for their basic survival; housing, rent, food, transportation is provided for those that are terminally ill. Our own hospital faculty here at Buena Vista is set on the other side of the mountain, this tour will be stopping their briefly for final medical checks. Our hospital is located near one of the more picturesque waterfalls in the Blue Ridge Mountains; the faculty is a stress free environment that has proven to prolong life for those undergoing the transformation. Those that live at the hospital are given the utmost care and when the time comes that the patient chooses not to live, an injection is administered during a farewell party. Death is only an extension of life.

"The body is cremated and the ashes are put to use according to their rank in life. This slave will have the honor of being buried with my Master or to be useful even after death, serving as fertilizer to a flower garden or added to concrete. We serve best by serving our Superiors; it's a fitting end for a slave. Even our collars and leg shackles are recycled; the only time they are removed once installed is after our death. Then the steel is recycled, placed in the forge and reformed for another slave's neck. Hopefully, then, some of the knowledge of its last wearer will pass to the new slave and aid with its growth. All ashes of handlers, slaves, unless unclaimed by outside families, are recycled. With exception of the Deus. Those ashes are entombed within a small alcove in a private open air chapel, if you wish to make the journey by foot it's about a three mile hike. Or ask at the main house for a pony ride, it's far more fun and gives a slave a lovely break from its boring life.

"The land upon which the house Buena Vista presently stands is my Master, our Deus' sanctuary, retired Major Bruce Hunter, Hunter to his friends. After his return from Vietnam he took refuge here on his family's tribal lands. Here he healed his sick soul of all the wounds that Vietnam inflicted upon a caring man. His other Number One, the second in command and lover in Vietnam, Captain Jonathan W. Hicks joined him a few years later bringing with him a pair of identical male twins who were his slaves. Both slaves are excessively handsome, blonde haired, blue eyed, almost hairless with well-defined chests from long workouts shifting pipeline in Texas where they lived with Cappy before coming to be with Hunter here at Buena Vista. Jonathan Daniels, known to us as JD, is the elder by one minute and mike is the younger, they with their Master have brought great talents to our estate and lots of happiness for both Hunter and Cappy.

"How did I come to serve My Master? Excellent question honored Sir. The answer is a long story about a hardheaded young stud that wanted more than anything to be owned by a Master. It is a long story about conquest but one worth hearing if all are so inclined. As you wish honored guests, as you wish.

"All my life I have dreamed of bondage, slavery fantasies, I even believed I was born at this time to serve others, those Superior to me. On a lark and a bet I became a contestant for a state title of Mister LeatherMan, I was shocked when I won the contest hands down. Hell, I was even more shocked to find out that I had to attend a national contest but I was hooked by the applause of my adoring fans. Initially, as a leather titleholder, one instantly becomes a spokesperson for the leather community and, by default, often pushed into the position of being a top, which was my case. I looked the part, was only 26 when I walked my first runway. Had the look, too. Painted on leather pants, knee high spit shined boots, nice hairy pelt of fur running up from my groin to curl across my well trained pecs, nice chiseled features with a handsome mustache, steel baby blue eyes hidden behind mirror shades, gauntlet gloves and that ever present chained visor leather Gestapo hat. I looked stunning, and according to the way people parted before me in a bar, I knew I was just that. Stunning. I loved winning the State Championship, loved the power it gave me. It was such a head-trip! The pillar grew to massive portions as my devotees lifted me to greater heights of domination. I felt complete; except, whenever I was working over a bottom in a heavy scene I wished I could have traded places with the slave at my feet. I was trapped in a fiefdom of my own making and when I won the National Title for Leather Men, I knew I was doomed. My dark secret had to be buried hidden for fear of losing the esteem of my equals. I had the world by the tail with a downhill pull. Or so I thought; until, I met Master Hunter. That meeting shook my foundation to the core. I did not go easily into slavery or submit to his will. His gentle persuasion won my heart and transformed my fears; still, he had to conquer the creature, my ego. This is our story, how I became the glove to his hand. I am his owned personal property, his slave and damn proud to belong to him."

Chapter 1

A journey of a thousand miles must begin with the first step.

Lao Tzu

I was once a bull headed, stubborn, arrogant, self-centered top that dreamed of being a slave. I loved to take men and boys, work them over, venting my pent-up frustration and anger upon them. I could not be both top and bottom to myself, so I worked them over pretty bad in the same way I dreamed of being treated. I did not care if some could not take it. Like a city bus, there was always another just around the corner.

The first time I met my future Master was at the Chesapeake Bay Run. Little did I know what a pivotal event that would be. If I had known then what I know now, I would never have treated him that way. Damn! I cannot believe just how arrogant an asshole I was that fated night!

He and his entourage entered the mixer; you would have thought the fucking Pope had arrived. All eyes turned on him. I was seething, all eyes were supposed to be on me. After all, wasn't I the fucking regional titleholder? I can still remember that night well; it's etched - if not burned - into my brain. He and two others entered, each with a boy in tow. They must have known every fucking one in the goddamn room! The men and women at the mixer lined up to greet him, "Evening Sirs, Hunter, Cappy, nice boys you got there!"

The big man was well liked by the reactions of the crowd, and those that he spoke to seem to genuinely happy he took time to speak to them. He definitely stood out in a crowd, at least 6'9" he stood almost touching the top of the tent with his head. Close-cropped hair with gray flakes only heightened his smoldering blue eyes, giving him an air of power. He had a hairy barrel chest shown by way he wore his leather shirt open to his navel. Very little fat on that man's body, muscles covered with a rich outcropping of black and silver daddy hair strolled over his chest and I really wanted to bury my face into it. His legs were wrapped in, of all things, deep bloodwine leather that laced at the sides of each leg showing off his well-defined body and his incredible basket. Knee-high motorcycle boots golden spurs covered the distance from floor to knee. If I had to be honest, I would not have kicked that man out of my bed even if his taste in leather were not to my liking. He stood out in a crowd on his terms. Not just his size but in his taste of wearing wine leathers to the mixer. The others were dressed in the official leatherman's outfit of the time, basic black leather just like everyone else in the room. Clone City! Did this Master Hunter impress me? Damn right, but I did not let on; instead, I became more the asshole than I was normally.

I should have kept my mouth shut, but booze and my own stupidity made me cocky. Oh Boy! I sure inserted my booted foot when I said too loudly, "Who let these leather queens into my party?" Those that heard my comment stopped dead in their tracks, midsentence, and stared at me. The sheep opened an unobstructed path between the Hunter team and me as heads turned - as if watching an invisible tennis match from one to the other players on the field. They first stared at me then to Hunter, waiting to see who was going to pick up the ball for the next volley. Hunter had his back to me when I lobbed that statement about leather queens into his court. He slowly turned his body and head to scrutinize me. His eyes bored a hole right down into my soul. I was prepared for problems but he took no action, his silence said more than words.

Deafening silence permeated the room and hung thickly in the air like a humid tropical afternoon. The silence made me nervous but I did not back down. Instead, it goaded me into some other form of action. Who does he think he is coming into my party and stealing the show from me, I was thinking in my ego-fed mind. His sidekick Cappy watched me intently. Casually, I worked myself through the milling crowd to get closer to Hunter. As I neared him, he turned to face me, saying "Greeting's, boy. I have heard so much about you from far too many sources. I see that it's all true! You really are everything they claimed you to be, an ass-Set to our Leather Family. Broken any more boys lately?"

He extended his hand for a handshake but I snubbed him by ignoring it. The very way he accented *asset* made me think he was meaning something else and the giggles of those around him confirmed my thought. His quietly spoken words fanned anger within me, why even now I do not know, I was angry with the way he upstaged my every move, how handsome he was, his quiet power and how I felt when I was near him. My knees actually shook while I stood in his presence, I so wanted to be down before him, serving him. No man had ever made me feel the way as did Hunter did that night, little, insufficient and out of place.

He continued, "My friends know me as Hunter but you can call me Master! Normally, I don't come to these events but I was told that you were the featured meat for tonight's events. I wanted to meet my new slave before I broke his will and reformed his thinking to my way. It will take some work, but I can make you into that creature within your dreams."

His words stung as if he had bitch-slapped me. *Who in the hell does he think he is?* My mind raced with furious turmoil and my anger rose into my cheeks reddening them with a flush anticipation. His next new slave? NO! I screamed in my mind.

Everyone around us was intently listening to our exchange. We were at one of those gravid moments in conversation that time felt as if it stood still. At that very moment, a man cut through the thong of people and deposited a slave at Hunter's boots. His attention moved to the bound slave but he continued to speak directly to me. "In less than one year you will be my personal property, my slave. Stop your pretenses of being a top, you can fool the crowd only so long, you are about to wear out your welcome in their eyes. You can fool almost everyone here part of the time but there is no way in hell you can fool me. I know how much you crave to be where this slave is, I know what you need to fulfill your destiny!"

Casually, the turned his back to me, dismissing me as if I was only a slave, not the National Title Holder. The bastard ignored me. The bound slave at his feet was far more important. I stood my ground, fuming as friends tried pulling me back into the crowd.

My anger grew the longer I stood there watching him toying with the slave and talking to the slave's owner. The room faded to red as the blood lust, my anger, took control of my body. He was rising from having been stooped over to examine the slave when I took my swing at his head, his face. He saw the movement and just moved slightly so the fist swished past him, not colliding with anything more than empty air. I looked more stupid for having thrown the punch than if I had just stood my ground. His eyes burned into my skull as his lips mouthed, "I will own your ass, slave."

He spoke audibly to the crowd around him, "It would seem your new sash-queen needs another drink or a boy to beat, someone take him away before I take what is rightfully mine." Turning his back, I was finally dismissed, friends handed me a drink and I allowed them to guide me away. I do not remember the balance of the party but I do remember his eyes drilling their holes into my skull.

Every time I saw him throughout the run, his eyes were always watching me. Every time I caught his eye; I seethed inside, his words held the ring of truth that set my soul on fire. A problem arose every time I was near him on under his watchful eye; my cock would harden, something I could not explain. Still, he noticed. Damn him, He noticed my cock's reaction!

A couple of months passed and I had forgotten the incident till we met again at an AIDS benefit. He had donated a shit load of artwork to raise money for the benefit. I had come straight from the airport and had no idea where I was to stay that night, hell, I had to change into my leathers in a men's restroom during dinner. Typically, a gay oriented motel would be appropriate lodging for those of use who were there to sponsor the event. When I found out that all of the guests would be retiring to Hunter's estate after the benefit, I damn near shit!

Four-wheel drive vehicles took us out of town to Hunter's country estate, Buena Vista. By the reaction of the other guests, they were looking forward to the quiet comfort of the estate. However, I thought I would have to put out to pay for these privileges, boy, I could not have been more wrong! Cappy recommended that I take the time to get to know the man all knew as Hunter, that weekend was a learning experience.

After that weekend I truly felt the fool as I found myself totally out of my league. I represented myself as a heavy player, but nothing prepared me for the scenes I saw Master Hunter take his slaves through. They trusted him totally. I envied him; but to a larger degree I truly envied his slaves. He had earned their respect and trust more than I could ever pretend to earn. It had become incredibly clear to me that I was only a great top in my own mind. I yearned to trade places with one of his slaves and would have done so in a heartbeat had the offer ever been made. I left that weekend richer for having learned more about Hunter, although totally sexually frustrated.

Over the following months, we exchanged numerous letters, e-mails and phone calls. I began to realize that what I truly wanted was to serve this man. Hell, his letters did things to me that no other man's ever could; they were like a lifeline to me. My ego fought me every step of the way. At last, I received my first set of specific orders from Hunter. I was nearing the end of my year as the National Leather Man and my newness had worn thin. The time had come for me to either shut up or shit out. I could still call and make an excuse but my rigid cock would not allow me. I read and reread every word and pondered the consequences of these next actions. I spent hours picking out my wardrobe for that night; even went to the gym that day to enhance my muscle tone. I wanted him to see me and know it was I.

These orders were my first test. I was to meet him at the Eagle in DC and go home with him to serve him as his slave for a week. I opened the bar, I was so anxious to be on time; however, the bastard made me wait. I was almost ready to go home, thinking he had stood me up, when he arrived. Not to look overeager, I grabbed a bottom that had been eyeing me all night long, pulled him aside and started a conversation. He entered, passed his motorcycle helmet to the bartender, grabbed a beer, and paused to light a big cigar before turning to rake the men in the room. He was wearing non-descript leathers, basic black, scuffed heavy leather chaps, well-faded crotch worn 501's, a heavy motorcycle jacket and knee-high engineers. Hunter took his own sweet time, chatting with friends, tweaking the bartender's nipples followed by his deep baritone laughter before he turned and walked my way, cigar smoke following in his wake. He slid in beside me, looked down on the bottom and quietly dismissed the boy with a curt nod; the boy smiled and withdrew.

"Boy, don't you have your keys hanging on the wrong side?"

I looked down at his boots, my face flushed bright red and I swear the temperature of the room went up twenty degrees. He had me dead to rights. I slowly looked up, "Yes, Sir," I mumbled.

"Speak up boy! I did not hear you! Fucking move those keys, shit head, now!"

His shout made the bar go silent; the music died, or so it seemed. All eyes turned on me. I froze and every second felt like an eternity. My head dropped and I stared at the floor. I was confused. Never before had anyone ordered me around in public. I slowly reached over to my left side and fumbled for my keys. As I removed them, I realized how badly I wanted to submit to this man's power, his strength and authority. I located the belt loop of my right side; I was surprised to realize that tears were welling up in my eyes. As the keys snapped into place I felt a strange combination of relief and pride. Tears streamed down my face.

"Come, boy, follow me!"

I hesitated only a moment before I followed him out of the door into the dark parking lot.

He led and I followed. Abruptly, he turned on his heels and ordered me to drop my pants. Without an ounce of hesitation I complied, I had hoped it would impress him with my desire to serve. He wasn't even watching; he had turned to unlock his silver and black Harley. While he stowed his chain in the saddlebags, my ass was turning blue due to the winter's cold.

He turned to me, "Grab your cock and balls and hold them out for me!"

I grabbed them in my left hand and held them out as far as I could pull them from my body. He approached me with a huge shit-eating grin plastered across his face. He cinched the frozen steel padlock around the base of my cock and balls and, with a click, set the lock. He held the key at eye level between us. "Watch the key, boy."

My eyes became glued to that key as I watched his arm extend his hand over an open steel grate in the floor of the city, his hand turned the key fell downward, clinked on the metal and was gone, swallowed into the maw of the underworld.

"My padlock is around your cock and balls, boy, that must mean I own you, doesn't it, shit head?"

"Sir, Yes, Sir!" I shouted.

"Ever ridden before, don't waste your macho image by lying to me, answer!"

"Sir, Yes, Sir!" I was about to say more when he cut me off.

"Get your ass on the bike!"

He climbed on before me, kicked the Harley to life, and sat down before rising to his feet and turning to me. "When I lower myself to the seat, I want your cock trapped within the 'V' of my ass crack." I did as he ordered, fitting myself on the seat behind him. "Yeah, that's better boy, but slide closer. I want you as my second skin, put your arms around my chest and I may allow you to play with my nipples while we are cruising home. We got a ways to go before we get home, so get as comfortable as you can."

That week was a transformational week for me. He pried open my Pandora's Box, which had always been sealed tight for fear that my fans would see the true me. Hunter put me through one scene after another, developing my trust in his talents till at the end of the week, I soared like an eagle after one of his whipping scenes. I was euphoric; at last, I was free to be the slave of my dreams.

During that week, I developed a whole new appreciation of what a bottom can and should be. I always treated a slave/bottom as a sub-citizen, not worthy of much care or respect. Hunter elevated my low self-esteem as he developed my need to bottom to him. Even though I served as his slave, never once did I lose self-respect. He pushed buttons I did not know I had and happily pushed my limits, testing me every step of the way. At times he made me delirious with pleasure; at others I would sob at his gentle caress. This week began the courtship that would eventually lead me to where I wanted to stand, an owned branded slave.

When I went home, I arranged for my boy to be taken by a friend. I knew then that I was happiest serving. Twice more did I go to Hunter, each time he used me harder, forced me to beg and humiliate myself for his pleasures. Attending his needs brought fulfillment and joy I had never found in the outside world. I worried needlessly about my adoring public, once a new titleholder had taken the sash; I was retired to the back of the line, just another muscle boy watching the sidelines.

Hunter's prophecy had come true. A new titleholder now took my place and in less than a year after I met Hunter, I submitted to him, made a commitment and became his property. Gladly, I signed the contract without even reading it, even though he suggested I read it carefully. I was transformed with my signature from a freely born man into that of an owned piece of human flesh, a slave. I was in lust to become Hunter's pet personal slave and never realized what changes I would have to endure to get from point A to point B. My fantasy world would be refocused into reality.

The night in celebration of my signature, Hunter had Cappy take me down into the underground dungeon. There Cappy spread and bound me eagle on an old wooden cross, hooded my head and left me to await his presence. Helplessly I hung, waiting the time when my Master would arrive. It seemed like hours till I heard the door open and felt his loving touch, the first of many whip strokes across my bound body. He warmed my back, slowly preparing to take me to heights I had as of yet not traveled. One flogger warmed me, another forced the air out of my lungs as it slammed repeatedly into my back and another burned a fiery path across my shoulders. It felt as if I was on fire, my cock never even lost its erection throughout the evening. I was lowered to the floor, blinders ripped off the hood, and watched as Hunter walked to a throne, sat, popped open a beer took a long swallow, lighted a cigar, drew the smoke into his lungs and snapped his fingers. I who had never, ever, crawled for another man crawled to the spot his fingers indicated; there I cleaned his boots of all dirt. I felt his boot resting on my head, had his piss trickle down my spine and loved every second I was with him.

Finishing his beer, he rose, walked across the dungeon, snapped his fingers, and again I crawled. I was lifted, slung over a sawhorse, bound legs spread, arms locked to the floor before me. His hands stroked my body, his paddle warmed my ass and thighs till they glowed a cherry red by the fire that I felt from inside. There still bound, he fucked my ass as if there was no tomorrow. Each slap of his thighs against my upturned butt made me more aware of his Mastery over his property. His scream echoed off the cavern walls as he blew his load up inside my ass and, while his cock softened, his piss filled my bowels. Dislodging his cock with a wet plop, he walked away; leaving me bound over the sawhorse, opened a beer and rested.

The following morning after a hearty breakfast, Hunter and I talked about the upcoming days and he gave me my assignment, "slave, you will sell everything you own to pay off your debts. You will return to me in 45 days, what you cannot sell you are to give away. Here is a suitcase and a one-way ticket for your return trip. In the suitcase you pack only that which you cannot live without, I will provide everything else when you are here. If you do not return or you cash this one-way ticket or fail to arrive at the location I have indicated on this map within 45 days, forget any future attempts. I do not need a slave who can not honor his Master's orders." With those parting words, a warm kiss and a hard slap to my sore butt I was dismissed. I climbed into a pickup truck that took me down to a bus, and from there home to my sorry excuse for an apartment.

My orders were to sell or give away everything I could not carry in one 12 X 30 flight suitcase. On my return to my apartment, I packed and repacked the fucking small suitcase trying to get in my most prized possessions. My beautiful trophy almost filled the suitcase that Hunter had given me; however, I could just wedge in the suitcase my titleholder sash, the highly studded harness, matching gauntlets and jockstrap that I had used for all my titleholder appearances. I chose to wear my "Official Leather Man's Outfit," black leather pants with studded cod piece, black Frye harness boots, leather button down shirt and my custom leather pride flag vest. I wanted to look hot for my Master.

It was easy to get out of the apartment lease. I had few household goods that I wanted having selected the contents from the Goodwill people. The only things that were my source of pleasure were packed in one suitcase as ordered with one big exception. Hunter couldn't have meant for me to sell or give away my beauty. He would just have to understand. I had worked many long hours for my treasure, sweated over him, had gone without food and a better place to live just to keep him the way I thought he prefers; but, damn he was worth the effort. Just to watch studs turn their heads as I rode down the road in him and the pick-ups I had taken home within him made him all worthwhile.

I tossed my one suitcase into my gleaming candy apple red Corvette. I knew that Hunter would let me keep him! Hell, he just had to! Wasn't Hunter a kind and loving man? When I won the Leather Man title, I bought the Corvette for myself and had the leather pride flag painted down both sides. I wanted people to know that my car belonged to a winner. Even had the interior customized to my needs with black leather interior and an added a custom license plate that read LTHRSTD.

My Corvette was like my cock - always primed. I keyed the ignition, revved the engine and slipped into a daydream. My cock hardened as I dreamed of Hunter's surprise at seeing me arrive in my Corvette instead of that smelly old dank bus. Stroking my leather-covered cock, I thought of how pleased Hunter would be when I lent him my Corvette.

It wasn't a long drive to New Market. I could make it in no time if I took the interstate highways; however, I thought I deserved better than that route. I left before

Portsmouth began the tube-steak boogie, morning rush hour through underwater tunnels, and a pure bitch! I was leaving my worries behind and as a reward; I took the Skyline Drive to New Market. It was longer but driving those curves at 90 M.P.H. was a major rush. God, what a power rush it was, and I needed it after the past months of hell I had been through. Besides, it would clear my head of the city smog before I reached Hunter.

It was a beautiful spring day. Just enough sunshine for me to lower the convertible top with just enough nip in the air to make my leathers feel wonderfully alive, and I loved this weather. The forest was just beginning to green as the trees broke out in bud. From a distance, the trees took on a greenish haze, the crisp air was cool and refreshing, yes, spring was in the air. It was a great day to be alive - or so I thought as I raced around one hairpin curve after another till I rounded a blind curve and damn near plowed over a bus full of mopheads making a mad dash to the rest rooms. Senior citizens were everywhere! Excellent brakes and quick thinking was the only thing that saved those senior citizens from rapid ascension.

Old fucking farts, teetering across the two-lane road from john to bus were taking their own sweet time. I was fuming, as they were making me wait. I revved my engine, it did no good and you would have thought they were all stone cold deaf by their reaction. When I noticed a bus leaving the rest stop, I nearly went nuts and began to ease my way through the wheel-chaired thong that were holding up my joy ride and were going to make me late for my appointment with Hunter. Two buses got out before I made it through the charge of the mopheads; now, I was forced to travel at the posted 35 M.P.H. speed limits, which was not my style! The rest area marked the halfway point between Elkton and the turn off at 211, which would take me into New Market and into Hunter's open arms.

I had been traveling at their snail's pace for too long when I overtook the second bus as they climbed a small incline. The mopheads got their underpants in a knot when another car had to take the curb as I passed. I fucking didn't care. I wanted around that damn smoky machine that was clouding my view with its belching black exhaust and I took the opportunity.

I had just hit the gas when I rounded a curve and had to slam on my brakes as the other bus' butt stared at me. While I waited for my next chance to pass, I flashed back to a time when Hunter and I had been out riding on one of his ATV's. His estate butted up to the Blue Ridge Parkway. We had stopped near a beautiful waterfall; he had ordered me to strip. One thing led to another and before I knew it he had me bound to a tree, had cut a sapling and caned my backside and ass hard. As usual, I had been giving him attitude, which he did not appreciate and went on to show me the error of my ways, the canning was necessary in his book to give me rightful thinking. When he finished, he released one hand and told me that if I still wanted to be a part of him that I would follow the cascading waterfalls down to the bottom. There he would wait one hour, eating our packed picnic basket. He left, taking with him all my clothes.

It was a struggle to get free. I followed the water downwards, running across slippery rocks and enjoying the feeling of being buck-ass naked and alone; me primitive man. I was not paying much attention to my surroundings until I heard a murmur of shock and surprise. Pushing back branches, I found myself standing in a group of Oriental tourists snapping photos of the water falling down the mountain. It was a few minutes before they noticed me and turned their cameras in my direction. I heard that bastard's laughter even over the waterfall; he sat calmly on the opposite side of the road, watching and eating a sandwich.

I gathered branches of leaves around me. Walking as if I had no cares in the world, I passed the camera-snapping tourists to stand before Hunter. Upon arrival, he only offered me a sandwich and to my embarrassment we had our picnic right then and there.

I had lost track of time remembering that sequence of events and failed to notice that my exit was rapidly approaching. I chose then to pass the lead bus - a bad move on my part. We both were aiming for the same exit. I accelerated, nearly side-swiping the huge mammoth of a bus that kindly took the ditch instead of ruining my Corvette. I saw in my rear view mirror that they seemed all right. Jesus, I had only 47 minutes to cover the balance of the trip and be there when Hunter arrived at the pick-up point. I put the pedal to the metal and my Corvette spread his wings, we flew!

I wanted Hunter to see me waiting for him at his bus stop in my Corvette. He'd get a kick out of my Corvette and can arrive in style with me driving him to his events in a leather pride decorated car. So what if I did not follow his orders to the letter by arriving on the bus that stopped at every little town from Norfolk to New Market? I would have had to leave at 5 A. M. to have arrived on time. My way, I would arrive with time to spare, more rested, and better able to please him once I was back on Buena Vista soil. I did get rid of everything and even packed the tiny suitcase to overflowing with my gear. I could almost see his big toothy smile as he saw me get out of my Leather Pride Corvette, dropped to my knees and submitted to him. Won't he be surprised!

I was absorbed in my make believe world when I first heard the high whine, I paid it no heed. I was driving a two-lane stretch of road; the route Hunter had told me was the best route into New Market. I had passed the bus a few miles back, having given them a scare as I passed like a fool on a curve. A tan and black sheriff car pulled along side of me in a straight stretch of road. From the loudspeakers, I was told to slow down and pull over to the side of the road or they would shoot out my front tires.

"Pull Over!"

As I complied, my mind raced over thousands of different scenarios, thinking the sheriff could not have known about the two buses unless they had reported me by radio. Nor did I see them along the stretch that I had just come, unless they had been hidden behind a billboard. I kept damning myself as I slowed my Corvette and pulled off the road. The sheriff's car followed me off. I sat, my palms sweating, watching in my rearview mirror as both doors opened on the sheriff's car. Out stepped two brown and tan uniformed cops with their guns drawn and aimed in my direction. Both approached my car cautiously till one had his gun pointed through the passenger side window and the other patrolman was off to the side, pointing his gun directly at my head.

I had rolled down the window while they were still in their car. I was screaming in my head, shit, damn, fuck; but turned to the older officer and meekly asked, "Was I speeding officer?"

A blue-tipped .357 was aimed directly at my eyes, sweat was rolling off my face and I dared not move my hands to wipe it or I'd have my ass blown away by these redneck cops. I damn near shit when I saw his gun waiver midair. I began to stammer and apologize while holding out my registration and license papers to the cop.

He took them in a quick snap, shouting; "Put both your hands on the goddamn steering wheel boy! We have been following you for the past nine miles with lights on, the past three miles with both lights and siren and were pulling around to blow out one of your tires when you finally noticed us. What's your hurry, boy? By the looks of how you are all dolled up, boy, I would say you are going to one hot date? Is that true punk?"

The sheriff that was holding his gun while talking to me tossed the papers over to his partner. "Go call this one in and see what they have on this sorry no good bastard!"

I was scared shitless, Barney Fife could just blow my ass away for sneezing and that would suit him just fine by the way he looked.

"OK, boy, we are going to open that door real slow-like. I want you to slide that sweet ass of your'n out of that car without putting your hands down where I can't see them. If you do, I will shoot and ask questions later, do you understand, shithead?"

I nodded my head in agreement.

He repeated himself, "Do you understand, shithead?"

Weakly, I mumbled, "Sir, yes, Sir. I do understand, Sir."

The sheriff laughed when I replied. "That's better boy. Now climb out of that fancy car slow and easy."

He backed away with his gun trained on me. Slowly, I reached for the handle outside of the car, lifted it and opened the door. All I could think of was getting the door open without making them think I was reaching for a gun. Using my left leg, I pushed out the door, turned and followed with my right leg. Keeping my hands above my head, I rose slowly to my feet and stood next to my car.

The tub-o-lard sheriff escorted me by gunpoint towards the front of my Corvette while his partner finished his radio report.

From what I could see, the sheriff's partner was a handsome full-muscled man. You could tell he was not a stranger to a gym just by the way his uniform stretched over his torso and filled out his pants. The older man, the sheriff, was the typical figure of a southern sheriff, fat gutted, smelly, tobacco juice running down the corners of his lips from the baseball sized wad of tobacco shoved inside his mouth. In my book, this sheriff was a troll.

The fat sheriff escorted me to the front of my Corvette, kicked my feet apart and pushed me forward; I made my first mistake by catching myself with my hands not wishing to ruin the paint job on the hood. Like a fool, I forgot where I was for a moment and whom I was with. I yelled out at the pasty-faced sheriff, "Stop that, you old fuck! My vest pins will scratch the surface of my car!"

I didn't think the old fart could move so fast, his lard gut hid his speed as my head was grabbed and slammed against the hood while my legs were kicked out spread by two brutal kicks to my ankles. "Move your goddamn arms out as far as you can reach, faggot! Open your fingers wide! Spread them like your legs, now! If you so much as twitch that ass of yours at me, I will beat the crap out of you! Understand me, shithead!?"

The bastard had caught me off guard, he moved so fast. I could have easily vomited, my head hurt so damn bad. I was spread neatly across the hood of my car with the tip of the sheriff's gun jammed between my ass cheeks and all I could do was watch and listen as the sheriff directed his partner to ransack the interior of my car before finding and dumping out the contents of my small suitcase.

"Hey, Jack?" yelled the old sheriff, his gun digging into my ass.

"Yeah, Chief, what you want?" answered the bastard who was rummaging through the contents of my suitcase.

"Find anything interesting, Jack?"

"Yeah, Chief. Found a bag of pills that looks suspicious and a bag of something that looks like homegrown. Looks like it's for his personal use, it's not enough for resale."

The Chief was talking, "I bet ya Jack, this shit is the drug dealer we got a call about this morning. He fits the description that they gave us."

I wasn't too concerned about what those two hicks were talking about as I had my own problems. I tried holding myself off the scalding hot hood as the heat of the engine was burning through my leathers and all my collection of run pin were gouging the surface of my pristine paint job. I was barely successful until the old fart noticed what I was doing. He leaned his more than ample weight on to me and my arms gave out as I went down onto the hood. I could actually hear my sweat drenched leather shirt sizzle on the hot hood and it only took a moment for my skin to be seared. I struggled to get off the hood; the old sheriff took my struggles to mean something else. Big mistake! My second and near fatal mistake in their books, resisting arrest.

My own stupidity sealed my fate. As I tried to push myself off the hood, my head exploded and I was dropped to the ground. All I knew was pain. I must have slipped off the hood in my struggle to get away from the blows that were raining down on my back, head and shoulders. There on the ground, both men began to kick me and beat me with their batons until I stopped struggling. Through bloodied lips I screamed for them to stop, begged them to stop and with a brutal kick to my head, they did. When I awoke, a booted foot was planted on my head and my face was being ground into the gravel. There I was held, cuffed and lifted to be thrown over the front hood.

"I am looking forward to taking your sweet ass back to town to my little jail. I have a private room set aside for trouble the likes of you, boy. There I can work you over real nice. You will confess to anything I want eventually, boy." Each sentence he pronounced in his long, drawn-out, redneck speech was emphasized with his gun grinding its way into my ass. "I will make you regret you were born, boy, don't fuck with me! Speak when you's spoken to, understand me boy?"

I didn't think the question needed an answer. He did, my face got slammed into the hood by one of his meaty paws.

"Answer me, shithead!"

I half nodded, half mumbled into the hood, "Yes, Sir!"

The chief changed places with Officer Jack and started ripping open panels within my Corvette, trying to find hidden drugs - or so they claimed. Jack grabbed my cuffed hands, lifted and replaced me on the hood and leaned his weight into my body.

"Don't even try nothing on me boy, I will just as easy skull-fuck you here as to have to drag your sorry ass back to the jail. No one will be the wiser that another dealer died in the county, they do it all the time." His deep bass laughter hinted at his hand in the drug dealers' deaths. I wanted no harm to come to me by this man; his heavily muscled body would have broken me like a twig. I had a handsome chest and cut stomach but would have looked like a weakling on the beach besides this man, he was massive!

Again he lifted my cuffed hands, repositioning them in the small of my back. "Don't move them again, boy!"

His threat kept me frozen in place as he kicked my legs to their greatest extension and began to pat me down. I got lost in the sensations of the pat down; Officer Jack's personal touch was something that I could learn to like. He draped his hard muscled body over my backside, pinning me to my car's hood. Was that his cock hardening or was that my imagination?

Officer Jack was one hot daddy bear! His uniform was literally painted on his muscled body. I have always had a thing for dark looks, a dark shadowed facial hair, mirrored sunglasses and big meaty hands. He took his time pawing over my body, grinding his nightstick into my asscrack. In a different location we would have the makings for one hell of a hot scene; here, on this God-forsaken backwoods road I became confused. He was doing his damnedest to get me excited, or that's how it felt. His hands swept across my chest, stopped long enough to roll each nipple erect before slowly allowing his hands to sweep over my hard stomach. He ground his hardening cock into my ass whenever he repositioned his hands. I became concerned when he called out to the sheriff, "This boy's got rings in his nipples. Shall I pull them out or let him keep them?"

The wheezing sheriff mopped his head with a nasty looking snot rag and blew his nose before answering, "Them rings either mark him as a biker, a biker's bitch or a faggot, can't tell which yet. I bet with this fancy-ass car he's the drug runner. I found some hollowed areas but I can't get to them here. I'm impounding his car and will allow Jim and Neil to tear into the bitch till we find them drugs. One way or another, that boy's gonna tell us what he knows."

The strong hands of Officer Jack continued their downward sweep, around my waist he found a small chain and followed it to my butt cheeks, "God, Sheriff this boy's got a chain around his waist and it looks from here that it dips down between his asscrack!"

Into my right pocket his hand descended. There he cupped my aching nuts and squeezed till I bowed over in agony, his chuckle at my discomfort gave me reason to worry. I thought his cock actually grew harder when he knew he had caused me pain. He increased the pain, unconsciously, I must have wiggled my butt seductively across his hard cock, and he drew up close to my ear and whispered, "Keep resisting arrest. I can't wait to get you back home to our private interrogation room. There your screams will go unchecked and I can have all I want of that butt, boy!" His laughter echoed in my head as I gagged on the thought.

"He's got roach clips on a chain, Sir, and here's his wallet, too." Officer Jack tossed the tit clamps along with my biker wallet onto the hood.

"Chief, he has something hidden under his pants, I think he is acting as a mule and is carrying the drugs inside his sweet ass. Can I strip him and see what's hidden?"

The sheriff walked the short distance to explore my wallet, while Officer Jack peeled me off the car. "Drop those pants, boy, or I will have to shoot your ass here on the spot. DROP'EM!"

I froze. Officer Jack, elevated my cuffed hands till I was standing humped over. It felt like my shoulder sockets were about to be ripped from their joints. His hand grabbed and ripped open the top buttons and, with a brutal jerk, my pants dropped down to my knees. My cock sprang to attention, saluting Officer Jack's handiwork.

The sheriff started laughing. "Look what you have gone and done to that boy Jack, got him all hot and bothered. His cock is so excited its dripping!"

I felt more than heard Jack's response, as two hands grabbed my butt cheeks and did their damnedest to rip them wide open. "Damn, Chief, that boy's got a plug or something locked inside his shit hole. My God, that thing's huge!"

Third stupid mistake, was finding my voice… "You can't do this to me, and I have rights!"

"Wrong!" Which was followed by a gut-punch that dropped me like a stone to the gravel. While I was puking they decided what was going to happen to me. I was terrified, scared half out of my wits! Jack was to bring me in and the Chief would drive my Corvette into town. Hearing the squeal of my car's tires on the pavement informed me that I was left with Jack. I knew then I was in big trouble.

I lay there; puke soaking into the ground where I had fallen, looking up at Officer Jack's legs and him smiling down at me. I did not like that smile; it foretold of future events none to my liking. I was cuffed, hurt, ass exposed to anyone passing on that road, scared to death and was worried sick when Jack turned towards me.

He approached me, leaned down, grabbed my cuffed hands and lifted just enough to help me understand how helpless I was. Holding my hands, he assisted me to crawl the five feet off the road to the backside of the cruiser before I was dropped. He stepped to the car, opened the passenger side door, sat down, fumbled with his shirt pocket and pulled out a cigarette, flipping the lighted match in my direction. He inhaled slowly savoring the smoke as it filled his lungs, pulled out the butt and exhaled in a deep sigh. Looked down at me, "Get your face up here, boy, crawl to me."

He sat there smoking, watching as I lay there before he began to speak, "The Chief can be a very evil man when he wants to be. His size hides just how cruel he can be, plus people underestimate his speed due to his bulk, plus hides a few other things till it's too late." His chuckle after pronouncing his little secret gave me more reason to worry.

"Boy, as I see it from my point of view, you are going to need someone on the inside that can take off the Chief's heat when he gets nasty, like I know he will. I can help you; but you are going to have to do something for me. Something that tells me you are willing to work on my behalf for my intervention."

Inhaling another long drag, he pinch-flipped the hot cigarette in my direction. Unzipped his fly and pulled out a hog of a cock that was hard, angry and dripping. "Crawl over here and make my boy feel good. Suck down this cop cock and I'll be there when you need some help with the Chief. Come on boy, I know you want it; I can see it in your eyes. Crawl to me, faggot, come on that's the way. Push your knees under your chest and push yourself forward, come on boy, come and get it. Hot cop cock waiting for you."

Slowly I moved, grinding my chest into the gravel along the road, each painful push forced me to hurt myself a little more till I was kneeling between the cop's open legs.

His legs opened wide, encircling my body and he placed his feet between my legs, thus pinning me from any thought of escape. His hand grabbed ahold of my shirt and, with a mighty rip, it was torn open to expose my nipples and abraded chest. He went to work, using the roach clips on my tits, pulling on them, tugging them while drawing me closer to him. Suddenly with a hard pull, he yanked them off. I screamed, which was followed by his laughter. *Sick bastard* is all I could think once the wave of pain passed beyond me. Still, my cock jumped within its confined space; trapped within folds of my leather pants, I was enjoying his heavy abuse.

Fingers like steel coaxed my nipples hard and erect as he expertly rolled first one then the other between thumb and forefinger. My body started the sex buzz that heralded rough sex coming my way. The clamps were reattached to my sore nipples.

My mouth dropped open to mouth a silent scream as he pulled and toyed with them, his hands pushed me lower towards his cock. It had a heady smell, rich, ripe crusty with smegma, ripe like a real men's cock should be.

He held me off it. "Beg for cop cock, boy, beg like the cockhound you are. Beg me to feed my monster down that throat of yours!"

One hand plastered to my forehead keep me away from his cock; while I mouthed the words he wanted to hear. "Please, Officer Jack, I need your cop cock. I have been very bad and only your cop cock can teach me a lesson. Please Sir make me suck it, please Sir!"

While I was begging to service his cock, I was totally unaware that he had pulled out his gun, had cocked back the trigger till he tilted my head and forced the gun deep into my mouth, silencing my begging. I choked in fear, gagged as he pushed his gun deep into my throat, moved it this way and that till he got most of his gun into my mouth.

"Suck on it bitch! Show me how you are going to make my cock feel good in that hole of yours! Work that tongue around the barrel, suck it down that cumsucking throat of yours bitch, or I'll just pull the trigger and be done with you now!"

I had no choice. I made love to his gun and his trigger finger till I felt him let off the cocked trigger and he slowly withdrew.

Slack-jawed, scared witless, I all but had pissed my pants while I sucked on his metallic blue cock and made it feel good, as I know I could. It seemed to please Officer Jack, his gun was removed and his cock was shoved roughly down my throat, which was followed by the order, "Lick my cock clean, pussy!"

My tongue rolled around the base of his cock, licking his balls and slowly ascending the hard veined shaft till I found a pocket of dried smegma which I tongued clean. God, Officer Jack's cock was wonderful! I climbed to my knees as he plunged his cock into my face, wanting him into me like I had never done for another. Jack would be my rescuer if I won him over to my side by making him and his cock happy. I was doing just fine till he rose, pulling his cock from my hungry hole as he stepped away. Like a dog in heat, my head followed that cock. I needed it badly! He stepped beyond where I was kneeling and I crawled after him. He slammed the passenger door, walked towards me, pinning me between him and the car.

His hand shot out and slammed my face with an open-faced slap. "Open that hole, pussy!"

My mouth dropped open. He planted his legs on either side of mine. His hands took my head between them and he held my face in place. His cock pushed past my split lip, past my teeth, pinning my tongue to the floor of my mouth as he did his damnedest to force his cock down my throat. His hips thrust forward as he leaned his body weight into his cock, forcing it to go deep into my windpipe. There, helpless, gagging on cock, starving for oxygen with his groin pressing my head into the cruiser door, I began to loose consciousness. Without any advance warning his cock withdrew, only to be slammed back deep into my throat. Again he waited until I was loosing consciousness, then thrust his hips forward forcing more of his cock deep down into my windpipe cutting off any air. He waited as I started struggling, pulled out, giving me a few seconds to inhale before he slammed that cock back into the depths of my throat. He took his time, repeating each step, making me struggle to accept his cock as he worked it deeper into my throat with each thrust till I became oblivious. Then he set up a pace that had my head bouncing between his cock and the hard surface of the door.

It was a brutal face fuck that, if I survived I knew I did not want repeated anytime soon. He rode my face till I became slack-jawed from oxygen deprivation; he rode it till he was damn sure and ready to cum. When he did, he forced his cock deep into my throat, inched it deeper and blew a load that just keep coming and coming. He withdrew his cock slowly, laughing sadistically when he felt my body go limp. His fist slammed into my gut, which forced enough air past my cumfilled throat, so I could suck in some air and swallow.

The bastard pried open my mouth, replaced his cock, soft as it was deep into my mouth and began to piss, cautioning me not to get a drop on his uniform. I was amazed that I got that load of piss down my burning throat, which felt like it was raw, and on fire from his cock.

Once finished, he pulled his cock back into his pants, zipped up, pulled out another cigarette, and leaned back on the car thinking as he smoked his butt. He thought in silence, rubbing his cock on occasion till his cigarette was finished; that he ground into dust beneath his boot.

I did not see it coming as his hand slammed into my chin. While I was stunned, he lowered himself to my level, grabbed my chin and started laughing, "Hot damn, and boy, that pussy of yours is a fucking gold mine! Sweet Jesus, can you suck cock! Maybe I can talk to the Judge get him to understand how nice it would be to have you do a few years of community service instead of sending you to the state prison. Hot fucking damn, boy, I can make me a fucking fortune off that mouth of yours, and I will, too!"

He pulled me up by my tit clamps, opened the back door and literally tossed my ass into the back seat before slamming the door. As he got into the driver's seat, he was speaking out loud to himself. "I can't wait to tell the chief what we got here. Shit, boy, the menfolk in this area will be lined up around the block to get at those pussy lips of yours. I wonder, if your mouth is that hot, if your ass is doubly as good. Is that the real reason you got that huge plug in your bung hole?"

His laughter filled my veins with cold water. My knight in shining armor rusted before my eyes. What I had just given to Officer Jack and what he was planning to do to me soon just added one more lump of coal on my scales of injustice by the United States Justice system. The past three months had been hell! I was now late for Hunter's rendezvous and would probably never see him again. A bomb went off in my head, I blew a gasket and I began cursing Officer Jack as if he was a whore.

Calmly he reached into the glove compartment, pulled out something that was short and black, stopped the car, hopped out and keyed open the door closest to my head. He jerked the door open pulled my yelling and screaming body out of the car. His first swing collided with my nuts; I went down hard, vomiting. While I was down on the ground, his arms made many blows connect with my body. I heard ribs crack, felt his boot slam into my stomach, felt the crunch as boots made fast work with a bound captive, then the lights went out and I lost consciousness.

Chapter 2

You can bear anything if it isn't your own fault –

Katherine Gerould

I awoke to the worst hangover headache I ever had. Then I remembered I had not been out drinking, but was beaten up by Officer Jack. Fuck! My head hurt, just turning it from one side to the other to see where I was made my stomach think it would be nice to vomit. By will alone I forced the vomit back down into my stomach, I would have none of that here. Opening my eyes only gave me blurred foggy vision. But by the smell of my new location I knew I would not like what I would see once my eyes cleared. Eventually, they did clear and I was right. I had entered hell! I was bound down to an army issue metal cot. My hands and arms were secured to the front legs and by the way my legs felt they were bound to the feet of the cot. Struggling got me nothing more than a shout from someone watching me.

"Hey, Chief, the faggot's awake!"

A door opened and I heard booted feet approaching. From my vantage point, the jail cell was filthy; it smelled of piss, shit, and fresh vomit (mine); it was below the cot upon which I was bound. Thank God, I was not bound on the dirty soiled, overly used mattress that was tossed on the floor when they cleared this cot for my occupation. It looked as if it crawled with lice and god knows what other diseases. Being shackled spread eagle by the police in a stinky jail was just one more weight tipping the scale in Hunter's favor. The past three months had been a trip through hell as one security after another was ripped from beneath me.

I thought back to losing my position at the 9th Avenue Clinic. It would have been bad enough had the inquiry remained private. Things got totally blown out of proportion when a reporter did an expose on the rampant use of Tina in the Bay area. All I did was write a few prescriptions for some recreational drugs that fisters liked to use, hell, I only did it once or twice. I had been a good LPN! No one would loan me any money for my defense; even those bastards who got the scripts turned their backs on me. Those that I thought were my friends turned out to be something other. I called Hunter in my desperation, he sent me bus fare; instead, I used the money for food and a good drunk. When I sobered up I realized what I had to do, I went to Hunter for help. Instead of cash, he gave me a suitcase, a one-way ticket by bus back to sweet Master and 45 days to return to him. Even that, I fucked up! Instead, my worst nightmare and darkest fantasy was happening. All due to my own foolish stupidity.

The door to my cell was keyed open, then shut. Boots stepped around my cot while dragging a wooden chair. They stopped, he sat and he began, "Damn, boy, you stink! What the fuck did you do to poor old Jack to get beaten up this badly?" He grabbed a handful of my hair to lift my face from the metal cot. "Shit boy! You're worse for the wear, those bruises and busted lips will take some time to heal."

Damn him, he laughed at my situation and how badly my face must have looked. When he lifted my head he let out a long slow whistle as if in appreciation for what Jack had done to my face. I couldn't see it but I knew just how it felt.

I tried to mumble an answer between split and swollen lips, but all I heard was a weak voice asking when I would get my one phone call. Who would I call? Hadn't Hunter said that if I didn't arrive on time not to call him, that I would be dead to him for all time? Why was this happening to me, I cried silently to myself. My tears must have been taken for a sign of submission to the Sheriff because he began questioning me almost as rapidly as my tears fell to the floor.

One moment my head was upraised looking at the troll of a sheriff through bloodshot eyes, and the next moment he dropped my head like it was a hot potato. It slammed back into the metal cot, reawakening every sore spot on my face. Then he began talking to me quietly. "Did you have a nice nap, boy? Good, good. What do you have to say for yourself boy? Who are you working for, why are you bringing drugs into my county, who hired you to be his mule? Was it this man you call Hunter, is he linked up to this? Talk to me, boy!

"Jack has been out front bragging to all the cops in this area just how good you can work your throat around a man's cock! He has plans to rent out that hole and I just might let him if I don't get me some answers. Hell, boy, he likes you. I just might let him soften you up some more. Are you ready to help me get those answers, boy?"

Weakly, I nodded my head yes. I wanted to help him understand what was going on. "Why am I being kept tied this way, Sheriff? I can't run away. Especially while I'm in this cell."

His low chuckle gave me reason to worry. "Being a combative prisoner, we don't want you hurting yourself none. Besides, boy, the charges against you are pretty serious; threatening a police officer, carrying a concealed weapon, being a confirmed drug dealer, handling drug paraphernalia, self-endangerment and being a cocksucking faggot! Reason enough to make me think it's best to keep you just as you are; bound till you begin to help me find some answers."

Clearing my throat, I grunted. "Sheriff, all those charges are trumped up and you know you can't make any of them stick. When can I make my phone call?"

"Boy, did Jack's slap-jack scramble your brains? You're in my turf! I am the law here! Hell, boy, the judge that will be hearing your case is my first cousin. Who do you think he'll believe? You're mine until I decide that you can go your way…and if that time comes I will gladly hold your leash and use my boots to get you moving!"

"Sheriff, I really need to take a shit, when can I get that chance?"

"You know, boy, shit in your drawers. You aren't getting off that cot till I have answers!"

He jerked my head back up by a handful of hair. He lowered his piggy shaped face till it seemed to be inches from mine. God how he stank, chewing tobacco juice had stained the corners of his mouth brown and extra juice was running down his face as he spoke to me. His face turned a bright red, then he opened his mouth and sprayed me with his foul juices as he screamed at me, "We found a stash of pills in your car when we tore your fucking car apart. We found a few bags of white powder which are being checked right now by the state boys. So you see, boy, your ass is in the wringer and I am in control of the handle. Talk to me now, or I'll allow Jack and his boys to have that visit."

What drugs was he talking about? I had a bag of vitamins and a bag of natural steroids that I put into a plastic bag instead of keeping in that huge container. I had no drugs; unless they were planted. He watched my face like a hawk, measuring his words for their greatest effect; each statement was like being slammed in the gut. If this was his attempt to get me confused he was doing a damn fine job.

"Don't think me a fool, boy. I may look like a redneck to you, but it's all a disguise. Who is this Master Hunter you've been writing? Nice letters, I might add. Loved the part about you craving his cock inside you, how you wanted him to string you up and beat you senseless and how you craved to bury your tongue into his ass! Gawd, boy! I got a hard cock that will make Master Hunter's pale in comparison. Those letters got my cock so hard, he has been begging for boy butt since I first saw that ass of yours. I will have it, one way or another. Before I'm finished with you, I guarantee you boy, you will beg me to fuck you senseless!" He laughed at his sick jokes while tears ran down my face in fear of what was to come from this brutal bastard.

My head collided with the cot once again as he rose from his chair and began pacing around my bound and helpless form. His fat sausage-like fingers grabbed my butt and found the plug; together they pushed it deeper into my hole till I cried out. More of his deep sadistic laughter filled my ears. Never in all my life had I felt so much revulsion from one man's touch as I did with that pig of a sheriff. Pockmarked fat face, triple chins, huge gut that overlapped his belt, meaty sausage-like fingers and hands, baggy dirty stained pants and those disgusting tobacco stains all over his shirt, mouth and chins. What a troll!

He was talking again. "You sure do have a pretty butt on you boy. Does Master Hunter like fucking that bubble butt of yours or does he like paddling it bright red before he climbs into that saddle and rides it hard? I take it from your letters that this man Hunter loves fucking your face and forcing you to rim his asshole too. Bet you love that, don't cha, boy? Yeah, just as I thought, you love burying your face and tongue into his butt. Tell me; do you do it willingly or does he force you to do his bidding? If he forces you, I can keep you safe from him. Believe me boy, if you don't start answering my questions, I can fix it that no one will want you beside me. No matter how badly you are beaten up, your Pappy will always take you home and to bed."

"Chief," someone called down the corridor, "there's a phone call for you. It's the state boys with the results from those drugs you sent Jack with!"

"Boy, think about what I've said. I'll be back to get some answers!"

His way of departing my cell was to brutally kick out, slamming my cot against the wall. The door of the cell slammed shut and he walked down the corridor bellowing to who ever disturbed him. "I told you assholes to leave me alone when I'm with the kid, goddamn it!"

While he was gone, I did some serious soul searching. I realized I knew absolutely nothing about Master Hunter with the exception that he was a damn fine lay, knew how to make me beg in four colors and how to make me do things I did not know I could do - and enjoy every fucking moment with him. Many times I was left in bondage while he attended to matters on the farm; but to what matters I had no clue. One day I did see a huge delivery of hydroponics equipment, which was an experimental way to grow plants in a gel, but I did not know how or for what he used them. It was not my concern; I knew that if it were, he would have told me. Did he grow pot for resale? Was he the dealer they were saying he was or was that just a way to keep me confused? Who was Hunter? Why did he know so many people at these huge leather events? Everyone seemed to speak of him with high regard. What had he done within the leather community that set him apart from all the other leathermen? My mind turned the sheriff's questions one way, then another. I kept at myself, working at what I did not know about Hunter till I was lost in my own confusion. God, how I hurt that first night I was bound in that cell!

I must have slept, as I awoke with a start. Something had cued me that I was no longer alone in my little cell. A baton striking my butt informed me I was correct and I bellowed out in shock and dismay that they were on me again.

"Glad to see you had another nice nap. Hope you got some answers for me, because I have some for you, shithead! Let's start again, shall we boy?" He sat down in his chair across from me with a clipboard and a huge mug of fresh coffee. He took a long sip from the coffee, sighed and sat it down on the floor. Its aroma was heavenly. "Ok, let's start at the beginning. Who is this Master Hunter you have been writing to, boy? Where does he get his money? Drugs, isn't it, boy?"

With a voice hoarse from too many screams and too little fluids, I creaked as I spoke. "Honestly, sheriff, I don't know a thing about who Master Hunter is or where he gets his money or if he sells drugs. All I had in those bags was vitamins, no illegal drugs. All that I know about Hunter is that he owns and runs a big farm. That he and his men work the fields daily. That he lives somewhere near New Market and I was to have met with him Tuesday afternoon at 3 o'clock at the bus stop."

He took another long sip on his coffee, listened quietly to what I had to say and countered with, "I know a lot about Hunter, boy. We haven't been able to pin a damn thing on him; he's a slippery son of a bitch, that one is. Help us and I can see to it that you are taken real good care of; he will do nothing to you. I know he's a slave runner and that he belongs to a secret underground society and belongs to something known as the Castle. Hunter even boasts of being a Shield, whatever that means. Tell me, boy, was he the one you took the rap for when you were caught selling prescriptions? See, I know you were a drug dealer in Norfolk."

"Sheriff, I honestly don't know a thing about Hunter. I just realized I know nothing about him, absolutely nothing. Please believe me, Sheriff!"

The sheriff rose from his chair so rapidly he spilled his coffee on the floor. He started screaming, "You're lying for that son of a bitch, boy! I'll teach you not to fuck around with me!"

He grabbed my chin, pinched off my nose and drew real close, watching my face as I struggled to fight for air. When he released my mouth it flew open and, in that millisecond, he spit one big glob of his tobacco juice right down my throat. No sooner did the juice hit my mouth, he forced it closed. He held it fast with his pudgy paws until the gagging and retching began. He stood up, removed his hands and watched as I went into dry heaves, trying to vomit up his tobacco juice and anything else left in my stomach. He patted my ass as he departed, his laughter hanging in the air. The door clanged shut and I heard him as he walked down the dark corridor barking his final threat; "I will have my answers one way or another, boy!"

I thought I was alone, when the gorge rose to fill my mouth and nose before it spilled out onto the floor. Tears were streaming down my face again out of fear and frustration. Will this nightmare never end? The pooling vomit lay right under my cot, its stink only added to the present smell of the jail. His laughter reached out to me and drove the point home. I was never as alone as I was in that cell. His parting words give me reason for increased fear, leering "No one will want that mouth or ass of yours after Officer Jack and his friends get finished with the interrogation that they have planned for you tonight; except, me. I like sloppy seconds. Or thirds!"

I lay there waiting, thinking of just how fucked I was. I had no one to turn to for help; by now Hunter had given up on me. Had I not failed to arrive by bus to at the appointed time? He would not have known to seek out my red Corvette, or to look at the local cop shop for my whereabouts. He probably thinks I had taken his bus ticket and run off with it. Or worse yet, drunk myself into a stupor.

It looked as if they had only one cell in this one horse town of a jail, and I was the only occupant. Lucky me! There were sawhorses with planking in one corridor and a heavy canvas sheet that covered another corridor. I wondered what was being built behind that sheet; a gallows for the next drug dealer?

I began yelling to the sheriff, "When do I get to make my phone call?" But no one paid me any attention. What the sheriff had said about just shitting where I lay? That I was not getting off that cot any time soon? I hated the thought of ruining my leathers, but I just could not hold it any longer. I thought maybe I could just let off a little stream to lessen the hurt till I could get to the john; but my body had other ideas as a gentle piss turned into a raging stream. It felt interesting to have the warm body piss saturate and drip from my leathered crotch. Now I could better understand the pleasure some men have when they get pissed on or being forced to piss on themselves. The piss traveled down my legs, then pooled around my waist before it dripped to the floor to mingle with my vomit. I had my own private cesspool forming below me.

Then the door down at the end of the corridor opened. I heard not one voice, but many coming my way. All my fears returned when they entered my little cell. I was shaking in fear, cold and uncertain as to what they were planning for my interrogation. The men stood around me, looking at me, commenting about my piss and vomit on the floor. Each of them was drinking a beer as if it was boy's night out on the town and I was just a sideshow. The men continued to tease each other, play with their crotches until Jack make an announcement that calmed their actions and scared the fuck out of me.

"Chief has gone home for the night. He said we could play with him some to get his tongue loosened up."

Another deep male voice spoke near the front of my cot, "Gawd, would you look at that mess he has made under his cot. Looks like Chief gave him a kiss or two and he didn't like it." The room echoed with their laughter.

"Damn boys, looks like I am going to have to get out the hose to clean up that mess before we can play with him. Or better yet, how many of you boys need to take a piss right now? Will you help me wash out the piggy's cage?"

By the grunts that came from the men poised around me, they were more than willing to help Jack clean off the floor.

"Hey, Rafferty, did you bring that chin strap? Here boys, you two hold this rope. One of you lift his head while I get the chin strap under his chin and when I say pull, both of you pull those ropes and tie them to the end of the cot. This will hold his head upright and give us all a proper target."

Jack lifted my head, positioned the strap and my head was bent back in a rigid curve before it was bound into place. I could barely shift my head left to right; lowering it was impossible. Jack looked down on me, patted my face and said, "That looks better pussy, lots better." Standing up to look at his men, he ordered "All right men, step up, haul out your cocks and, on command, fire at will! I want to see every inch of this pig's body soaked in real men's piss. Hose him down, boys!"

Officer Jack stood right in front of my face, hauled out his cock and aimed the head right at my face. The stream of hot piss hit me in the forehead, was played across my face, down over my lips and back up to soak my hair. The other men were playing their hose streams across my leather-covered body. God, how they laughed as they pissed! My handsome leather outfit could never be worn again after this pissing; I knew it would hold too many bad memories. When everyone finished, it was suggested that they go for another round of beers and let me soak. As they were leaving the cell, the ropes were suddenly cut and my face slammed into the springs, again the lights went out for me.

I woke with a start, something smelling like rotten eggs was shoved under my nose. My eyes burned and made my heart raced as if I was running a hundred yard dash. Officer Jack and another cop were studying me.

"See, I told you those poppers would do the trick, Jack, I told you they would." The new speaker was a motorcycle cop - or at least that was how he was dressed. He turned to an orange tackle box and retrieved another snap capsule when my eyes fluttered open.

The motorcycle cop continued talking to Jack, "Looks like you captured us a nice fuckable piece of meat there, Jack. What's your Pappy's plan of action? When do I get to snuff him, I do love a good snuff-fuck. Best to ride them to their last breath. Man, I am so horny for this hot boy butt, I could ride it for days!"

"Damn it, Carl," snapped Officer Jack, "Pappy says he needs him to testify against Hunter. As if it will do Pappy any good. Seeing as Hunter pretty much owns the whole town with exception of the police department. Still, Pappy says, I got to keep him alive so the judge can see him. So, no snuff-fuck tonight Carl."

Carl was speaking to Jack, "Let's see what he's hiding under them piss soaked leathers of his. He looks hot the way they cling to his body. Hot and sweet, just ripe for the plucking."

"Reach into that tackle box of yours, Jack, and hand me one of those cuts-anything scissors you're always boasting about. On second thought, drag out two pair. We can make it a game to see who can cut them leathers into the smallest pieces." Carl laughed at his private joke while Jack did as he was told.

I found my voice when they approached, both with shit eating grins plastered across their faces. "Please, Sirs, don't cut off my leathers, let me peel them off for you. Please, Sir, I will do anything for you, just don't cut them off!"

Both men laughed at the way my voice cracked while I was begging. "Listen to him, he wants us to release him so he can strip and probably try to run. Ain't no way, pussy. You're not coming off that cot any time soon," chuckled Carl as he winked to Jack.

Both men took positions on either side of my body. Each of them took turns cutting off sections of my beautiful handmade custom leather titleholder uniform. My leather pride vest was first to be hacked to death. They sliced it up my spine and across my shoulders, two hands grabbed a side each, and the vest was history, torn and thrown on the floor. These butchers transformed my hard won leather uniform into nothing more than scraps of leather on their nasty floor. I began to bawl like a baby as these dimwitted bastards cut more of my leather into pieces. My shirt was cut up the arms, across the shoulders and down the spine before they ripped it from underneath me. Each piece was first ripped from my body and tossed to the floor where I could see the tatters of my world class uniform.

"Would you look at that Jack? Look there, the baby's crying! What a fucking fool he must feel like as we cut off his hides? Shame we couldn't use the video recorder to tape this session, I bet we could sell the breaking of this fake to his adoring audience.

Yeah, boy, I read your letters and looked at that pretty scrap book of yours. You sure did think highly of yourself. Kind of a shame, 'cause after Jack and I have turned you out there ain't no man - especially Hunter – who'll want your busted up hide no more. You really are a dumb fuck, boy! Real dumb!"

My titleholder belt was jerked from around my waist and Officer Jack laid claim to it, saying it would fit well into his eagle collection. Carl and Jack took their fucking sweet time cutting off my leather pants. First they exposed my ass cheeks, cutting the seat right out of my pants. Then they pawed at my buns, slapped them some and one even licked them before stating they tasted mighty fine. My legs were split down and pulled out from under my body one at a time. They took great pride into cutting those into pieces, allowing each shred to fall before my eyes. Together they hacked their way, first with the scissors, and then with a knife to cut through my waistband. Another piece of leather joined the heap.

One of them let out a loud catcall whistle. "Would you look at that huge plug in his ass! Christ almighty, I've never seen one that big shoved into a hole that small. Bet that thing has to hurt you, doesn't it, boy? Look how it's chained into his ass! He must have one fine piece of tail there - and someone didn't want anyone playing with his property. Damn!"

"Jack, Pappy has bolt cutters in his office. Go fetch them so we can get this plug out of him and see if he has any drugs hidden up that hole. While you're gone I'll get prepared for a cavity search."

Carl must have been the top ranking officer in the cell the way Jack jumped at whenever Carl spoke. Or was I reading more into their relationship? Jack returned, panting from the short dash up the hallway. He held the chain while Carl cut and removed the chain slowly, a section at a time as if it was connected to a bomb.

I brooded about Hunter while those two morons hacked the chain between my asscrack. Hunter had started my butt training by making me wear a butt plug while I was with him 24/7. He liked having me beg him to take a shit, he liked watching me humiliate myself and he liked having that control over me. It seriously cranked his knot into overdrive to listen to me beg. However, I had grown used to having that full feeling that only a plug can give a body. It was comforting and very secure to one whose world had been turned upside down due to too much turmoil. So I wore the plug whenever I could, even while at home alone. For my birthday, Hunter had given me a whole set of plugs ranging from tiny pinkie sized plugs up to Oh-My-God plugs. I had been working on stretching my hole for Hunter. He had once said that nobody has ever been able to take his hand or arm and he wanted one of his slaves to be just that - his glove. I wanted him to own my soul with his fist plowing my ass. I remembered, as I dressed for my road trip, how I wanted to fit that last plug into my hole and surprise him when I was undressed by offering him my well plugged ass. Instead, these bozos would get the spoils of my stupidity.

I screamed from the depths of my soul when these baboons in uniforms pulled the huge plug out of my sore butt. I screamed not so much from the pain as I did from the emptiness that would grow in me with the absence of Hunter in my life. I screamed because no one was at fault except my ego and me.

"Fuck, Jack, that sound brings back memories! I do love to hear a man scream out in pain and fear of the unknown, don't you, buddy?" Carl laughed quietly to himself as he studied the size of the plug that had been too long in my hole. "Jack, look into the kit and give me a pair of rubber gloves those in the paper wrappers, one of those small flashlights and that thing that looks like a duck bill."

Rubber gloves snapped over his hand, Carl straddled and sat down on my legs. He ordered Jack to pry open my ass cheeks with his hands on the outside while he worked his hand slowly inside to see if there was any contraband hidden within what could have possibly been a mule. Carl announced to the room that he felt nothing out of place, meaning no balloons filled with heroin or Tina were shoved up my butt. I could have told them that, but they weren't listening to a prisoner.

"Break time," Carl proclaimed and ordered Jack to go fetch them a cold one from Pappy's refrigerator and bring back a bottle of cold water for the prisoner. I could have kissed that man's boots when he said that till my thoughts froze midway, "He'll scream better if his throat is wet!" Carl sat down in Pappy's chair, hiked up one boot and placed it on my cot in what would have been kissing distance if I was so inclined, and I wasn't.

Carl was a handsome man, neither he nor Jack would I have tossed out of bed had we been under different circumstances. Where Jack was dark, Carl was light. Sandy blonde hair, clean-shaven, steel-like features of the true Aryan bloodline with cold, blue, eyes. He was wearing a black and blue uniform, knee high Dehner's, short leather wrist length gloves and a huge black belt that held numerous leather pouches for ammo; as well as cuffs and a baton clip. His pant legs seemed to flow from boot to leg up to heavily muscled thighs, the tunic he was unbuttoning as he sat there watching me watch him opened to reveal a nice tight hairless chest with beautiful saucer like nipples. He almost had angelic features if it wasn't for the horn sticking out of the fly in his pants. Damn, his cock was almost as handsome as was he. Big, thick, mushroom shaped head, heavy veining down the shaft, with the girth at least six inches or more by the way his hand wrapped around while he was stroking it.

He caught me watching him stroke his cock and winked. He fucking winked at me as if to say things would be alright then Jack took that time to return to the cell with beers for them and water for me.

Jack laughed, seeing him playing with his cock. "Put that thing away Carl, first we use wooden sticks before you can use that fleshy one of yours, he'll split better that way and spill his beans for Pappy."

They made me watch as they slowly drank their beers. The sweat that beaded up on the can would run like rivlets down the side and drop to the floor. I must have licked my lips a thousand times while they were drinking in silence. When they were almost finished with their beers, Carl cracked open my jar of water, took a big long gulp and put it down beside me. He hauled out his cock, lifted the jar and placed his cock just over the edge of the jar and let his piss flow into that water, all the time starring down at me. Once he was finished, he looked at me and chuckled, "Thirsty boy?"

I nodded my head yes, being unable to speak clearly. He put the glass jar up to my lips and slowly fed the contents into my mouth. At that point, I didn't care if it had been horse piss; I needed fluids badly so I drank my fill. Jack giggled like a schoolkid while I was drinking Carl's piss till Carl backhanded him into silence.

"You stupid fuck, Jack. If you take care of your prisoners they'll take care of you. This boy has to testify against Hunter, we want him kept alive till that time. Break time is over," announced Carl. "Let's start with towels. Remember to soak one towel and wring it out a little before you put the second towel around the first. The weight of the first towel will create more pain and deeper bruising, which won't show up for a few days. We want him to look good for his appearance before the judge."

Carl and Jack took opposing positions and began to beat on my back. At first, it felt like a beginner using a heavy flogger for the first time, then all too quickly it became brutal! I wasn't given time to adjust to each blow. It was a body numbing pummeling that I was receiving from those bastards and they laughed overhead insanely.

Carl spoke to Jack over my body while they were beating me. "I was reading his last letter to Hunter. We wouldn't be having this much fun if the boy could follow orders. Can you believe Hunter detailed to this piece of shit just what to bring and when to arrive and even gave him a ticket for the trip and this fuck up still couldn't get it right?"

I tried biting my tongue, then my lips, to maintain silence not wanting to give them any pleasure. But eventually I broke and screamed and begged them to stop. They didn't until I was a blubbering idiot!

The two men walked away from me, Carl sat in the chair while Jack had to sit on the floor, and they opened two more beers and drank them deeply. I was a mass of hurt! Breathing came in short gasps like I had been running uphill for too long. I was sweating, oblivious to the world around me. Little did I realize till I heard that familiar weak voice that I was begging for more water. Jack stood up, picked up a slop bucket and tossed the contents of the nasty bucket over my bruised body; I had my drink and more!

"Hey, shit head! Yeah you, cock sucker! Hey, boy, I am talking to you! Look at me, boy!" I tried to raise my head. Instead Carl propped his huge boot beneath my chin so that I could see Jack speaking to me. "You're a regular gold mine boy! Once I told everyone how good a blowjob you gave me alongside that public road, everyone wanted to ride that face. Carl and me sold fifty tickets for that pussy of yours at $20 a pop! Are you ready to start earning your keep, pussyboy, or must we keep beating you till you are? Which is it, boy?"

I only heard a part of what Jack was mumbling. I looked at Carl but spoke to Jack, "Fuck you, asshole!"

Carl's laughter filled my soul with dread, "I hoped you would say that, pussyboy. When you beg to suck those cocks, I'll stop whipping your ass. Let's hope there's some meat on those handsome bones by the time we're in agreement that you're ready for dinner." Carl looked to Jack. "Help me readjust his feet. I want him welted from his shins to his chins!"

Both men worked as one, as they released one shackled foot, removed the boot and rebound the leg in rope before inserting it below the metal bar at the end of the cot, and binding them together securely. These men were a team; you could tell by the way they worked together for their common goal.

Carl dropped two-foot long garden hose chunks down before my face just before they went to work on my legs. Once done with my legs they retrieved the hoses and returned to their positions on either side of my body.

I heard only a low hum as the garden hose cut through the air before landing on my calves. Jesus, I thought I was experienced in pain by Hunter's hands, but nothing prepared me for what was slowly crawling up my body inch by cutting inch. I was being laced with angry red welts from my calves upwards. Each cut felt as if it took away chunks of skin, and lay in its place a fiery blood flecked space of pure pain. My screams started with the first blows, never stopping but gathering in intensity with each passing strike! I felt like a thermometer swelling and rising as heat was applied, and knew at any moment the mercury would blow out the top of my head. The fire in my body gained in strength as the calves gave way to the thighs, which gave way to my buttocks which fell before their assault to my mid back and up to my shoulders; they jumped over my head and finished off while beating my arms and hands.

They laid one welt upon the other as they climbed my body, pouring flame onto a body that had been locked in darkness of my own making. I felt as if my life was being beaten out of me and I knew as these bastards laughed and swung those hoses that they could kill me this way! Their clubs were driving all my stubbornness out of me. I broke and begged them in a scratchy screaming voice to service their cocks if they would only stop beating my poor body.

I felt lost, confused. Somehow I found myself on the floor, my shoulders, ass and legs a living hell! I struggled to lift my torso off the ground but instead I rolled over onto my side. Officer Jack and Carl were standing together, laughing about what I was going to do for them. Periodically, I would mouth off to them, resulting in another beating. Each time they made me into their drum; beating me with their mallets till my tight voice drummed out their song. From my position I could look up Officer Carl's boots to catch a glimpse of my tormentors. I was unbound, held in place only by Officer Carl's boot planted on my chest. As I lay there, I saw Officer Carl take Jack's face between his gloved hands, pull Jack's face towards his and they kissed. This was not the kiss of two straight men sharing a common bond but a long fevered kiss of two men who were lovers. Was this just another whip-induced hallucination or something played out for my benefit?

In the blink of an eye it seemed as if scenes unfolded around me. First they were sharing a hard kiss; blink, then Carl is sitting and shirtless Jack is kneeling before him. Carl drinking a beer while Jack has his ass upraised and his face down sucking at beer being spilled down the shaft of Carl's black motorcycle boots. Like a dog, Jack was lapping at the beer that Carl poured down one of his boot shafts. Carl caught me watching them, winked again, lifted his boot from my chest and spilled some beer down it as if to invite me to his boot for libations.

Blink, blink, I was lapping like Jack at the puddle of beer gathering around Carl's big black motorcycle boot while Carl sucked on a huge black stogie. The fresh smell of the beer and his boots helped me revive more quickly than I would have been able to do on my own. I don't remember how I got to his boot. All I do remember is how great it all tasted. How wet the beer was on my parched tongue and how it bit into the cuts in my lips. It was all good. How good the beer looked as it cascaded down that black boot shaft to collect in a puddle around the boot heel and how greedily I sucked that nasty concrete for every drop I could find. Even to the point of lifting Carl's boot and sucking the moisture from under his boots before I went to work licking them clean of any beer residue. I loved it! I didn't think of how it might look, only that the beer was helping me revive and how good it felt to suck it off Officer Carl's boots!

Carl stood, using the toe of his boot to roll me onto my stomach. He reached down, took my arms in his hands and elevated them. Jack knitted my elbows together with rope. Pulling upwards, Carl lifted me to my knees and, using my arms, steered me crawling across the small cell.

Together they flipped me onto my bruised back, bound with my head touching the steel bars, which left my elbows supporting the weight of my torso. More rope was wrapped around each ankle before they walked in opposite directions, wrapped the excess rope around the bars and pulled my legs open wide and knotted the rope. My body was a rhapsody of pains.

Carl walked up, straddled my torso and squatted down till he sat on me. My dazed eyes turned to look at him and I saw in his mirrored shades, my own image looking back at me. He spoke over his shoulder to Jack, "Damn if you weren't right, Jack! This boy is a leather freak; he's probably liked everything we've done to him. Hell, he's fucking loved it, look how hard his cock has gotten while I've been sitting here."

Who wouldn't be happy as a pig in heat with a hot motorcycle cop straddling your hips, playing with your cock and feeling his hardening cock locked within his black uniform breeches and boots? I was turned on by Officer Carl's close presence. Yes, they had just brutalized me but it had been for my own good - or so I rationalized. Hadn't I failed to answer any questions? So why did I feel so confused, I wanted Carl to hurt me more; I knew I needed whatever he was going to do to me. I was wrong, my thinking was wrong. I was a total fuck up! Besides, any moment now I would wake up and find myself asleep in my bed at home, this being nothing but a hard-on dream.

Carl began by gradually slapping my face harder and harder while screaming, "Loosen up them jaws, pussyboy! Dinner will soon be served, and it's liquid. You'll learn to love it after tonight's activities, I guarantee!"

Blink, blink, Jack passed my titleholder belt into Carl's hands. "Make him kiss the belt. That'll change his way of thinking and help him get proper attitude."

My belt was pressed hard against my cracked and split lips. "Kiss your belt, cock sucker. Kiss every inch of it. That's a good boy, do it for Officer Carl." Carl smashed the hexagon studs into my lips before he handed it back to Jack. "I bet if this belt could talk it would tell an interesting story. How many boys have felt this on their backsides, cock sucker? Just how many have you bloodied with this belt?"

What he just said registered on me and again I found that weak voice speaking where once had been a strong powerful commanding voice. "Please, Sir," I cried, "I'll do anything you two want, just don't beat me any more, please, Sir, please!"

"God, Jack listen to him whine, he's actually begging you not to beat him no more. What you say Jack, are you going to stop this beating?" Carl laughed.

"Fuck no! I got my orders! No can do, Carl. I was told to break this piece of shit. Break him hard. He has to be punished for fucking up; besides, the Chief will have my hide if he doesn't testify against Hunter. After a taste of his own belt I bet he will sing loud and clear!"

Jack went to work on the soft tissue between my inner thighs with that damn belt. It was weird, I could watch his arm swing down with my belt, feel it hit, even know it caused me lots of pain. But it was as if my pain centers no longer felt anything as they were already overloaded. All my attention was focused on Carl, who was removing the cellophane from another cigar, spit slicking and then lighting it. I was transfixed as that cigar glowed a bright cherry red. With each suck to the opposite end, when he blew smoke in my direction I could not suck enough in to fill my lungs. That aroma smelled wholesome and spoke to my old self of manly men; hadn't my dad smoked an old stogie often enough?

Carl enjoyed his smoke while Jack worked up a bloody sweat beating the hell out of my inner thighs. Carl made me watch him as he sucked in a nice long draw on that cigar, held it in the cavity of his mouth before inhaling it, pausing a moment and exhaling the blue white smoke in my direction. I actually think my cock got harder as I watched Carl enjoying his cigar. "Open your mouth boy," he demanded.

Without so much as a moment to consider what I was doing, my jaw dropped open and my tongue slipped out, waiting, waiting as I drooled and watched his cigar go from brown tip to gray-white ash. With the flip of his gloved finger that ash hit my spit slick tongue, sizzled and was drawn back into my mouth in less than a second. "Swallow," came the command. Without a thought, I swallowed his salty ash from his cigar. Casually, as if he had all the time in the world, Carl would place that cigar shaped penis between his lips, draw on the cigar, the cherry head would glow bright reddish orange and the smoke would be sucked into his lungs before it was blown into my face. Whenever he needed to drop the ash, my tongue was waiting. When I was ordered, I would swallow his gift of hot ash. Slowly the cigar burned just like Jack was burning my open legs with my belt. Once again, Carl flipped the ashes but this time instead of replacing his cigar between his lips, he blew on the hot end, blew so I could feel the heat coming from his cigar. The cigar descended, coasting like a cherry-eyed monster over my heavily panting chest. Yes, I knew what he was going to do. He, like Jack, needed to punish me for yet another fuck up on my part. Someone had to be blamed for not paying attention to Hunter's orders; Hunter wasn't here so Carl did the job.

Another draw on the cigar, he pulled it from his clenched lips and a bridge of saliva formed from his lip to his cigar. He blew on the cherry orb, his hand descended, found his target and singed off all hairs around my right nipple before it coasted over and repeated the process around my left. I felt only a slow roasting sensation which grew in intensity the longer he held it in place. He laughed on some private joke, applied the hot tip to my right nipple and watched as the skin bubbled, blistered and I released the most god-awful scream as all the pounding of Jack's belt and Carl's cigar came rushing home! My scream was primordial from the deepest depths of my core and when it ended I was babbling stupidly and begging them to stop. My resolve broke as I underwent their agony!

This was not loveplay, this was abuse by Officers of the Court. These fucking policemen were going to beat me senseless till I gave them what they wanted; answers. That's when all of it hit me. Right then at that moment, I realized I was doomed! If I had only followed Hunter's orders and not second-guessed him, I would not be undergoing this rough treatment, but would be locked within his arms.

Jack and Carl helped to reposition me, I no longer cared. My legs were fed through the iron bars of the cell walls and locked in place by heavy leg irons around my ankles. Together, they lifted me and roped my bound elbows to the bars at my back, causing me to slump forward, my face at crotch level. I remember staring down at the floor, not caring, blank minded, not even wondering what was going to happen next.

Carl came up to me and slapped my face till he got my attention. When I looked up he winked, smiled, and ordered me to open my mouth and swallow. I was fed one beer at a time until I seemed to come to my senses. Jack walked out of the cell on an errand. One beer down my burning throat another popped open, callously another was used to pour over my head and face, his hand washing it down. A third was forced down my throat; any refusal to drink got either a slap or him holding my nose. Rapidly, I was fed a six-pack, the beer was all I had to drink or eat in a day, and it sent my head reeling with an alcohol buzz that would not stop. The room actually seemed to spin out of control as the alcohol daze took control over my senses.

Jack returned carrying that little suitcase that Hunter had given to me to fill. Carl greeted him, "What you got there, boy?"

"Hey, Carl, I found his scrap book while going through his belongs and some other shit that I just don't understand," replied Jack as he set down my suitcase. "That boy must have thought awfully high of himself by looking at this here scrap book of his. Damn! Almost all the pictures in the book are of asswipe there, strutting his stuff at beauty pageants and shit. Damn few pictures of him and friends. I wonder if he has any friends? Well, I can bet no one will miss him. That's for certain."

Carl laughed deeply before he replied, "Well Jack, Pappy has one hell of a new incentive plan to get new recruits to join his team. Add a tattoo to shithead that says Official Police Equipment, and he will make one hell of benefit package. What do you think about that Jack?"

Both men chuckled at their own thought.

Carl had been rummaging through my suitcase when he pulled out an old beaten up leather hood. "Here, Jack, put this on him, tight!"

Jack worked the leather hood over my head, pulled it in place and laced it tightly around my head.

"Wow! Jack, would you look at all these bits that go with that hood? Here, snap on this eyepatch and force this rubber cock in his mouth, strap it nice and tight. Let him get ready for what's coming his way," Carl's laughter was joined by Jack's heehaw braying that reminded me more of a jackass than a man.

The leather hood was almost as old as me, having purchased it just after my first contest, and the penis gag I had stolen from Hunter's bedside table after he used it on me one night. I had been talkative, wanted to chat the night away; whereas, he had a long day working alongside J.D. cutting down some trees. When I did not shut up after his repeated attempts to silence me, he rolled over, opened a drawer, pulled out the penis gag, forced it between my lips and strapped it tight. With my hands cuffed to the headboard there was no way to dislodge the gag and I had to endure it the whole night while he snored in my ear.

"Carl, that hood makes a change in him, makes him look less like a man and more like a thing," Jack was laughing again. "You know, Carl, I like it!"

"Shut the fuck up, Jack," Carl bellowed. He was growing tired of Jack's acts of stupidity, sneering "Go get the men that won first dibs to crack his cherry, and bring the next twenty or so men back here. It's time to start this bitch earning some money."

Their new nightmare began to unfold. I could have shit when I heard the clamor of men as they walked down the corridor towards my cell. What they had promised was about to begin and I was helpless to stop anything as men filed into my cell. Dear God, they were a horny sounding crowd.

Carl stepped forward, "Jack, hand me those fucking alligator clips. We got one more thing to do to that piece of meat before we put our peckers in its hole. Pull the gag, Jack."

Without much fanfare, Jack ripped off the blindfold and opened the buckle and tore out the penis gag. Carl stepped forward, handed the alligator clamps to Jack, and told him to get my nipples erect before he set the teeth to flesh. Carl stood to my side waiting, watching and seemed disappointed when I did not open my mouth to give voice to another pain. For reasons beyond me, this silence seemed to piss off Carl something awful.

"Jack, grab those clamps and roll them till shithead opens his mouth. Make him open that clap trap, do it for me boy, open wide!" Jack did as he was ordered, took my sore tits between his fingers and ground them into a bloody mess till I opened my mouth to scream. Carl jumped at that opportunity. His gloved fist pushed its way between my teeth, holding my mouth forcibly open. He inserted two black rubber wedges between my back teeth before removing his fist. My mouth remained open and no matter how I worked my tongue against them, I couldn't get them to budge. Bastards!

"Is it ready, well, is it?" A huge greasy looking man was fighting to the front of the line and calling to Carl as he drew past the men milling around my cell. By his looks, he could have been an outlaw biker. Dark smoldering eyes starred at me through filthy long hair and matted beard. He was covered in oil stained leathers that looked as if he lived in the damn things. He turned and I caught a glimpse at the colors he was wearing on back of his denim vest. I knew right then and there I was in for a seriously rough ride. His biker patch was from the Iron Skulls, an outlaw biker group known for being drug runners, extremely sadistic and on a mission to fuck the world. He looked like he could do it all by himself; he looked mean, real mean.

"Well, Jack, is it ready?" Jack just stood there nodding his head till Carl stepped forward.

"Hell, yeah, Bill, that pussy is as ready as it will ever be," Carl said as he backed away.

The bastard leaned down, grabbed my tit chain and lifted it watching me moan before he laughed, "I won the right to first fuck on this bitch, move back you fucking hicks, give me some fucking room!"

Bill's hand cupped my chin, tilting my head upwards as he looked down and spoke with Carl, "How did you find this pretty boy? It's not your normal bill of fare, now is it, Jack?"

While the biker was opening his belt, unbuttoning his fly and hauling out a sizeable piece of uncut meat, he was half listening to Carl. "This boy is one stupid fuck, Bill. He has done this all to himself. Yeah, hard to believe ain't it. We got a call this morning from a friend who tipped us off that this swinger was skipping town, Portsmouth, leaving friends holding some chips. They wanted him to learn the error of his way."

Bill was manhandling his cock as they talked, worked it slowly as it grew in length and girth to fill out his massive hand. He seemed as if he was thinking as he fisted his cock, helping it to grow to full extension before he spoke to Carl. "Tell ya what I will do Jack, Carl. When you are finished with your fun with him and gotten all you want from him, I will buy him from you guys. I could use him. I could sell his pussy to my brothers at the clubhouse or just keep him at home to take care of my needs. By the looks of his hard cock and your whip strokes he kind of likes this party. I know after I feed him a bootie-bomb his holes will want anything I can give them."

He talked while he played his cock's head around my torn and cracked lips. He seemed happy when my tongue took a stroll around his cockhead and actually tasted his pre cum without his order. He rested his cock on my lower lip, pushed his hips forward and eased his cock into my mouth. There, resting on my tongue, it lay as if waiting for some sign. Both of his big hands closed around my head and with another push he forced his cock into my gag zone, there he stopped, letting me choke on the size of his cock before he inched it forward. It seemed as if he wanted to see if I could deep throat his cock like Jack had been bragging; eventually I did. Slowly, he fed me the whole of his cock, my choking and spluttering only seemed to make his cock grow harder and press deeper into my throat until the room started spinning from lack of oxygen. Only on the verge of passing out did he withdraw his cock. Then he paused a moment so I could catch a gulp of air before his balls kissed my chin and he was deeply in.

Using my head and shoulders, he stood planted in one spot, rocking me back and forth on his cock. He seemed to work his cock in and out of my mouth for an hour or more before he increased his tempo. I was praying at that time that he was getting tired. I know I was exhausted by the time he began to pile drive his cock into my mouth. With his balls slapping my chin and the bellow of a raging bull he shot his load - and what a load! He filled my mouth full of his hot jism before his cock withdrew to the applause of all the others still waiting their turn.

Once the biker dismounted, I was transformed into an assembly line fuck. A large cock followed by a small cock which followed a pencil dick which followed a stubby which followed a shrivel dick. On and on they came as they walked up, made a deposit and departed. I have no idea how many men mounted and used my mouth. I was thankful for the hood which hid the tears and snot that ran from my eyes, nose and joined the cum dripping from my chin.

Throughout all the torture from Carl and Jack I had held an underlining hope that Hunter would rescue me. All hopes were trashed when the gang rape began. No one except biker Bill or Pappy would want me again, especially with all the diseases in the world today. No one was to blame for what was happening to me but myself. I was the stupid fuck-up that brought all of this on myself, I deserved these punishments, and I needed them.

Cum dripped from my open maul. At one point I screamed, which only excited the men still waiting for their turn. Hell, if I heard them correctly extra money was paid if Jack would help me scream when it came their turn. Jack was more than willing to give his paying clients their money's worth. Besides a quick pull down on my tit clamps made me both scream and more willing to please.

God, how I wanted to die there in that cell that night! To drown on their spent jism. I even prayed silently in my head for some form of a rescuer to come to my aid. Someone or something must have heard my silent prayer, because I heard a scuffle and then a familiar voice bellowing at the remaining men who were standing in line for seconds.

"What the fuck are you bastards doing to my prisoner?" The cock that was just about to cum in my mouth was jerked out before it shot its load as the bellowing voice drew closer to where I hung limply in my ropes. "Get your fucking asses away from my prisoner! Go the hell home! Where in the hell is Jack and Carl? Anybody know?" Bellowing transformed into a grumbling, "Wait till I get my hands on those two!"

Chief drove the men out of my cell as if he was herding a herd of cows, and then slammed the door of my cell. He literally walked the men out of the jail and returned a few minutes later.

I felt more than saw his presence when my shackled legs were released from the leg irons and the rope that held me to the bars was cut. I fell like a stone to the concrete floor and lay there as the cum pooled out of my open trap. Time stopped and the lights went out again.

When I revived, the sheriff was sitting a few feet away from me, watching. "Crawl your ass over here boy. I'm just too damn tired to come to you, boy. I'll take off your ropes and let you rest. Come on boy, move it!" He continued to talk more to the room than to me as I struggled to get my body to move in his general direction. Movement of any type was hard, this seemed to be the hardest thing I had ever done in my life.

"I'm just too damn tired for this bullshit, boy! Wait till I get a hold of Jack and Carl, both of them will suffer for leaving my prisoner alone with those crazy fools. The boys know my rules during an interrogation of this type; a cop in charge must always be on guard for any hanky panky. Damn those boys, they left without paying me my cut!"

Struggle! It was a major struggle to get my legs to push me forward towards the general direction of the sheriff. It took what seemed like days to get my body moving. Once I did get going, each kick of my legs seemed to push me closer to the old fart sitting in the chair across the room with his legs outstretched towards me. I felt like a snail crawling the distance and leaving a trail of slime in my passage. My laughter caught me unaware as I cackled at the absurdity of the situation. Nevertheless, I continued my slow journey as I dug into the depths of my core for energy to move - inch-by-inch - closer to my savior.

I got one more kick in before I slammed my head into the pavement. Pappy rose from his chair, knelt at my side with a grunt and crack of old bones hitting concrete. I felt the knife cut the ropes that had pinned my elbows across my back. Those arms dropped to my side, numb and lifeless. I felt him gather my hands in his; I thought he was going to pull me closer to him. Instead, he just cuffed them and let them drop. In his defense, he said "Can't have your arms regain too much circulation and you try to do me harm. You could take advantage of an old man like me and try to escape."

I chuckled at his sick humor, knowing that there was no way I could hurt him in my present state. He did, however, grab my ankles and drag me the short distance to his chair before he sat, lifting his feet and planting one boot on my butt. Interestingly, his boot resting on my butt gave me a sense of security. It was as if he was claiming me for himself. Odd, as I lay there regaining some strength, actually drawing it from him, I wondered about the gang rape. How many times had I jerked off just thinking about being gang raped in such a setting as this jail cell? Too many years of using the gang rape as a jack off fantasy almost made this evening's rape seem hot in my mind. It all changed when the men kept coming and coming and wouldn't stop, that I really started fearing for my life! I was totally helpless at the mercy of two sick sons of bitches that eventually left. Before, my street savvy kept me out of situations like what I was undergoing, why didn't they help me now, what was different?

A wonderful smell entered my desperate state, a smell that invoked memories of such goodness that I was disturbed by a scent in the air. The chair above me creaked as the Chief leaned forward and rubbed something cold around my still open and badly bruised lips. I licked those lips, finding a taste that was wholesome and sweet. I could not raise my head due to my exhaustion; however, I did extend my tongue silently begging for more juice. Drops of the precious liquid fell with a splashing blow on my lips before it dribbled into my raw cavern of a mouth. The acid bite, the very taste of the juice helped me revive quicker than if I would have been left alone to recover.

His boots shifted as I rolled to my side and curled inwards towards him. I found myself lying between my savior's short legs, the outline of his ample cock and balls trapped within folds of well-worn khaki pants. His gut filled my vision as my eyes searched higher till I saw the Chief's toothless grin smiling down at me. He leaned forward and placed an orange section in my mouth and ordered me to chew it slowly. Only then did he realize why I could not close my mouth. With a curse hurled at Jack and Carl, his fingers reached into my mouth and removed the rubber wedges, allowing me to close a mouth that had been open for what seemed like hours.

Again, he leaned forward, cursing under his breath, grabbed my shoulders and pulled me upright. There I sat between his legs, one leg serving as my back rest, the other tucked neatly between my legs and pressing against reawakening cock. His fingers worked slowly on the laces that fused the hood like a second skin to my face. Slowly he peeled it free and tossed it across the room in a fit of anger for what his boys had done to me. "That should make you feel better."

I distrusted him and yet he had come to my rescue and was my savior. A cold bottle of clear liquid was pressed to my lips and he ordered me to drink. Ice cold water flowed into my mouth. He ordered me to swish it around and spit it out. I followed his directions to the tee. Another sip was granted for having obeyed him that went chokingly down my raw throat. He let me hold on to the bottle and drink as I felt necessary, as long as I drank it slowly.

"Here, boy," he placed another section of orange into my mouth and to my own shock, I licked the juice off his fingers before I began to chew slowly on the burning fruit in my mouth. Damn, it tasted great! Slowly he fed me the whole orange, section by section while I regained strength. "Eat the orange sections slowly, boy. Got to get some energy back into you if you are going to be able to walk to where we have the phone, that is, should you still want to make that phone call."

The promise of a phone call perked me up. Each section of that orange burned every inch of my mouth and all the way down my throat to my stomach, it seemed. I could not have had a rawer throat if I had gargled acid and, in a way, I had.

"Who do you want to call," he asked me quietly. I did not give it to him but waited to see what he would say or do. "I have to go fetch you a pair of prisoner overalls and shackles before I can take you to the phone, boy. Rest here by the chair till I return." He rose to go and turned back. "Here are more orange sections, eat or suck them all dry, you need the fluids in you, boy."

I actually thanked the sheriff for his kindness and the oranges he was feeding me. I could not believe my ears. Now my only concern was if Hunter would receive my phone call and come rescue me from this hellhole.

The sheriff was not gone overly long before he returned whistling, carrying an orange jumpsuit over one arm and a handful of steel shackles clanking in the other. He ordered me to come to him, had me place my cuffed wrists through the bars so he could remove them and passed me the overall.

"Wiggle that cute butt into those, they are the only ones I could find," the sheriff actually apologized. Something was up or the winds had turned in my favor. Maybe Hunter was looking for me? Anyway, there was promise in the air.

As I wiggled my 'cute butt' into those coveralls, I realized they were not just a little dirty - these things had never been washed. These coveralls were still warm from the last person who was wearing them and that person was somewhere within this jail. They were a size too small and I must have scraped off all the scabs on my back, but I did finally get them on. They left nothing to the imagination and, by Chief's reaction, he liked how they showed off my basket and my butt.

"Ok boy, hands through the door bars." Chief had turned all business-like as he cuffed my hands, opened the cell door and dropped to encircle my ankles with leg irons. One cuff was opened, pulled past the door and recuffed. Chief, with his gun drawn, marched me down the corridor to where I would make my phone call. Each step of the way, I prayed, Hunter or Mike or J.D. would answer the phone because I knew if Cappy got the phone the message would not get to Hunter. Cappy hated me!

The Chief escorted me through a doorway into a small cluttered office that was being shared by another cop. Chief ordered him out of the room while he marched me up to the phone on the wall. He removed the cuff on my left wrist and reconnected it to a solid looking bar sticking out of the wall near the phone. While Pappy fished out a quarter from his pocket, I was praying silently to God that Hunter would pick up the phone.

"What is the number you want to call, boy?" I told him and he wrote it down on a clipboard then deposited the quarter and dialed the number. He listened to the dial tone before he handed it to me and withdrew a couple of steps. The phone was ringing in my ear. I was sweating blood and praying that someone would please pick up the phone. The ringing continued. It seemed to go on forever and ever before I heard a double click as the phone call was being transferred. I was holding my breath and shouting mentally, YES! Yes! Yes!

My hopes crashed when the metallic voice answered indicting an answering machine. I cursed the world and myself while the machine droned out its message. I spoke over my shoulder to the Chief, "Where am I, Sir? What are my charges and what is the name of this jail, Sir?"

"Boy, you are in Monroe County Jail, located behind the courthouse. If you are speaking to Hunter, he knows the location well enough. Charges: dealing drugs. Tell him you will need a good lawyer because I got the case sewn up tight!"

"...at the tone, please, leave you name, number and message."

"Master Hunter, Sir, this is your new slave, David Greenberg. Sir, I am sorry for failing to follow your orders to the letter. I have screwed up! Please, Sir, give me another chance, please, Sir! I will do anything you ask if you can help me this time, anything! I am at the Monroe County Jail. I have been sorely beaten. Please, oh God please, rescue me, Sir! They say you will need a good lawyer cause I supposedly have been caught trafficking drugs but did not have any on me, honest, Sir! Please Sir, I will do anything if you will just help me get out of here before..." The machine turned off and I stood there holding the phone in my hand, tears streaming down my face when the Chief hung it back up.

My hands were reconnected, this time at my back. Quietly, Chief walked me back to my cell. Removed the leg irons, opened the cell door, escorted me back into the cell, slammed the door and removed the cuffs. There he waited and watched as I worked the overalls over my shoulders and off my body before handing them back to him. He cuffed my hands at my back before he tossed the coveralls out of the cell before he spoke.

"Think he will come after you boy?"

That's when I broke down and started crying. "I don't know, I just don't know!"

The Chief actually pulled me to his chest and wrapped his arms around me, damn him! I fell into his trap, as I released all my pent up fears through my tears into his big chest. I became a sobbing mess and failed to hear what the Chief said; until, he repeated the order followed by a slap on my naked butt.

"Drop to your knees, baby. Lick my cock and balls through my pants like a good boy who wants daddy to feel good," he spoke quietly.

Startled, I looked up to him, thinking, would this nightmare ever stop? I hesitated just a moment before I sunk to my knees. He grabbed my head and pushed my face into his khaki pants.

"Open your face, boy. Let me feel your tongue outlining my cock. I want my pants soaked with your spit. Come on, boy, I know you want to make daddy feel good, go ahead now, do it!"

Numbly, I tongued his cock through those nasty tasting pants; it hardened as my tongue played around its edges, growing to massive proportions. A size queen would have been in heaven with this daddy's cock but I did not want any more cock in me. All I could do was try to get my lips stretched around the fucking pole that was growing in his pants.

He pulled my face away from his spit-wet crotch, having me sit back on my thighs and commanded me to watch. He opened his belt; I flinched as he unsnapped the buttons on his waistband and pulled down the zipper to his pants. Beneath the pants was a second belt of tiny spikes that caught the fabric of his pants to help him hold them closed around his ample waist. He pulled my face into the opening of cloth, placed my nose between the folds and ordered me, "Breathe in deep, smell your daddy getting excited. Use your tongue and lips to pull out daddy's toys, pull out my cock and balls, boy. Don't let me feel any teeth either, boy, or they'll be knocked down your throat."

I tried, sincerely tried, to get my chin down inside those pants to get at his cock, but it was no use, there was just no spare space. In disgust, the Chief pushed my head away and pulled out his cock and bull-like balls. As he held his penis in his hands, the damn cock began to engorge itself with blood. The head purpled as his cock became rigid like a fucking pole! I was transfixed by its width, the thickness of a damn beer bottle. I knew I was in trouble when that monster began to grow. It was huge. God, I thought, how am I going to get my cracked lips around that head? My jaw would have to be dislodged just to take that bastard's cock down my throat. My mouth dropped open, awaiting the order to suck him off, the order never came.

"Your mouth is a fucking cesspool, boy! Disgusting! When I saw that plug in your ass I knew you were made for my baby here, I am going to fuck that ass of yours, boy! You're going to love this ride; I have lots of practice getting my big beauty into tight places. And believe me he loves nice and tight places. You would be amazed how many love to service him."

There was absolutely nothing I could do to stop him from fucking the living shit out me, not with my hands cuffed at my back.

"I bet those tit clamps have made your tits real numb by now, huh, boy? I have a way of waking them up and using them to get you into the mood to service me and my cock well tonight." I watched as he drew a piece of leather lacing from his shirt pocket. He attached one end to the center of the chain that ran between my two extremely sore clamped tits. Even those minor movements of securing the leather made them catch fire across my chest. Odd, how they remained dormant when I was putting on the coveralls and now they were angrily mad as they ached. The opposite end of the leather lace was pulled behind my neck before being reattached to the chain in front.

"Now, my pony has his reins. They'll help you to give me the ride of my life and spur you to improve as my cock inches into that sweet ass of yours, boy. You'll just love my ability to fuck butt, boy! I can fuck non-stop for hours! The doctor says it's what keeps my heart so damn strong, all this fucking!"

He stepped away. I wanted to run, run somewhere, but there was absolutely no place to flee that he could not lay hands on me. That nasty mattress in the corner was drug over to where I was kneeling. He whistled as he caught sight of my back as if it was the first time he really saw it. "Damn boy! You made Jack and Carl really work up a sweat by the bruising that's beginning to show through. No wonder they went home early, you wore them both out. Damn boy, you are fun!"

Pointing to my chest, "Those reins on your tits will give me just what I want from you and that sweet ass. I don't like climbing into a saddle of a young cock sure stud without a few bucks from the horse, and baby, you will buck for me! I think I am going to be good to you boy, seeing as all that you have been through with them boys. Crawl over here, I got something for you."

Using his reins, he helped me to my feet, pulled me to stand before him. A piece of twine was used to bind my cock before he bound my nuts deep into their sack. Once done to his liking, he pulled me onto his big meaty thigh and ordered me to sit. He opened his shirt, removed it to reveal a huge pair of fat flabby breasts. He grabbed my neck and moved my face into one armpit and told me to lick. His pits were ripe, smelled of Old Spice and tasted bitter. Still, I complied with his wishes with no hesitation on my part. My face was lifted and my lips placed on his nipple. I tongued them slowly listening to him moan in my ear, "Yeah, baby, make daddy feel good. You do know how daddy likes his boy to behave, good boy."

Two nipples, two pits later and I was tonguing my way across his chest, bathing him with my tongue, anything to delay his cock from plowing my butt. He knew what I was doing and just went along with the ride, allowing me to give him pleasure knowing all along nothing I did would stop what he wanted, boy butt, mine! I was tonguing a fold of his stomach when he started talking, "I bet I could get the judge to see just how useful you would be to have around all the time, an asset to our little community. You would make one hell of a benefit package for my officers. Besides, I know a few state boys that would love to join my team with you here to help them with their daily needs."

I stopped my tonguing when he made this statement and got a slap up against my head till I went back to work, his sadistic laughter echoing in my ears. I was sucking on his balls and thinking, how great a family vacation this would not be, pussy face toy boy to a group of small town cops and a town full of horny pricks. God, please send Hunter!

"Crawl up here boy," he pointed where I was, so I rose up on my knees and his fat legs closed around me. "You are so good, I think I will help you get into the proper headspace for what I want from that boy butt of yours." He leaned over, picked up his shirt and pulled from his pocket a hand rolled cigarette, put it to his lips, lit it and took a long drag before placing it to my lips. I was not a stranger to the use of Mary Jane and had no problems sucking in as much as my lungs could hold before exhaling. Damn, that was sweet pot!

The Sheriff chuckled as he took another long drag, "I got it out of the evidence locker. Pays to be a hard-ass cop some days. We can grab a few kids and take their pot. Little do they know we destroy it our way, by smoking the damn shit! Yeah, boy, this is mighty fine stuff ain't it? Ok boy, it's time for you to earn your keep. Crawl over there to that mattress and wait for me."

As I crawled, I heard him rise from that old chair, chuckling to him self as the pot went to work on the old man. I was kneeling in the middle of the nasty mattress having searched for an area that I hoped was less dirty than the others. His boot caught me unawares as it hit my back and I tumbled onto the mattress; god did it reek! I heard him grunt as he knelt behind me. How I dreaded the next moment. His huge paws grabbed my hips and lifted me to my knees, another hand pushed my cuffed hand up onto my back and he landed a slap to my upraised butt.

"Damn boy that is mighty fine looking!"

I heard him grunting around behind me, getting into position, but I was not prepared for what happened next. His hands pried open my ass and his tongue dove in! I damn near jumped out of my skin with the suddenness of his attack! Then I settled in as the pot and his tongue made me into a quivering fuck hole wanting more than just his tongue. I was shocked to hear my own voice begging him for more.

"Daddy, please, fuck me!"

His tongue worked deeper into my hole and it opened to him. I felt him reposition himself, felt his finger teasing my horny hole and felt him lean into me. His cock wormed its way in past my opening gate and crawled up deep inside me, what a feeling! He took his time inching it forward as the massive girth of this cock forced my muscles to relax and accept what he was forcing in my hole. Eventually his cock found its depth, he sighed, I sighed and we grew calm together. My heartbeat raced with excitement, never had my hole been this filled with exception of course to Hunter's cock, but I dare not say anything to ruin Pappy's pleasure now. I felt his deep chuckle and excitement that he had gotten the whole of his cock into my butt hole and he loved it, a lot!

I felt him shift his weight, felt a tightening on the reins that ran to my tits as he lifted them. I thought I had prepared myself for what was to come. His cock slid, slowly gaining momentum as my own body began to lubricate that cock's passage. I gave myself over to the sensations my body was being given by this gruff old sheriff. My chest bellowed flames and I screamed as my ass was rammed with the full length of his huge cock to the hilt. I reared off the mattress screaming from the combination of pain and pleasure and the old sheriff voiced his pleasure, bellowing "Ride'em cowboy!"

That old man sure did know how to fuck! He had the uncanny ability to twist his cock while it was within me. My hole was being ridden by an expert and I knew it each time he pulled all the way out and slammed it to his balls. Damn, that man did know how to make his boy ride. His hold on my tit reins kept me bucking, the pain making me do more for him than it ever did for me. Forcing me to writhe and scream as his cock drove my body and him across the mattress on to the concrete floor. When he didn't pull on my reins, he slapped my butt and ground that damn pinprick belt that held his pants in place into my bleeding backside. He had been fucking my hole steady for what seemed like an eternity when he called a halt and withdrew his cock. I all but begged him to bring it back as I had become sex crazed while he was fucking my hole.

He walked over to the chair, sat down, peeled off his pants and put his boots back on his feet. "It seems, boy, that I am doing all the work here. You are going to crawl over here and do something for me that I have not had done for a long time. Crawl over here and get your head down between my legs like a good boy."

I did as I was told and was shocked when he rose, pushed the chair away and squatted over my face. Oh God, I thought not this, not eating his ass, oh, please, God, no! His ass reeked of unwashed body for days; it smelled of rotting flesh, it stunk of caked shit of brown hash marks on the inside of his boxers. I began nodding my head back and forth refusing to do this disgusting act!

His hands closed around my bound nuts, the pressure began to build till I screamed and his ass connected with my lips. Pressure remained on my nuts till my tongue dove into that unholy crusty shithole. My tongue danced across his anus, teased around that hole, its taste was nasty as my tongue moved in and around his poop shoot. The pleasure he was getting seemed to make him weak-kneed, he was chuckling as I ate his ass, then I felt his sphincter muscles tighten. His pimply ass rose from my snaking tongue as he giggled and announced to the room, "Got something for you, boy!"

The shit flaking fart tore out of his ass, blasting a methane rich air that got me. One hugely loud fart followed by a rapid machine gun fire that ended on an untuned note. The air in the cell had turned poisonous, each gasp for air I got more methane till I was buzzing as if I had way too much poppers during a scene. Again he moved, his huge bull like balls hanging down in my face, he ordered me to open my mouth, it dropped open, those big meaty balls were shoved in with not so much as a howdy do, they filled my cheeks like a squirrel with nuts.

"Make them feel good boy, you know how daddy likes it." His balls were pulled from my face, his hand closed over my chin and I could see a mischievous smile cross his face. I knew something was up, that twinkle in his eyes foretold something evil was about to happen to me. Holding my chin he forced his fingers into my mouth, a goober of his spit was dribbled into my open mouth, followed by his shit stained boxers. The bastard sniggered while his hand held the boxers in my mouth as I gagged on their foulness.

"Don't go getting sick on me, boy, you'll choke to death and no one would be the wiser." He stood, began pumping his cock as he looked down on me. "Gawdam! You sure are a pretty sight laying their boy, all cuffed, open and waiting for Pappy to come home! You look almost as good as my boy, Jack, yeah, he is my real son. Loved coming home and finding him just where I left him, cuffed to our bed. Yeah, it is a shame they grow up, a real shame."

Pappy dropped to his knees, grabbed my hips and pulled me to him, and using one hand he guided his cock into his boy's butt. Using the other, he drew me to him, impaling me on his huge cock. My legs were bent up, resting on his shoulders as he worked his magic, plowing my furrow.

It was a trip watching him making faces as his cock dug into my bowels and turned them to mush. I loved the determination he had when he was drawing near the end of the ride. Sweat was dripping from all over his face and body; his tongue was being whipped back and forth over his lips as if he was eating something he really enjoyed. Actually he was, my ass, and I hate to admit it, that man could fuck ass!

But when he neared his climax, he turned mean. His fucking motion was no longer fluid but harsher, like gut punches as they were pounded into me. Not needing his other hand to hold me to him it closed around those tit reins. Each thrust forward went with a tug on my tits till, with one mighty pull and thrust, his cock blew. I reared off the floor before dropping to the concrete and the alligator clamps broke free. He followed my descent when he collapsed over me. Together we lay on the floor me struggling to breath, and him wheezing like a broken vacuum. His breathing returned to normal and, with a mighty effort, he pushed himself upright; his cock was still buried within my sore butt. His eyes twinkled, his cock stirred the mud that had once been my guts and slowly began to withdraw. Then it stopped.

I could see his concentration, willing his cock to do what? Another ride? No, I felt a trickle out of his cock turn into a flow that filled my lower bowels. The bastard was pissing in me, and the fucker was laughing as he did it, too!

"Those nipples are looking really bad, the bleeding will stop soon; by God, boy that is a great piece of ass you got on you! I just might keep it for my own private use! That is a really nice piece of equipment you have on you boy, that ass is sweet! Mighty fine!" His cock pulled out of me with a wet sounding plop. "Don't worry about that damn mattress; it's had other piss fucks on it. So if you gotta, you gotta. Cause I ain't letting you out to use the john till tomorrow sometime."

Pushing himself upright was a three phase maneuver. Crawling to the chair on his knees, using his arms to push himself up to his legs, slowly straightening his back and then using his hands to push himself fully erect and standing tall. He was one hell of a sight standing there in boots and a huge watermelon shaped gut, big ham sized breast, triple chins and an overly pudgy face. Not my idea of a real man at all.

While he dressed he chatted with me, "Once I get your sentence commuted you can join our little team. You can have your own coverall, too. Have Billy Bob come here with his tattoo kit and get that ass tattooed as Official Police Equipment. Yes, boy, you are going to like it here! I will see to that."

I yawned wide and loudly, I was so tired and so fucking sore. He seemed to catch the hint. "Let me make you more comfortable boy so you can get some shut eye before the morning shift hits here and wants their portion of your hide. The judge will be in his office on Monday, and its only Thursday. A few more days and you can put your case before the judge unless I get him in here early; do you want me to do that for you boy?" Once dressed, the Sheriff stepped closer, opened one cuff and repositioned my arms from the back to the front of my body. He found a pair of the leg irons, set them around my ankles with the chain running through my handcuffs. He exited the cell and returned to drop a blanket over my shivering body, patted my cheeks lightly and said good night. I passed out before he left the cell.

I slept fitfully, perhaps due to the position. It didn't matter as exhaustion had a stranglehold on me. Hell, I didn't even awaken totally when someone fucked my ass, shot his load and departed. I was nothing more than a new very accessible hole, which had a sign hanging over it; *caution: police crime scene.*

However, I woke up when Officer Jack made his presence known to me. His paddle blew my body into full alert as first one than four more blows landed squarely on my upturned ass. When he got my eyes fully opened and my ass burning, he drove his cock into my hole. Pantingly, he spoke over my shoulder, "Pappy said you had one hot ass, by God, you do, boy! That paddle is going to stay with you till you get it in that head of yours that you belong with us. Hunter doesn't want you or he'd be here, wouldn't he, boy? You fucked up when you blew him off, no one but Pappy and I can help you now, boy. Eventually, boy, you're going to learn to appreciate our ways. You'll learn to love the way we treat you, crave it when we leave you alone, and beg for it when we're with you. Believe me, Pappy and Carl know how to train to do their bidding. You're going to learn that when we beat, slap or whip your sorry ass that we are saying we love you. Boy, you are going to get more use than a pair of shoes."

Jack rode my ass until he came. What he thought was me groaning my compliance to him using me was my crying, deep chest sobbing tears streamed down my face as I gagged on my defeat. Carl joined Jack as I was cleaning off his shit stained cock. Together they escorted me to the nastiest looking crapper I have ever seen, locked one hand to a ring in the wall and closed the door, giving me a chance to take a much needed crap. Once done, I was escorted back to my pen. Once there, I was force fed a bottle of orange juice and a jar of applesauce. At least it was something in my growling stomach besides cum.

Carl held my hands behind my back while Jack roped my ankles and thighs together. Both men pushed me down to my knees and secured my hands to each ankle. More rope was wound around my chest just below my sore nipples and another length locked my ankles to my thighs. The penis gag was shoved into my mouth and buckled tightly around my head. Carl checked my bindings, looked to Jack and declared I was ready for the inspection. Just before they departed, a leather bag was slipped over my head.

When the bag was lifted and I blinked at the sudden light, two men stood before me, Pappy and another gentleman who was introduced as the judge. The judge fucked my face hard, shot his load down my throat and laughed at the Sheriff's idea of keeping me around. I mouthed off to both of them, which was a major mistake. Pappy's nightstick made quick work to cut off my words. The penis gag was reinserted and his boot kicked me over on to the mattress. I cursed my own stupidity.

There was an open house of sorts in my cell to all available policemen in the area. Throughout the day, I was used in more ways than I thought imaginable. Cops loved to inspect the new equipment; they tried every hole, some twice. My fantasies of being used by cops turned sour as I was beaten by nightsticks or had them used to ream out my holes. Some cops were gentle with me; most were not.

I had given up all hope of release from this sadistic cop shop when I heard someone shouting in the office as I lay beneath some sweating motorcycle cop's heaving hips. The voice was screaming that I was being held without just cause. My cop blew his load, got up and left. The yelling became louder then the door opened and Officer Jack escorted a Virginia State Trooper down the corridor to where I was being held. Jack opened the cell, the trooper entered.

"Get those bindings off that prisoner, you moron!"

Jack scurried to do the trooper's bidding. I was released for the first time since the judge had been there this morning. The trooper sent Jack for a jar of water while he spoke quietly to me. He actually seemed apologetic for the behavior of those that had used me. Water was given to me to drink quickly then Jack took the jar as the trooper dismissed him. I should have seen it coming, but I so wanted to believe that this trooper was a godsend.

He asked me how they were treating me. I told him everything that they had done to me. He seemed perplexed, even took notes in a small notebook. He ordered me to stand and place my hands at the back of my neck. I complied. He looked over my body; touching deep bruises watching me flinch, writing down things in his notebook. He made me turn and I obeyed. More notes. He checked my wrists for bruising, then my ankles, all the time writing things down in his notebook. I opened my mouth, his gloved finger invaded and checked for missing teeth - or so I thought. More notes. He pushed my body towards the cell bar wall, ordered me to put my hands up as high as I could reach, I did. His hands reached up and I felt that familiar metal click that said I was fucked again. He had cuffed my hands high above my head. He walked back to study me hanging there, standing on my tiptoes.

He was all spit and polish, crisp uniform, knee high motorcycle boots, which was my first clue that something was bad wrong. No Virginia State Troopers wore motorcycle boots! He had a square jaw, black smoldering eyes and a wickedly crooked smile. His hand went to his black pants and grabbed his hardening cock. He removed his Sam Browne belt, letting it slide down to the side. Then he began to unbutton his navy blue shirt, slowly peeling it off a deeply tanned muscular torso. When he turned a glint of light caught my eye, his left nipple with pierced and held a big silver ring. The Sam Browne belt was pulled back into its rightful place before he walked to where I hung.

Hand and Glove: The Path

He was my last patron of the day. He beat me senseless with his lead shot filled gloves; he opened my ass with his nightstick and made me beg for his cop cock. Gladly I begged over and over till I gave him what he wanted. When I did not beg loud enough for his pain his boots found flesh more to their liking and I was kicked all over the cell. I mouthed his balls, chewed his cock like he wanted and when he came before he wanted, I was knocked out for disobeying an order. I didn't remember him leaving.

Chapter 3

The damned don't cry. The Haunted
Eugene O'Neill

Some time in the morning, I was taken from my cell. Marched bare-ass naked to the can and supervised while I shit cum from my raw if not bloody asshole. Humiliated? You have no idea. Like a school kid. Jack laughed when I released a low rumbling wet fart. I wasn't even permitted the privacy of the shitter! Having my hands cuffed while trying to wipe my ass was a bitch, but I think I did a passable job. Luckily, I was taken from the can into a small room, given a bar of soap and a rag before the cold hose was turned on. It was their idea of a shower. It felt great to be clean again. I dripped dry as I walked back to my cell and found not only a brand new orange coverall that actually fit waiting for me, but a tray of food, the first real food since Thursday.

While I was eating, a thin man wearing a shirt and tie was let into my cell. He reminded me of an accountant by his slim frame and thick glasses. He told me he was Mr. Derek Compton, a lawyer. He had come on request of Mr. Hunter. I nearly choked on the mashed egg and grits I had been shoveling down my face when he said that name. He waited patiently while I finished eating and asked me for my part of the story.

I told him that I had been set up by someone and explained my reasoning to him. He told me the horror stories about this jail and other inmates that were not as lucky as I was; to have survived a week at the Monroe County Jail. He made the Sheriff and his boys sound like Hitler's own.

It was his answering machine that had received my message. When I did not report as ordered, Hunter went ballistic and began searching the area to find me. He had even traveled to Portsmouth to see if I'd left. Hunter had to come to a conclusion one-way or the other. Friends found my Corvette (or what was left of it) behind the jail and reported it to Hunter, who called Mr. Compton. Mr. Compton had been trying to get me released since I had left the message.

"Son, the charges these bastards have against you are real serious. I honestly don't know if I can get you off, but I will do my damnedest. Still, you may have to stay here another day or two before I can get enough clout to get you out of this hellhole. I will have to pull in some really big favors to get you away from Pappy and his thugs. I will return."

No sooner than Mr. Compton departed was I stripped of my coverall and returned to my shackles and cuffs. My public service continued throughout the day and late into the night. There seemed to be an urgency by the way everyone wanted a piece of me; an odd feeling to have when the situation felt hopeless. Still, Hunter had gone out to find me that was the most wonderful news Mr. Compton could have told me.

To Jack's dismay, Mr. Compton posted my bail on Monday morning bright and early, or so he told me while he stood outside of my cell. He finally cut through the political bullshit, calling in more favors and a Federal Judge that was more than the sheriff had at his command. However, I had to forget everything that I had undergone while in the sheriff's care. All the police brutality was going to be swept under the rug and forgotten. It was simply a case of mistaken identity, nothing more. Plus, for as long as I lived or Pappy lived, I could not come back into Monroe County without being arrested. I just about refused to sign the contract that was put before me; but Mr. Compton helped me see beyond my anger.

I had been in a living hell since Thursday afternoon. Been beaten, gang raped, fucked by God only knows how many men, a continuous line of men and they expected me to forget it! Forget Hell! Somehow, someday, I would get my revenge on each and every bastard that hurt me while I was in this Goddamn cage!

I was forced to wear a filthy coverall issued to me since they had destroyed my only clothing. Again I was shackled, handcuffed like a common criminal. Barefooted, Jack and Mr. Compton escorted me down the corridor. Just before we reached the outer door, the Sheriff stepped out of his office and halted our little procession. He wanted to speak to me quietly on the side out of earshot of Mr. Compton.

"Boy, if I see you unescorted, off Hunter's estate anywhere in this county I will have you picked up so quick your hat will not have hit the ground before you disappear. One day you will be mine. I will keep you and no one will take you back from me again, no one! You may think Hunter saved you this time; but there will come a day you may wish you were back here in my cell where you are safe and secure. You hate me, Jack and Carl right now, that's not a problem. I guarantee you, boy, one day soon I will look real good to you. Remember boy, I want you and I will keep you safe from the likes of him." He turned to Jack, "Take him to Hunter. Return with all my equipment or I will tan your hide raw!"

Carl only snickered and gave me a push forward, down a few steps into the fresh air of freedom and into a waiting police cruiser. There Mr. Compton said his farewell.

"They will take you to Hunter's estate, he knows you are coming and is waiting for you. They will not try a thing knowing that Hunter is aware of everything they have done to you. I need to stay here to finish up some paperwork and will bring by the final papers."

He closed the door to the cruiser and waved a warm good bye. Our car moved slowly forward past a secured lot that Carl pointed out. I noticed in one corner of the lot what looked to have once been my Leather Pride Corvette. Ruined! Even its doors were ripped off their hinges, all the painted panels were scattered everywhere, and it had been taken down to the under frame. All in search of imaginary contraband, they had destroyed the only thing I loved, my Corvette. I hung my head and seethed inside.

Never in my life was I so happy that a wire screen was there to keep them safe; I could have strangled them both and truly been lost to Hunter for their deaths. Carl was laughing through the wire screen that separated front of the car from the back, "Yeah, your car is ruined. Shame we didn't know what we know now - that you were the wrong guy we were searching for. Sorry about that! Oh, we'll sell the remnants of your car for scrap to help defray the cost of having you as our guest. It costs a lot of money to have extra police officers on duty and to guard you."

They drove me in relative silence the rest of the way to Hunter's estate; the only sound other than the wind whistling through a cracked window was some county singer twanging a song. We must have driven the greatest part of two hours before they turned off on to a gravel road and stopped at a pretty white and red guard house. An Afro-American security officer with a shaved head stepped out of the guardhouse with a clipboard and approached the patrol car. Jack rolled down the window.

"Got a delivery for Mr. Hunter, here, boy," said Jack as he jerked his finger towards me in the rear of the car.

Jack statement of 'boy' seemed to make the handsome black man's hackles rise a touch but he must have known the source. "I have my orders too, boy!" replied the black man. "Leave him here with me and I will make certain he gets to the home safe and sound."

"I have my orders," Jack bellowed to the security guard, "I am to make certain Hunter signs his own John Hancock on this clipboard before I release this valuable piece of property to him." Jack emphasized his words by revving the engine and making as if he was going to crash through the wooden pole hanging over the private entrance.

The security officer backed away from the car, looked at Jack and called to him, "Go ahead asshole but we added more tire cleats in the road. You won"t get very far. Just like last time you did something just as stupid!"

Jack began slamming his fist against the steering wheel in a fit of anger. Carl got out, opened the back door and pulled me out of the patrol car. Carl all but pushed me towards the guardhouse. He handed the security officer the clipboard, snorting "Here, sign this damn thing so we can get this all done and over with!"

"No problem. I will sign while you remove his cuffs and irons. He is not going to run from me like he will you two. Here he is welcome, whereas neither one of you are."

Carl released my cuffs and leg irons then ordered me to remove the coverall. I hesitated until the security guard turned to me and snapped "Get out of those smelly rags, boy! The sooner you are out of them rags the sooner you can report to Hunter. Strip, now!"

I all but ripped them into rags as I clawed them off and left them on the ground. I heard a whistle of disbelief as I was stripping. The security guard's arm encircled me protectively. "You officers can leave now. He is with me and in good hands!"

I watched from within his warm arms as those bastards pulled back on the highway and drove off. For the first time in a long time, I felt really secure in a man's arms.

"Damn, boy! You are black, blue, yellow and green damn near every-fucking-where on your body. Those bastards fucked you up something awful!" Once we were certain that the cops were gone. His arm dropped and he walked back to his guard post. I was left standing in the middle of a gravel road, stark naked, not caring about anything in the world except I was free and soon would be going to Hunter.

I walked over to the guardhouse, asked him if he was going to take me up to the main house. Was told that I had to walk because he knew, like I did, that Jack and Carl just might try something. He did call them in the main house that I was in route and on foot.

I set out walking on the creek gravel road, found that too hard going with bare feet, and stepped into the fallen leaves along side of the road. It was much easier traveling. It was such a nice feeling to be free. How lightly we take our freedom until it is taken from us. It was a nice sunny day. The walk the guard suggested did me more good than I realized as it helped all my soreness to fade. I sung out to the world around me, I am free! Thank God I am free. Each step drew me closer to that man I loved, that man who would make me his slave. I would be in his arms tonight, wearing his chain collar, having just eaten a huge meal. Life would be so good with Hunter as my Master. I kicked at the leaves as I walked, hummed and dreamed of our time together.

Through the trees I could see our house, Hunter's, two-story log home. It was so beautiful to see as each step drew me closer. It was a magnificent house, set on the edge of a cliff over looking a beautiful valley. Hunter's house held many secrets, some dark and sinister, but none as dark as from where I had just come.

Master Hunter and his friend Cappy had transformed their simple log home into this two-story version from a simple farm into a great big estate with hundreds of acres of land. Hunter once said, no farm or estate knew its equal. He was proud about what they had created, rightfully so! My pace increased the more I thought about Hunter and his happiness to see me. Never did I think he would refuse me after all that I had undergone, it just never did cross my mind. I was here to serve him at last, wasn't I?

I ran the short distance to the house, up the steps to stand panting as I pounded on the front door. No one came to open the door. I pounded harder thinking they could be in the back and had not heard me. Still no one appeared. I stood before the massive oak door with hinges that Hunter had made himself in his shed out back behind the house. Big beautiful steel dragons were the hinges to this special door.

I picked up a rock and used it to pound on the door thinking my hands were too soft to be heard upstairs. As I stopped and waited in a deeply growing silence, fear crept into my soul; and then, I heard a small portal open in the massive door. There was a face behind the grillwork and a voice, "May I help you?"

I nearly cried, my voice cracked when I spoke, "Oh, please let me in. I am Master Hunter's new slave reporting for duty."

The voice behind the grill spoke in a cold tone, "You were expected on Thursday of last week."

"Yes, I got arrested by the police. Mistaken identity and Mr. Compton just got me out. Please," my voice broke and I must have sobbed.

The voice spoke again, "I will tell the Master that you have arrived. Servant's entrance is at the rear. Come around the porch. He left instructions should you appear." The grillwork closed and he was gone.

I stood there rooted before the door for a long time, in shock at how I had been greeted. Why wasn't this door opening to let me in, why did I have to go around to the back door? I felt totally betrayed, then my mind went blank. I turned and walked slowly around the side porch to the back of the house. I thought to myself, if this is the game he wants to play ok. I would prove myself.

As I was walking around the big porch, memories of better times began to surface. That was the swing we took down when a heavy petting session grew more amorous. Hunter and I laughed so much we woke the whole household. When we did, Cappy blamed me for the noise and bound me to one of the log columns and then gagged me with his underwear. My hand was playing on the banister as I walked around the side of the big cabin, yes, this was the spot where Hunter had bound me, bent over the banister, spread eagle and took my ass. Damn! My cock was hardening as those memories flooded me with warm fuzzy feelings about Hunter. Rounding another corner, I saw the coffee stain still imbedded in the wood and remembered that morning with Hunter as well. My steps hastened, and before I knew it, I was standing before the screened back door. Hesitantly, I knocked. A boy wearing a leather harness and steel collar encircling his neck came to the door. It was mike.

"Yes, may I help you? He spoke as if he was totally devoid of all emotion. We had become good friends - or so I thought - when I was last here.

"I was told by a voice at the front door to report to the servant's entrance. I am not a servant! I am to be Master Hunter's personal slave! Let me into that house to see him this instant, please?"

"Are you hungry, boy," asked mike from behind the locked screened door.

"Yes, hungry and thirsty. Is Hunter here, mike, please tell me?"

"I have instructions for you. Wait, I will be only a moment."

Slave mike emerged from the house carrying a metal bucket, "Per my Master's instructions...should a boy come to the door asking for him, feed him. Here's a sandwich. Eat it now! When you are finished, take this bucket, soap and brush," mike pointed to the bottom of the steps, "and go to that pump, fill the bucket and wash yourself till you turn pink. When you are finished, kneel and wait, head to the ground, arms locked at your side. Do not move once you are in position. Someone will come for you. Follow that person's instructions as if they are from Hunter. He will prepare you for your meeting with Our Master."

I took the bucket, turned to follow the orders but mike touched my arm as in confidence. He spoke in a whisper, "Pssst...you must pass these tests if you wish to see Hunter! Do not screw this up, too! He is giving you a second chance, something no other has ever received. He must really love you, boy!"

All but dancing down the steps, I skipped to the pump. This was my chance to prepare for Hunter and to scrub off the stink of that damn jailhouse. First order was to sit down and enjoy the country ham sandwich that mike had made me on two thick slices of his homemade bread, which was better than any cake. It hit the spot! It took both hands and part of my body weight to get the old rusted handle of the pump to move, and once it did the water just kept coming. First bucket took my breath, it was so cold. The lye soap felt good as I lathered up my head and face in hopes of killing any pets I may have picked up at the jail. I scrubbed my whole body briskly with the scrub brush mike had provided. Skin could have been ripped off, I no longer cared, I wanted to be clean again even if I had to peel a layer of skin from my body. I took perverse satisfaction in cleaning myself using the homemade soap and the heavy bristled brush. When I was finished, I shone a bright radiant pink. At least one layer of flesh had been scraped off my body along with any disgusting pets that may have climbed on board. I was tempted to ask mike for a razor but thought better, knowing that later I could shave and eliminate the fur forming on my face.

I walked around on the green grass testing to see if I could find a soft spot; there weren't any. So I settled for a grass knoll nearer to the water pump. I folded my knees beneath me, looked longingly up to the house hoping for a glimpse of Hunter and sighted someone looking through a lace curtain. I smiled as I tucked my chest, dropped my head over my knees and wrapped my arms down to the sides of my legs. I made a couple of adjustments until I settled down for the stay and settled in for the hopefully short wait. I would play his waiting game as long as it took and prayed silently that the wait would be a short one.

This was not the way I had seen within my head that Master Hunter would receive me. Why was I being treated like a common slave, wasn't I to be Master Hunter's personal slave, his property? In my mind, it only meant that I had to wear his chain collar around my neck and his padlock. He would control my sexual needs and control when or where I ate, maybe what I wore but other than that I could come and go, as I wanted.

Hunter must be furious with me to hold me away from him this way. Treating me like a common dog or some beggar at the door. Making me wash before I even entered his house; but then, I wanted to wash off that grime from the jailhouse. It honestly felt good to be really clean. The sun on my back and the breeze helped me enjoy my newly won freedom.

I had worked out all the problems in my head while I waited for him. I was getting cramps in my legs and back. Hell, I was ready to get up when I heard in the distance crunch of boots on gravel, the same gravel path that ran around the outside of the house. No matter how much my body ached I knew now that I had to stay in place someone was coming to me, was it Hunter? Oh God, please let it be Hunter!

Whoever was approaching was taking their own sweet time about it. I so wanted to move my head and look to see whom it was but did not dare. "Do not move once you are in position," mike had said. I froze in place and almost held my breath. The boots drew closer step by step, no hurry, not in any rush, just constant movement in my direction. The sound of walking on gravel gave away to the silent whisper of walking on grass. He walked around where I was kneeling. I was afraid to lift my head in fear that I would screw up the test and be forced off the estate and into that bastard Sheriff's hand. The boots paced around where I was kneeling, circling around me, studying me as I knelt so perfectly obedient to his orders. The boots stopped just to my right, shifted and I heard his knees connect with the ground. Shit, I said mentally it was only another slave! Where there was once one there is now two slaves kneeling awaiting the presence of the Master.

It felt like an hour or more had passed before the screen door opened and slammed. Bare feet hitting wood, running as he took the steps down, it had to be mike. Pantingly, he ran past my kneeling form, past the other slave and he, too, dropped to kneel beside the other slave. Damn, I thought what the fuck is happening in that house of Hunter's?

Kneeling there, I first tired to speak in a whisper to mike. He told me to shut up without mincing words, be quiet, and listen. I really wanted to look up but I felt someone's eyes burning into my back. I knew someone was looking at me.

I heard a door slam inside the house, someone cursing loudly then silence. The screen door was slammed open and forcibly shut with a loud bang. Boots paced up and down the wooden porch almost as if someone was trying to control their anger before he came down the steps. A decision was made by whoever was pacing the porch. He began to descend the steps and hesitated at near the bottom step. The boot crunched into the gravel and began its slow measured steps towards three kneeling slaves. His boots swung into view. From what I could see they were spit shined combat boots. Their owner spoke to the two slaves kneeling beside me. I was disheartened that the voice was not Hunter but his friend Cappy. "J.D. you and mike take this screwup into the shed. Place him in the horizontal pillory. Make certain his head; arms, and legs are well secured. When finished, J.D. you start the forge, lay out our tools and drop in three spikes. Slave mike, you will prepare a medical tray. We need to draw blood on this one and give it the necessary shots, make all preparations. Only when all is completed, buzz me on the intercom. Dismissed, slaves!"

I looked up while Cappy was issuing orders to see that it was Hunter's foreman, the twins' Master, who was issuing all the orders. Both slaves jumped, came to stand next to me and lifted me to my feet. I was about to open my mouth when mike realized what I was about to do, his hand over my mouth cut off any attempt to be a belligerent ass. If I had spoken what I had thought in my mind I probably would have been dumped in the Sheriff's lap before nightfall. Luckily, mike had silenced me and the boys literally dragged me into the shed.

Once again, I was confused, as things were not going as I had planned them to go. Hadn't I knelt as I was ordered, wasn't I clean and pink as he wanted? What the hell was happening to me? Hope drained from me as the boys took me into the shed and locked the wood pieces around my neck, hands and feet. I was like a balloon which had all its air escape or a rag doll without enough sawdust, they could have molded me anyway they wanted. It just seemed as if all of a sudden I was tired, really butt-dragging tired. I would have sat down and had a good cry if I had been permitted; instead, they pulled on a rope that passed through a block and tackle, hoisted me to my feet and tied me in place. Then the two men set about their own individual tasks, none of which were to my liking.

The slave known as J.D. was busy at a huge stone oven, the fires were ignited; steel bars were dropped inside a metal caldron that he placed inside the fire pit. Tongs, hammers, pullers and pliers that had long blackened handles were set out and he filled a barrel with cold water taken from a pump. Slave mike was in another room. I could hear him opening cabinets, closing them. The door opened and he stepped out carrying a covered tray. He carried the tray in my direction, unfolded legs from under the tray and set the tray down. All I could see was a linen covered tray which held long bumpy items and smelled of antiseptic. I knew I was not going to like those items one iota. Once again I was at the mercy of others. Is this to be the reality of my world, having no more control of anything? Only following orders and obeying blindly? Right then, I began to have my doubts about being a slave to Master Hunter.

I really never paid much attention to the boys till now. Anything to take my mind off of what was about to happen to me. I was horribly scared because I knew Hunter was insanely pissed for my failing to follow his orders. Why else would he treat me like this?

The slaves, J.D. and mike, were identical in every way from what I could see physically. What did set them apart was their slave harnesses. Both men had beautiful, short, blonde hair, greenish blue eyes, were tall, muscular, yet built like swimmers. Both wore a harness like I had never seen worn on the boys in the bars.

One of the slaves, J.D., was a little more heavily muscled; his harness looked to be designed for hard labor. Two straps ran over his shoulders, two sets of straps ran over his rib cage and attached to a single strap in front and back down his spine. Heavy straps encircled his thighs and it looked as if the harness was riveted on his body, as I did not see any 'O' rings. Both boys had steel bands around their necks and, by the way they moved, it looked as if there was no key to remove the circle; but why? They both had a weird little hopping walk until I looked down at mike's leg and noticed they both had steel shackles that wrapped around their right ankles. Odd, I thought to myself, why hadn't I seen these items before, they have always had them on by the looks of the scar tissue that was present on both men's necks. Was I blinded by love or just a fool?

The second of the two slaves, mike, wore a simplified harness compared to his brother's. One strap ran from the steel collar banding at his neck, down his spine, between his ass cheeks and caught on another steel shackle that encircled his cock and balls. He caught me studying him and bent over to show me that his ass held a plug and his cock was padlocked like J.D.'s to a ring inserted in his flesh.

Both boys were busy filling and adding water to a barrel when Cappy entered the shed. Cappy stood there watching as they finished up their chores a big smile plastered across his face, his well veined arms folded across his chest, waiting and watching.

I was the loud mouth that made them aware of his presence. His riding crop across my stomach helped me realize my mouth was not appreciated.

Meekly I spoke to Cappy, "Sir, could you please ask Hunter to forgive me."

His reply was angry, "You should not have returned here! Not after what you have put him through. He would have been better off if the Sheriff and his boys had kept you as their own!" Cappy stepped closer to where I hung, put his face closer to mine, "I would gladly cut off your nuts just to watch you bleed to death. I do not like you. Never did. We have taken care of his needs better than the likes of you ever could. What he sees in you I will never know!

"You beg him for forgiveness; he will be out here eventually. You will have your chance with Our Master, but I doubt if anything you can say will change his mind. Fool that you are! You are screwed royally and nothing he can do will change anything that must happen to you!"

Cappy was spitting his words out at me. He stopped, thought a moment, having decided to tell me something that I knew I would not like. "Remember that day that you begged Hunter for a slave contract? He tried to get you to read it, didn't he, shithead? I know he did, I was standing there when you signed the contract without so much as reading what you signed. Fool, you thought you were in control of Hunter, you tired to manipulate him and you got out manipulated by him!" Cappy was laughing at some joke that I wasn't quiet catching. "Oh, you still don't understand, do you, boy?" He could barely stop laughing long enough to tell me what he wanted, "You failed to even read the bold print! Buena Vista owns your hide, not Master Hunter! All you had to do was follow his orders, arrive on the goddamn bus and you would have belonged to Hunter. He knew you, knew about your fucking Corvette and your goddamn ego!" Cappy fell forward in a fit of insane laughter, "You could have waltzed into this house and become a house slave, his personal property; but now, you are going to be trained like a common slave as Buena Vista owns your stinking hide, not Hunter! If he wants you after your training is complete, he will have to purchase you off the block like any other slave owner.

A low moan, which rose to a high scream of anguish, came from the depths of my soul and filled the shed with sound till a gag was inserted and bound in place. Still my voice could be heard beyond the rags that had been shoved into my mouth and buckled in place. I wanted to kill Cappy and his fucking honesty.

Cappy leaned in real close, he had been spraying me with spittle as he talked he was so angry with me, "You hurt my best friend, asshole. You will rue this day, I guarantee." Then turned to the slaves, "Shave him from the top of his head downwards, I want no hair on his body, none! Collect all that you cut, it will be needed later for this binding ritual to hold true."

I struggled as mike started the electric clippers - that is until J.D. locked his strong arm around my head and held me in place. First to go was my eyebrows, next came the hair on top of my head and then my face. The boys busied themselves with cutting away one patch of hair after the other. Once I had been clipped, mike added water to a whitish powder in a bowl. With rubber gloves and a spatula this goop was applied to all sections that had once held hair, as the goop dried it began to burn. The acid was literally burning away any residue hair that the clipper had missed. One moment I was screaming, the next, buckets of cold water washed the goop away. Cappy ran his hands all over my denuded body and pronounced the job passable. His hand told me I was smooth as a newborn baby's ass.

Turning, Cappy began directing J.D. and mike to complete their tasks. "Before we summon him, let's get the medical done. Mike, draw the vials of blood Doctor needs so it can be tested properly and you, J.D. run to the house. In the foyer, there is a small suitcase and a brown paper sack. Bring it back here. Is everything ready at the forge, boy?"

One arm was withdrawn from the pillory. That arm was strapped to a wooden board that was attached to a section of the wall near where I hung. Blood - five big vials of it - was drawn before they marked each vial and inserted them into a big envelope with a number on the outside. Four shots of god knows what were stuck into my butt, and my gag was ripped out of my mouth. A tube with a funnel attached to it was inserted halfway down my throat. A pill was inserted into the tube and with the aid of a bellows the pill was shot down my throat, mike's hand helped massage the pill down my throat while I was choking, water followed. They were making certain if I picked up any germs from those men at the jailhouse that they would be stopped rapidly. No one gave me any explanation; it was as if none was needed and I was only a dumb animal. Tube removed, gag replaced and mike took the envelope and tray back into the medical room.

No sooner than he had gone and Cappy had muttered about where in the fuck was J.D. then did J.D. hit the wall opposite the entrance of the shed. The slave cowered on the floor as Master Hunter in all his splendor entered the shed shouting, "I told you boys I did not want to be disturbed!"

He was a sight for sore eyes. His anger was like a wave that washed the room in fear; it seemed as if for only a pregnant moment that everyone, including Cappy, was fearful of Hunter's anger. He stood there, his face beet red, chest heaving as if he had drug J.D. from the main house to the shed, his fists balled up as if he was in the mood for a fight, but found no one deserving his anger. Till his eyes lighted on me. He rushed me, crossing the room in a few short strides. "Why didn't you stay with Carl and Jack?"

I so wanted to say something, but was thankful that I was that I was gagged. I would have only made the situation worse by speaking. He took my chin in his hands. I felt as if he wanted to put his fist into it, "Did I hurt you so badly, boy, that you had to treat me this way?" His steel blue eyes raked my eyes, face seeking an answer but finding none. He tossed my face away and turned to his men. "Boys, it's time we mark this piece of shit and make it ready for the slave pens. Is everything ready?"

Cappy stepped forward; his head was bowed a little. Or was that just a trick of my blurry wet eyes? "Sir, yes, everything is ready and it has had its shots, Sir!"

The door opened into the medical room and mike stepped out, Hunter grabbed him, pulled him in his arms, laid claim to his chin and turned his body so I could see as Hunter raped mike's mouth with his. When he released mike an order was issued, "mike, undress me and prepare me for the forge."

Damn if J.D. didn't crawl behind where Master Hunter stood. Without even looking, Hunter sat down and connected with the slave's waiting body. Quickly and quietly, mike began removing Hunter's shirt, boots, and pants and while mike took these into the room, Cappy approached with Hunter's work clothes. A heavy bibbed leather apron was bound around Hunter's torso, leather slippers were fastened over his feet and a leather bandana was tied over his hair. He stood, clothed on the front of his body but naked at the rear. Handsome and barbaric; that was Hunter at his finest.

He rose from J.D.'s back, ordered the slave to stoke the fire and walked back over to where I hung in abject fear. He spoke quietly, yet everyone in the shed heard what he said. "Why must you always choose the hardest path, boy? You really fucked up this time; there are no more outs for you! Carl, Pappy and even that dimwitted Jack did nothing to you; leastwise, nothing like I am going to do! All your games die tonight because tonight all that you hold dear and even you die tonight! No one, not even I want you like you are, so tonight, you die by my hands!"

I had gone ghostly white while he talked. I thought I had known fear in the jailhouse. Nothing, nothing compared to how scared I was when he said I was going to die tonight by his hands. I was so afraid I literally pissed down my own leg and when he saw that he only laughed.

Hunter began talking again, "I know more about you, shithead, then you probably remember about yourself. You learned to be a cold hearted manipulating little bastard from the best, your mother and your dear old dad, who is rotting in a Georgia pen. He told me just how much he loved tying you to his bed before he went out to be with his biker buddies. He liked coming home drunk, beating your ass and then fucking it, didn't he? He claims he taught you that love meant a belt, his backhand across your sassing lips or his dick down your throat! He even said you got tossed out on the streets after he caught you doing his best friends, his biker brothers. After that you turned tricks, did dumpster diving and used your talents at manipulating men to get your way! That boy will die this night! He will no longer exist! All those manipulating ways will go into my forge fires and will be burned away for all time. May God help you boy, cause I no longer care! Listen to this Cappy, this piece of shit had a great job as an L.P.N. till he got greedy and sold prescriptions for recreational drugs to his 'friends'. The same friends that - when he got caught - walked away from him and left him hanging.

"And that damn Corvette that he was so proud of was basically stolen from the Chesapeake Federal Land Bank, he left town owning them $9,000. Outside and off this mountain your life is fucked, boy! The world will be better off without your kind in it. So I am taking it on myself to end it for you tonight!" He crossed the room from where he had been standing while he lectured the room about my misgivings, grabbed my head and directed my face to stare up at him, "Don't you try to look away when I am speaking to you, boy!! The games that you have played have hurt more people than you care to even realize. Your tricks have been hospitalized, some damaged beyond repair! You are a bad Top. You have left a wake of broken and battered boys wherever you have been. You are a hazard to everyone that practices safe, sane and consensual SM. Did you ever wonder why you were not invited to runs and leather functions anymore? Because you were unfit company and there were too many complaints about you!

"Well, tonight reality is going to hit you square in the face! There is only one person in this room that likes you as you are and he is bound and gagged into silence, his vote does not count! I do not love you like you are, never did, but I do see a great potential within you to be a worthy slave. That slave, I do love; but he is not you! I am REAL, too real for some! My world is real! Here, we do not put on leather and parade around like peacocks. Even naked, our leather shows through by the way we handle our lifestyle and ourselves. Here, we do not pretend but live 24/7, 365 days of the year in the SM lifestyle! Here everyone practices that old time SM religion. Work those bellows J.D., and mike, run to the house and bring us an ice chest with beer. It's going to be a hot night."

His anger had not abated as he shouted at me. Again he turned, laughed a deep sadistic laugh that made me wish I were back in the jailhouse with Pappy. He leaned forward, "Hell, boy, I even found your mother. God rest her soul! I know your real name and how you were dropped like a sack of shit at of all things, a biker run. She named you for the things she liked in her life, Harley's and Jack Daniels, isn't that right, Harold Daniels? And her nickname for you was, 'Boots'. Tonight your past history dies, all of it gets dropped into that hot furnace over there, and from that forge I will make a slave worthy of serving Buena Vista."

I had seen Hunter in a few of his moods. This, however, was not just a mood. Tonight, I had no doubts that I was going to be killed by his own hands, by the one and only man in this world that I really loved beside myself.

Hunter turned as mike returned with the ice chest; he spoke to Cappy, "Is everything ready for this butchering?"

Cappy nodded and spoke, "Yes, Sir. Where do you wish to begin?"

Hunter walked to the forge, adding more metal to the pot. "Bring me his hair."

My hair fried midair as it was tossed in the general direction of the melting metals. It smelt like burning flesh, mine.

"Bring me the suitcase and the brown bag," Hunter roared over the noise of the working bellows, which was with each downward pull flamed the fire in the forge hotter.

The boys all but ran and returned to where Hunter and Cappy where standing. "Open the brown bag first." Out of the bag came what was left of my beautiful cherry red leather pride Corvette, the license plate, LTHRSTD. Hunter held it up so all could see; Cappy took it in his long handled tongs and without any ceremony dropped the metal plate into the melting pot.

Cappy kicked out and struck J.D. who was kneeling beside him with the suitcase, "Open the bag, slave! Hand out the largest item, first." Cappy turned to Hunter, "I heard that the boys in the jail really loved his scrap book and they quoted passages of your love letters to him while they were fucking his ass." Cappy held a small neatly bound package to Hunter, "Mr. Compton said this is all that he could salvage from his car. It seems that when the police were denied their new toy they destroyed what was left of his Corvette. Oh, look Sir; it's a plastic emblem, just like the slave. Shall I toss it in the fire with the other parts? Yes, Sir, done!"

Sick laughter was issuing from Cappy's mouth when J.D. placed my title-holder trophy into his open hands. "Oh, God, Sir. Can you believe he packed this damn trophy? Would love to see what he would have packed if he had been given a larger suitcase." They both loved that idea by the way they laughed. Cappy studied the trophy before he spoke to Hunter, "So much plastic goes into making these damn things.

Once the title was an honor, now it seems it has become more of a fashion show. Does this follow the license plate, Sir?"

It did. Although I could not see it well, as my eyes were blurry from the tears streaming down my cheeks. How I wished I could have broken free just to stomp their asses. How dare Hunter pry into my past history, how dare he destroy my trophy, and who did he think he was?

Out from the bag was pulled the remnants of my handsome leather pride vest with all its pins and the logo of the contest worked out on the back panel with small studs. God, how I felt the cock of the walk when I wore that into bars. Cappy's only comment is that it was a touch flashy for his tastes, Hunter laughed telling him that you could not go wrong with basic black then he added at least it would add some metal to the pot. It did too.

Hunter turned and stirred the melting metal in the bottom of the pot. He seemed satisfied by the way things were looking till he looked down into the case at his feet, "Hand me that plastic bag." He held the bag of vitamins before mike, "What are these boy?"

Mike opened the bag, sniffed them, rolled a few around in the bag before pronouncing them to be nothing but vitamins, they, too, hit the fire.

Another larger plastic bag was pulled into view, nothing that I remember having placed there. Once opened by J.D. he informed his Masters that the contents were wet and stank of piss. Dumped on the shed floor, I realized it was what was left after Jack and Carl had taken their scissors to my wardrobe. My leathers were tossed on the back of the fire; however, my custom made codpiece of chain male joined the other metals in the pot.

Hunter was talking to J.D. "Toss all this shit into the pot. I don't want a fucking thing left that might remind him of his past, from this day forward he has nothing but the future to look towards."

They loved my sash. Actually they laughed their asses off about sash rash and how dumb it makes some men. It died in the fires like all the other possessions I once considered to be of great value to me. All the stuff could be destroyed, still I had my memories of the event. Those were safe - or so I thought - for the moment.

My wrist gauntlets that were heavily studded were tossed into the melting pot, as were the rings off my harness boots and the buckle from my belt. The belt with its eagle done in studs was not present; Jack had it in one of his gruesome collections by now. All my leather cock rings and cock sheaths had disappeared; the metal ones fell into the pot.

From the front pocket was pulled a ring that I had worn on my finger. Hunter grabbed it and walked towards me, Cappy following in his wake, "Sir, they removed his tit rings and Prince Albert while in the jail, shall I ...?"

"Yes, Cappy, all of it goes in that damn pot, all of his crap! Even this fake class ring, I know you did not graduate from high school, shithead! Lies, so many lies, they stop tonight along with your life!"

He wanted nothing that connected me to my past. While my life was burning in the forge, J.D. and mike half-dragged/half-carried a huge tub of water in my direction. It was dropped near my legs. Hunter tapped both boys lightly on their butts, tilted his head towards the private room and called to Cappy, "Let him watch his life go up in flames. It's time for us to have a cold drink, C'mon, get your asses in here."

As the door opened a cold blast of air conditioned air washed over me. The door slammed and I was locked into watching my life go up in fire. While they enjoyed a nice cold beer, I chewed on myself. Why had I failed to see the harshness that existed in Hunter's world? Was I so blind that I did not see or that I did not want to see? Nothing had ever been hidden from me. I had seen Cappy take a whip to mike when he fucked up his steak. I even watched Hunter beat J.D. for failing in some minor planting. Hunter had taken his bullwhip to my back because I foolishly mouthed off to him. Why did I think I could manipulate Hunter like all the other johns in my world? Why was it that every time that I came to be with Hunter that I hated to return home to the outside world? Did he have additives spiked to my food so that I was addicted to something? My only addiction that I could think of was my addiction to his touch.

No matter how dark my day had been during the trial, when I called him, my burdens were lifted. When we were apart, why did I crave his touch, his cock or the way I felt when I was kneeling before him? What had changed to make him so cold and impersonal? Was it just that simple? That I had displeased him by not following his orders, by arriving on the bus, could it be that simple? Why did my cock get hard when he found me playing alone in the room with his collar snapped around my neck? Why did my cock stay hard no matter how hard or rough he played with me? Why did it not matter if I did not cum when we were together?

He knew I was a gold digger from the get go. I thought at first, I could fool him. If it took his collar padlocked around my neck; then, I would do just that. Get him to place it around my neck like others before him and I could live in the lap of luxury and top from below. It worked on others, why was it different with Hunter?

Oh, Shit!! What about that day we were sitting on the back porch drinking coffee after an all night session that involved a major flogging? Hell of a nice way to see in the New Year all proper like. I was sitting between his legs, while he sat above me, his hand resting on my shoulder. We were enjoying watching the sunrise. I turned to him, looking up and begged him for a slave contract. He tried to tell me that at Buena Vista, slavery was not a game, that it was the real thing. Once owned, forever owned. I shushed what I thought were his fears. He told me I was not ready for this level of commitment, which only made me want it more. I laughed when he told me I would have to sell everything. He wrote a date on to the contract, gave me a suitcase that would return with me. He read the contract before he signed it and he even urged me to read it before I signed, I like a fool didn't! Cappy witnessed the signatures on the contract. Hunter even gave me a copy of the contract and told me to read it when I got home but did I? No! I had 45 days to read the contract and realize just how serious the contract was; instead, I played that time away bragging that I would soon be living in the lap of luxury. My friends laughed in my face. They knew what I now know, once I signed the contract, I was no longer the Master of my own fate. With my signature I had given away my freedom.

A blast of cold air hit my face as mike ran out of the room and over to the forge. He stirred the bubbling brew, added metal and something that flashed blue flames. I giggled to myself, as it looked as if he was making candy. A witch's brew would be more likely for this crowd. He ran back into the air-conditioned room while I was forced to endure the growing heat. It would probably get a lot hotter before Hunter killed me. He did say that he wanted to make my death slow and extremely painful, just like he had suffered when I did not show up at the appointed place or time. Jesus, what type of torture can a sadistic bastard like Hunter do with hot metal? Only the devil himself would know, and too soon I would learn it first hand.

The door slammed open, Hunter and the boys went towards the forge whereas Cappy came to me. He walked behind me; let his hands stroll across my hairless chest till they found my nipples, those he rolled expertly till they were hard. As he played with my nipples, rolling them between his thumb and forefinger he began to talk in a whispered undertone, "You probably think the sheriff and his goons did a lot to you?"

I nodded my head yes.

He continued whispering in my ear, "Nothing has prepared you for what we have intended."

My body stiffened and I started to loose my hardon, but his fingers on my nipples put that idea out of my head and my cock began to regain strength. "It's a funny relationship we have with the Chief, Carl and Jack. They know we're slave traders. Carl and Jack bring us some of their used meat hoping to make a trade or bring us one that has gotten too hot to handle. Meaning someone like a momma's boy has been picked up and is wanted back. We take them, train them and sell them. You would be amazed how much we get for our trained slaves." Cappy hesitated. "Why am I telling you this? In a few minutes it won't matter what you know. One thing for certain, if you want to survive these next few minutes you follow Hunter's orders to the letter or you will die only due to your own stupidity." Cappy turned his head and answered a question from Hunter. Dropped my nipples, leaned closer, "If you screw this one up like you've done with most of your life, you will not get a second chance."

Damn if that fucking bastard didn't laugh as he walked over to where Hunter was lifting a sparking crucible out of the heat with a heavy pair of thongs. Sparks arced all over the room as he poured the molten liquid into a mold that Cappy was holding beneath the stream with other tongs. Together, the men worked in unison. Snapping the molds apart, releasing glowing curved shapes that were dropped into bucket of cold water before being returned to the fire pit. When they backed away from the fire pit, their skin had darkened a shade due to the hot ash. With a laugh and a pat on Cappy's bare butt, the two men returned to the air-conditioned room while mike and J.D. came to where I stood.

The boys went to work. They pulled from the water filled tub what looked to be two-inch wide strips of very wet leather. Mike drew one huge piece up my chest, while J.D. placed two strips across my shoulders. Each section was brought into alignment, cut and riveted in place. The cold of the wet leather seemed to go directly into my soul and once they got started I couldn't, even with all the heat in the room, stop shivering. The thickness of the leather that they were working with looked to be almost as thick as a boot sole. I knew just by its feel that this harness, unlike mikes or J.D.'s, would be sheer hell to get broken in properly. Hunter's harness was to make me suffer as much has he had, bastard!

Since I was unable to view the harness while I hung in the pillory, I had to use other senses to guess what it looked like once the boys had finished my fitting. Two heavy straps ran over my shoulders, connected to 'Y's' at the front and back of my torso, two heavy straps ran over my rib cage and down on either side. The one central strap parted and became two that ran between my legs on either side of my cock and balls, rose up to frame my butt checks. A smaller strap connected to a cock ring that encircled my cock and balls and felt way too small for my endowment, that strap ran under my body and up between my ass cheeks, it was the only one that had a buckle and would later hold a plug securely in between my ass cheeks. Wide straps encircled my upper thighs and were connected by smaller straps to the main harness, then they added 'D' rings so I could be attached to various things or my body be bound to numerous items.

While the boys worked on my harness, Cappy and Hunter were hard at work beating metal on an anvil. Sparks rose every time the hammer struck the white hot metal. Cappy held the hot metal to the anvil while Hunter slammed the hammer down heavily. The hammer pounding the anvil was deafening! Together they formed two rods of glowing metal.

I damn near shit when it dawned on me, those rods would be used to encircle my neck like mike and J.D. The other would be the shackle on my right leg; both permanently sealed just like my fate had been sealed. Hunter would make me his slave if I passed the next few minutes.

Cappy stepped away for the hot forge, wiping the sweat that was streaming down his face and came towards where I hung as Hunter pounded a piece of metal on his anvil. Cappy, turned and yelled over the din, "Looks like the animal finally realized where that hot metal is going," his laughter was blocked out by the increased fury of hammer strikes on the hot metal. Hunter's face shown like a devil, bright red and hot as he worked those sparking bars of metal.

The hammering stopped; looking towards Hunter I could see his arm over a rising boiling mass of steam and hissing water. He looked so damn evil. The soot of the forge had darkened his face, his sweat had cut white pathways through the dark surface and the red from the glowing embers gave him an evil grimace. I knew he was the devil himself and I cried out in terror. Nothing would stop till I died by his hands tonight and there was nothing I could say or do to stop what was drawing to a close.

Hunter spoke in a stage whisper, "Put the slave clout on his cock and balls; then, put his arms in the binder. This time boys, make it secure. I do not want him breaking free like the last slave that was burned horribly!"

Cappy turned to mike, "Fetch my bag." He stepped closer, eyed me, looked down and laughed, "Good, your cock has shriveled in fear, which is just how I want it. Makes it easier to stuff into the clout." Nodding to the slaves, he instructed, "Hold his cock head, pinch it if you must, boys, but hold it tight." Cappy pulled something from his bag and began lacing my cock into a sheath lined, by the way it felt, with tiny pinpricks. The sheath covered from the base of my cock up and over my cock head. A belt of sorts was cinched around my waist, my balls bound deeply into their sack and tucked into a small leather bag. Together my sheathed cock and encased balls were forced into a steel cage that forced my cock to remain erect. The device was lifted, two padlocks sealed my family jewels behind iron gates and the clout was set. Once set in place, Cappy began laughing as he noticed a pained expression on my face. He laughingly shouted over his shoulder to Hunter, "Your pig likes the clout and is ashamedly getting a hard on, now he will really hurt himself!"

Hunter and Cappy withdrew from the fire pit to the private room for what I could only assume was another beer break while I was left with the boys. They had been ordered to place my arms into a leather binder that would encase them and keep them out of harm's way. I was quiet while the men were present, even allowed the slaves to think I was one with this project. I stood still while they lowered my arms, unlocked the pillory and removed first my left hand, my neck and then my right hand. No sooner than both arms were out I put all my effort into gut punching J.D. The punch knocked him back and he fell to the floor holding his stomach as he gasped for air.

Mike on the other hand was working to get both hands of mine under control without much success. I was fighting to keep one hand free and working on the snap hook that would release my feet from the other stocks. I was doing a hell of a job trying to keep mike down. I had just gotten the snap hook free and was opening the stocks when a viciously swung boot nailed my newly bound cock and balls. I choked as I sucked in air, bowled up as I grabbed for my aching nuts. I wanted to puke, scream and flee. One boot followed another boot until I was subdued by pain and the sheer weight of two slaves piling on top of my struggling body.

When the dust settled, Hunter had his boot resting none to gently on my throat. Like a volcano, Hunter's anger had blown. If looks could have killed I would have exploded in flame. Instead, he held me till J.D. flipped me onto my stomach. With J.D.'s knee grinding my face into the dirt and muck covered floor of the shed, Cappy and mike took their level of revenge by patiently working each leather sleeve up my arm before cinching them together. Neither seemed to care if my shoulders popped out of their joints, they were so intent on making me hurt for having struck J.D. Straps running over my shoulders locked my upper arms to my spine. Still they added an extra set that locked my bound wrists to my cock and balls. If I attempted to flee again, I would damage my cock and balls beyond repair.

More carefully than before, the boys removed my left leg from the stocks. It was bent in upon itself till they could bind my ankle to my upper thigh. Two heavy straps locked my bent leg in a very uncomfortable position. Then they removed the right leg and began its preparations. Burlap strips were bound from the arch of my foot upwards to mid-calf, three layers deep before they were finished. Over that, they laid a very wet, thick, piece of tanned leather, this was held in place by simple rope. Bound as I was, arms locked behind me, one leg cinched up to my butt, no matter how I tried there was no way for me to escape the next phase. Cappy looked it all over and nodded his approval.

Hunter sent mike to fetch what he called the helmet and collar. The boy returned with a bucket filled with sloshing water. I wondered was everything alright with the boy mentally, Hunter, did not seem to pay any attention but looked to mike and spoke, "Ah, good boy. How long has it been soaking?"'

"Sir, about 24 hours, Sir!"

Everyone began to mill around me, waiting for some command, "Ok, mike you hold his head, J.D. get his mouth open by whatever means. We cannot have another failure like last time."

I would not have thought mike's hands would have been as strong as they were. I mean, hell, he is nothing but a cook and house cleaner for Christ's sake. Both boys got down on my level, J.D. straddled my chest as mike grabbed a hold of my nose and locked my chin closed by leaning his weight backwards. I had gone wild eyed in fear of what was rapidly coming my way and I really did not want part of this slavery routine any more. Would have backed out if I could have walked but that was not happening. I tried to buck J.D. off as I struggled for any air that my body could give me. Black stars had been firing before my eyes, my struggles had become real intense when mike released his hold on my mouth and I opened it wide in hopes of sucking in a huge lung full of air. A heavy rubber bite guard that held a rubber hose, about the size of a dime, was forced between my teeth before I could close my mouth. The bite guard held some type of crème that squished around my teeth and grew warm as it set. My mouth was actually glued shut! Now I could breathe or scream but not both at the same time. All laughed at my predicament. I, on the other hand, was wide eyed in fear.

The very same chinstrap that had been used on me by the boys at the jail was shown to me, and then installed. Straps ran over my face and were tightened at the back of my head, thus locking my jaw into silence. Hunter looked down on me speaking, "Good, you do remember the chin strap. Where do you think they learned how to use it? Jack was once my guest as was Carl. Jack was sold to me by his Pappy and Carl rode in with the other Shield mates."

Hunter dropped to one knee turned to look me straight in my eyes, "Listen to me, fuck fart! We have come to the crucial part of your transformation. When I come to you in a moment I will be carrying an extremely hot piece of metal. If you so much as wiggle an inch you will be burned horribly! I will first apply the metal to your neck then I will do your ankle. The metal will burn away all your lies and bullshit. From this day forward, you will be held answerable for everything you say and do." Hunter turned to the boys, "Bind his neck."

The boys took from the cold water thick strips of cloth. Then a silverish white cloth was wrapped first around my neck before they applied thick strips of cloth pulled still dripping from the tub.

"Now, give me the collar, mike."

I had seen one of these before in a leather catalog; it was a posture collar. The only difference is I don't remember having seen one this thick. One tilted my chin up while the other slid the collar around my neck and buckled it on either side just below my ears. My neck was locked into a position from which I could not, even as I tried, move. My eyes filled with terror. I began to pray that I would not die by Hunter's hands, that I would do anything if I only survived this ordeal. I so wanted to beg Hunter to forgive me, to say anything in my behalf but he had taken that time to go to the forge. There he pulled from the flaming embers the cherry white steel and began shaping it with his hammer into an open 'C'.

He barked at mike and J.D. to drag me closer to him. The heat in his area was breath taking; it sucked the life right out of your lungs. On the floor where I lay, it was unbearable. I dare only imagine how hot it was where he was standing, sparks cascading off his anvil to fall near where the boys had dropped me.

"Ok, boys, here we go."

The boys lifted me up and lowered me slowly into a mass of heat that was encircling my neck. His hammer hit the steel once, twice and the heat engulfed my neck. I was on fire; the heat was unbearable! My screams could be heard over the din as he worked to close the metal before it burned through the leather around my neck. His hands lifted and gallons of water were steadily poured over the steaming metal. Still the heat penetrated the leather, that damn silver cloth and burned into my hide. As the steam cloud diminished and my eyesight cleared mike was working the hot fabric from underneath my leather posture collar. The leather was removed when Hunter proclaimed it cool enough to his touch. I should have realized that his idea of hot was not mine. The metal touched my sensitive flesh scorching and blistering the areas it touched.

Cappy broke the silence, "Turn him around. Next comes this animal's leg shackle."

In turning me so that my right ankle could be shackled, I noticed a unique anvil that was split. The metal bar would side down into a groove and assist with bending the bar around whatever was placed over the groove. Still the heat of the collaring would make a lasting impression and healing the blisters around my neck would help me remember my hour of transformation.

Again the process was repeated, this time around my right ankle. Twice my ankle was taken to the anvil. Once to secure the metal shackle around the ankle and the second time to seal a link of handmade chain between the two ends, thus locking my shackle in place till death do we part. The metal was cooled with water and the rags removed. Once complete to everyones' satisfaction, the room sighed one big communal sigh of relief. No longer was I a freeman. I had survived rebirth and was to be known as nothing more than a slave, human property, a thing, and a base animal till I could begin my training.

Once the job of banding me was completed they all seemed to move as one. The boys moved me out of the way and my left leg was released from its position before being reconnected by way of a leather shackle to my right. The wind seemed to go out of my sails with the completion of the banding. All fight was taken from me with the banding of my neck and leg. Totally exhausted from all my ordeals yet relieved that I had survived what could have easily killed me. Never in my life was I so thankful for them caring enough for me to have bound me solidly so no escape was possible.

Hunter spoke to everyone, "Well done men, well done! Ok, let's finish up and stop for the evening. You know the routine."

Cappy went about relocating tools that had been used around the forge, J.D. set about banking the coals and shutting off the gas so the forge would cool slowly, mike moved all the tubs he could lift or upturned the contents making certain no spark was left that would catch fire. Hunter walked over to stand, then squat, beside me.

He shifted his weight, reached over and unbound the lacing that was wound around my cock and balls, relieving some of the pressure on my bound arms. Another adjustment to a strap up on my shoulders allowed my arms to regain some circulation. With returning circulation came pain as my shoulders awoke to sensations that had been halted by the bondage. He leaned down on one arm, ran his hand over my face almost gently, looked down on me sadly, "Now you will learn what it is to really be a slave, and not totally by my hands." He pushed himself up to his feet, staggered and caught himself. "Men, it is time for liquid refreshments, mike is there any more pot roast left?"

They withdrew into their private room while I lay back and tried to get comfortable. At first I wanted to be in that room with them, resting besides his boot. Then I realized that would come when I proved myself worthy. The lights went out in the private room and they were gone. I was left where they lay me, as it was impossible to escape. The moon came out while I lay outside in the shed. I was warm enough but I could tell the room was slowly loosing the heat of the forge as night settled down on the Blue Ridge Mountains.

I must have dozed off, but was startled when a lone figure entered the shed with a flashlight. The figure was nothing but a blackened blob behind a tunnel of white light. A match was struck, a kerosene lantern was lighted, the glass shade lowered and the flame adjusted. The warm glow of the lantern revealed Hunter had returned to me. Something hit the floor near me; I ignored it preferring to stare up at Hunter. He turned as if to go, I cried out, "Please, stay, Sir!"

The lantern was hung from a hook in the ceiling, its low warm light filling the area in which I lay with a soft golden light. He looked extremely tired, his eyes had dark circles beneath them; still, he looked good as he leaned back, raised a boot and propped himself against a wall. Looking. Just looking at me. Mind made up, he lowered himself to lie beside me. I was rolled over onto my stomach, the laces that held my binder were released rapidly and the binder was all but ripped off my numb arms. Hastily he pulled each arm out from under my body, each was extended outward and with a click, and my hands were secure once more. I could recline but not move my arms to protect my face should there be a need. Anything was better than the damn binders, at least these shackles gave me limited freedom. He ignored my bound cock and balls and increased the chain links between my bound legs; some movement was better than none.

He slipped forward, pulling himself up next to my body, placed his left arm over my right one, pinning it down with his weight, thus holding me in place. I was incapable of scurrying to the other side of the shed if I had wished to do so. He reached behind him and found whatever he had dropped to the floor when he had entered. The brown bag was placed on my heaving chest, opened and waxed paper was pulled into view. He broke off a chunk of bread and placed it to my bruised lips. I all but bit his fingers off in the rush to get some food into me. Slowly he fed me bread, meat, cheese, grapes and water. From his fingers to my lips, he whispered, "Not unlike an animal, a slave eats what his owner provides. First from his fingertips, so trust is born."

I was amazed at his level of self-control; he did not try to kiss me once. Any attempt I made he brushed off or placed his hand in the way and pushed my head back down to the floor. He wanted none of that tonight. Or so I thought till he pushed himself up on his knees. Releasing the chain holding my legs together, he elevated them, spit on his hand and planted his cock deep into his slave's ass. It was a brutal fuck...or was it rape or was it a Master taking what was rightfully his? When he came, he collapsed over me, pinning my heaving body to the floor. He rolled off, wiped his cock off with his hand, shoved it back into his pants and climbed back to his feet. Before he left, my legs were reconnected by a few chain links; he lifted the lantern and departed. Dawn was beginning to color the sky outside of the shed.

Chapter 4

In fleeing the ashes he's fallen into the coals.

Apostolius: Proverbs

I was shivering from more than just the cold air when J.D. entered the shed with a bowl of hot watery mush. I had to eat it like a dog, since I could not reach the bowl with either hand. I found it to be amazingly good. Of course, it could have been my nearly empty stomach that made almost any food taste good. Cappy stepped into the shed, snapped his crop to his knee high boots and declared it to be a great day.

Cappy held a leash in his hand and flipped the leash to J.D. He pointed in my direction; J.D. scurried to follow unspoken orders. The leash that Cappy had held in his hand was attached and I was pulled to my feet and led in his direction. Once before him, J.D. dropped to his knees, I tried to stand upright and had my knees kicked out from underneath me by a brutal blow from J.D.

Cappy turned, gave a tug on my leash and would have drug me if J.D had not risen to his feet. I followed suit. Together we walked towards the house. I thought to myself smugly that Hunter was going to forgive me and take me back. I laughed silently, thinking the collar and ankle shackle was only a ruse, a means of proving to Cappy and the others that I was his property. God, I thought how good it would feel to climb into Hunter's hot tub and soak away the aches in my body.

His boots were making crunching sounds as each step ground into the lime-stone gravel. It was going to be so good to be home with my man tonight. We walked right past the back porch entrance; past the area that I had knelt awaiting Hunter after I had scrubbed my body pink. I balked, tried to slow down by holding back my steps till Cappy tugged hard on my leash. J.D. slipped behind and struck my ass with Cappy's crop. I cried out from the sudden strike, jumped forward and would have fallen if Cappy had not stopped abruptly. Together they drove me, with crop on my ass, beyond the house and across a wide driveway to stand before a hand hewn stone building that Hunter had said was the springhouse.

A key was produced and given to J.D., who stepped up to open the oak door. Once unlocked and opened, the key was returned to his owner. The air that rushed up from the depths below smelled horrible, it reminded me of the jail cell, just only a hundred times worse. The air was vile! I tried to back away; neither Cappy nor J.D. would permit that action as I was driven forward with Cappy yelling and pulling on my leash and J.D. setting my ass on fire with that damn crop.

We stepped across an old log doorjamb and began the descent on what felt like a spiral staircase of rough stone. Torches burned in brackets above the stairs as we dropped down what felt like a hundred or more feet. The cold air grew damp as we descended the footing on the moist steps; still we turned as we dropped into Hunter's hell. The curving steps stopped, then leveled out as we found ourselves in a rock-lined corridor. There, at the foot of the steps, stood a black uniformed guard. He led us deeper into the corridor until we rounded a stalagmite and walked into a well-lighted room. Two guards jumped to their feet and saluted when they saw it was Cappy.

"Thank you, gentlemen, for meeting me here. This is our newest addition, 9-745. I know each of you have your own slave teams, but I would appreciate it if you would accept this honor by breaking this creature down to the level of slag. Teach this animal house rules, obedience and do your damnedest to destroy its ego. Standard training procedures; no food till it learns its lesson, only water. Please direct your reports to my desk, as this one will be getting preferred treatment. As you were, gentlemen."

My leash was handed over to the same man who had met me at the guardhouse. The same Afro-American man who had wrapped his arms around me, protectively keeping me safe from Carl and Jack, now took the leash from Cappy. He looked as if he had been poured into the black uniform. I turned my attention to him, hoping that there would be some of the same kindness he had shown me earlier at the gate. Instead, his fist slammed into my stomach at least a half a dozen times till I had fallen to the ground, he leaned down to me and screamed, "Let's get something perfectly straight! From this moment on, Master Hunter is God, Sir Cappy is the Lord Himself and I am one of the demons in their private Hell! Misbehave and I will make you wish the fuck you were not born! Obey and you will be fed! Now get up on your feet, slave 9-745!"

Weakly, I crawled to my feet. He grabbed my leash and all but pulled me down the corridor as we ran to the next station, which doubled as the guards' recreational room. My guard ran into the room; when he stopped, I toppled to the floor winded. Two guards jumped to their feet. "Why are you bringing that piece of meat here, Jim?" said a big bear of a man.

"Sir Cappy just sent it down. He wants it to have preferred treatment and to be taught the rules and regulations of our little compound here."

"Let's put him on the rod in the booth. That way if he falls, we'll hear his blood curdling scream and the doctor is not too far away for repairs." They all laughed at joke. "Dan would you do the honors and prepare the bottles for this jailbird?"

"Sure not a problem. How many do you think it will take?"

"Break about a case, that should do the trick and keep the shards small. More are better than less for this one."

My leash was tied to a rusty ring in the wall and I was ordered to stand in place. Nearby, I heard the breaking of bottles, as they were systematically shattered. I stood, resting my forehead against the stone wall, till someone walked up behind me. My hands were released from the cuffs J.D. had placed upon me and held together while rope was wound around them and cinched tight. More rope was wound around just above my elbows and cinched like the wrists. What was it about his place that liked slaves' arms knitted at their back? It must have been a favored position for ease of handling.

A door next to where I stood creaked open on rusty hinges. I was escorted towards it. Standing at the threshold, I saw a tiny room much like a long closet, it looked to be about four feet long and 3 feet wide. However, where the coat rod should have been at eye height this one had it located about a foot off the floor. I was helped to climb upon that steel pipe and turned so I could look out the door. They took their time with making adjustments; that is, moving the pole more forward so I could turn my bound arms and walk back and forth on that damn steel rod. Thankfully, I was barefooted. I thought this session would be a breeze. Heavy leather soles would have made me fall off this rod in no time, barefooted I had a chance to hold my place for however long they wanted. Once they had me comfortable, they increased the danger to this session. The broken glass shards were tossed in and repositioned till they covered the floor of my tiny cell. The door was closed, locked and I was ignored.

I paced back and forth on that damn bird perch; I tired putting my foot out to the door and damn near fell off. It wasn't so hard to pace back and forth on that damn rod, it was hard to turn and remain balanced. After a few minutes I realized this lesson would be hell, I had to remain awake or I would slide off the bar and have my feet ruined by all that glass. The reality of this hell was to remain diligent, awake and constantly moving, because when I stopped to stand still my feet really started hurting. I also knew I was doubly damned. By having not had much sleep the night before; I would have to fight to keep awake and off the glass on the floor. Damn Hunter! He must have known this would be my first lesson in his private hell!

Thankfully, the jailors ignored me while they busied themselves with a couple of other slaves in the recreation room. One slave walked behind his handler, crawling as if he was a dog, damn if the slave did not bark and sniff the ground like any other dog would have done. The animal wore a standard slave harness, heavy leather paws on his front feet, modified boots on his back, walked on both hands and feet his knees never touched the ground. It was interesting to watch the handler and the dog interact as the handler went about the room.

The third slave in the room was a creature who crawled on the floor quite possibly due to the weight of his chains. The slave looked as if he had three full sets of chains running between his feet to each arm and up to his collar. When he stood, he couldn't stand straight due to the tightness of the chain, and he had to do a jump step to move about the room on errands. When he was ordered down, he lay down before his handler, raised the Handler's boots and placed them on its own body, where he seemed to be at peace.

My handler Jim caught me watching everything and came over to my cage. "Like what you see 9-745? Yeah, I bet you do!"

He wheeled over a tray of items, pulled some wires from the tray and opened my cage door; he was talking rather matter-of-factly as he stepped in to work. He released my cock from its cage, whistled in appreciation when he removed the pinprick sheath before he began applying rubbing alcohol to the tiny cuts and laughed as I danced up and down my bar. They are all bastards I thought.

He pulled me to him and even held me in place as he put self-adhesive pads to each of my balls, another was placed on the underside of my cock and tape was firmly bound around each to make certain they held in place. Wires were connected to each pad by alligator clamps and those wires were attached to a small black box he pulled from the wheeled tray. He turned on the device and began fiddling with the knobs till I jumped and nearly fell off the perch. He thought it was funny. I did not!

Pulling a stool up to the door, he sat. Taking up the box in one hand, he turned to me with a smile, "Alrighty then, let's begin your education, shall we?"

"Do I have a choice," I sarcastically snapped.

"No, none!"

I screamed as he hit the buttons and my family jewels caught on fire. I began jumping around on the damn pole and would have fallen if I had not caught myself with my elbows. Damn that bastard and his fucking toy!

The lessons began. He picked up a clipboard, What is your name slave?"

I replied in a quiet even tone, "David Greenburg."

He blasted my nuts and screamed, "Wrong! What is your name slave, 9-745?"

"David Greenburgggggaaaaaaahhhhhhhh!"

"Wrong again, 9-745! I can keep at this all day till you remember who you are slave 9-745. Again, slave, who are you?"

I wanted to shout my name but gave in and responded with what he wanted, "9-745."

He smiled a big white-toothed smile that made his whole face seem to light up and did not depress the button. "Good boy! Now comes the hard part." Jim stepped forward, looked into my cage and ordered me to repeat what he was about to say, "When speaking to any superior, a slave starts each statement with Sir and finishes each statement with Sir. Repeat and apply what I just said slave."

So I repeated the first lesson, "When speaking to any Superior, a slave starts each statement with Sir and finishes each statement with Sir."

He held down the button which made me scream, jump and run back and forth trying to avoid the fucking pain in my nuts and cock, "Wrong slave! Repeat and apply the lesson!"

Again I tried to please him, "When speaking to any superior a slave starts each statement with Sir and finishes each statement with Sir."

He shook his head, hit the button and held it down, then stopped, turned one of the small knobs and hit the button again.

I all but doubled in pain, fell forward and caught myself with my head on the wall. My feet were slipping off the perch when he stepped in pushed me back upon the rod. "We will have none of that, next time, you will drop. So don't do that again, 9-745."

I was stuttering and stammering trying to think what he wanted through all the pain in my feet, neck, shoulders and now my balls.

He looked up from his position, spoke over his shoulder, "slave 9-342, bring me a beer." He sat there comfortably on his stool, reading and writing something on his clipboard while I moved like a caged bird back and forth on that damn metal perch. The heavily chained slave crawled up and offered him the beer. Handler Jim opened it, pointed at his boots and snapped his fingers; 9-342 crawled to Jim's boots and began licking them clean. Jim did not even pay any attention to him as he drank his beer slowly then turned to me, "slave 9-745, how do you address a superior?"

I was watching the slave 9-342 as I listened to Jim's question. The slave looked up and replied for me, "Sir, a slave always begins and ends each statement with Sir, Sir!"

Jim laughed, leaned forward and patted 9-342 then looked up to me, his fingers moving towards the button when I shouted out the reply he was seeking, "Sir, a slave always begins and ends each statement with Sir!"

Jim leaned forward, patted 9-342's head, "Maybe you would make a good trainer shithead, but that's a long way off. Move to the other boot, pig!"

He was looking at his clipboard when he spoke, "What's your name boy?"

Stupidly I started to say David; no sooner than I got out the D then the button was hit and held. My cock caught on fire and nothing I could do would stop it till I started screaming "9-745 Sir, Sir 9-745, Sir, Please SIR its 9-745!!!!!" The pain stopped.

Jim looked up at me, "David Greenburg is dead. In his place is 9-745. Remember this lesson well. Till an owner purchases you, everyone will call you by your number. Fail to respond to it, fail to answer when that number is called, and pain will help you remember. David Greenburg is dead to everyone, even to your family in the outside world."

I began crying, "No, no, no, no, no, no!!!" My nuts and cock caught on fire and I had to use my arms braced against the wall to keep my footing. When he did stop, I was sweating profusely from every pore. Each drop that had fallen from my body while I was screaming my denial seemed to have fallen on the metal perch. Traveling it back and forth was now more dangerous due to the slippery rod. I knew eventually, I would be lying in the glass cut beyond recognition or my crotch will blow off just from the amount of pain he was injecting.

Jim looked up, "Again, slave, what is your number?"

Again, I replied, "Sir 9-745."

Again, a short blast of pain hit me. Hadn't I said it right?

"Repeat the first order slave, what is it suppose to do at the beginning and end of each statement?"

"Say Sir, Sir!"

The scream left my mouth before I even finished the answer.

Jim rose from where he was sitting, stepped in to my cage and backhanded me in the face. He leaned real close as if I was deaf. "Listen to what I'm saying cock sucker! Listen, apply and learn to live without the pain! I do not like giving you the pain as much as you think I do. But it is necessary for you to understand that we hold you accountable for every screw up you do! Now, one more time, slave!"

"When speaking to any superior a slave starts each statement with Sir and finishes each statement with Sir."

"Repeat it correctly or so help me, 9-745 I will burn those things crispy!"

Again I repeated his lesson this time with a subtle change, "Sir, when speaking to any superior a slave starts each statement with Sir and finishes each statement with Sir, Sir!"

Jim's only reply was, "Good going slave, you got it right. Repeat it again."

My voice cracked as I said it again," Sir, when speaking to any superior a slave starts each statement with Sir and finishes each statement with Sir, Sir!"

"Again, repeat it again, slave 9-745."

"Sir, when speaking to any superior a slave starts each statement with Sir and finishes each statement with Sir, Sir!" My voice was becoming raspy as I spoke.

"Again, repeat it again, slave 9-745."

"Sir, when speaking to any superior a slave starts each statement with Sir and finishes each statement with Sir, Sir!"

One more time so that I know you have it locked into that thick slave head; repeat your second lesson.

"Sir, yes, Sir. Sir, when speaking to any superior a slave starts each statement with Sir and finishes each statement with Sir, Sir!"

He stepped into the cage with me, ordered me to tilt my head upwards and open my mouth, I obeyed and he poured a mouthful of warm beer. I held it till he ordered me to swallow, gladly I did. The bottle was empty; he tossed it to the ground - adding another to the floor at my feet. 9-342 was sent to fetch another one. Again my head tilted back, this time Jim inserted the whole longneck bottle into my mouth and slipped it down my throat, the contents were swallowed rapidly. I did not realize it was not beer till he pulled the balance of the long neck from my mouth and some of the liquid filled my mouth. That was when I realize it had been recycled beer from one of the handlers in the adjoining room. Jim watched for a reaction, got none - to his dissatisfaction. Besides, I thought to myself, Hunter had been the one to introduce me to piss and piss parties; this bottle full was nothing but refreshing.

They left me alone for the most part of the day; that is, when one of the handlers was not questioning me or grilling me in some manner. I did finally learn my new name and number, 9-745. I did learn to start and end everything with Sir. It was a very hard lesson, but I did finally grasp the fact that I was not to speak till I was spoken to directly.

Just before they were to remove me from my perch, they pulled all my strings and made me fall, I was descending and screaming en route down when with a jerk I was halted mid air. They had attached a chain to my pinned elbows. There wasn't any way for me to fall the short distance to the floor. All of it was one very major mind fuck; still, the lessons had been ground into my core. I now answered to 9-745.

I hobbled like a man with both ankles twisted. I could barely walk when they took me off my perch. My feet hurt more than my balls and cock, but not as much as my shoulders. I was crippled when I hit the solid stone floor; both feet were severely swollen and bruised. Once unbound and seated on the floor in my ever-present chains, a doctor checked both my feet, shoulders and proclaimed me fit for duty. Two handlers helped me to my next station. One ran with my leash in hand. The other, a cute female, used a thin leather strap to burn my legs if I so much as faltered. We moved beyond the corridor into a small darkened room. There they bound me in a tall wooden ladderback chair. Ankles, calves and thighs were strapped together while I stood panting before they pushed me down onto the chair. My arms were elevated, rolled back and slipped over a bar before the wrists were pulled forward and strapped to the back of the chair. Additional rope locked my back to the chair and secured my legs. Before they finished, a posture collar that forced my head to look down at the floor was locked in place. The room was warm, quiet, and I was exhausted from the rigors of being in that damn cage. I must have fallen asleep.

I could see no one from the corners of my eyes, nor did there seem to be anyone present in the room. That was when I heard the chair scrape across the floor, wood against stone and my mind flashed back to the time I heard the Sheriff enter my cell. Sweat began to run down my face and drop from my nose. The silence in the room was deafening.

A match flared into being, the fire was cupped and a cigar was puffed into being, the cherry tip was a dead give away. Was Hunter looking in on me?

A voice spoke, "Who are you?" To my dismay it was a female voice.

"Sir, I am 9-745, Sir."

She purred, "Yesss!"

"What are you?"

It was going to be simple questions or so I thought, "Sir, I am a man!"

I jumped even within my bondage as my nuts caught on fire, "Wrong!"

"Shall I tell you just exactly what you are slave?"

"Sir, if it pleases the Sir!"

"It is an inferior being, a sub-human, a thing to be bought and sold. You are only another person's property till that person finds displeasure and it's sold again on open market. It's only a commodity. Merely an untrained slave, the lowest thing in these caverns. Who are you?"

God why was I always so damn dumb. Like a fool I held my tongue. My screams had to have echoed down the corridor. Sadly no one came to my rescue; my song mingled with others songs of lament. The questioning went on for hours, each time I held my tongue I was electrocuted slowly. She smoked at least three cigars before she was finished with this session. A leather bag was roughly pulled over my head and I passed out in total exhaustion. Time had no meaning, I was awoken by a jolt of electricity to my sore nuts, the hood had been removed, a slave in chains stood near me, "Thirsty aren't you, 9-745?"

Weakly I replied favorably.

A black rubber cock that was attached to a bucket was presented. My puzzled look must have said it all.

"Open your mouth and suck the cock like it belongs to its Master, reviving liquid will be sucked from the bucket and you will feel a lot better. Drink all you want but do not take your face off of the cock. Once your face is removed I must, by rules, move to the next slave."

I sucked and sucked on that rubber cock; whatever the goo was that slipped down my throat, it was good. It filled my empty stomach and quenched my thirst. The slave at my side was kind enough to hold the bucket at face height and allow me to drink as long as I wanted. Amazed, I thanked him properly, "Sir, thank you, Sir"

The old slave chuckled and shuffled out of the room.

The interrogation was renewed this time, with two sitting in the dark asking questions, stupid, dumb questions.

My stomach was full, I no longer was thirsty and it felt as if I had a little buzz creeping up my spine while I sat bound before my captors. They knew so much about my old life it scared the shit out of me, as each question directed my mind to turn back and look through their eyes at how miserably I had failed in the outside world. The interrogation could have been for an hour or two or days. I had no clue, nothing that showed me passage of time. I was moved on occasion, rebound, and the questions began again. There was always a light above my head, nothing told me except the flames when someone lighted a smoke that they were there. Questions followed more questions, a shock then more questions. It was as if they were pulling everything they could from me, drawing my past life out and trashing it, showing me how incorrect had been my assessments. I was fed again from the bucket, this time it did not revive me as fast. I got more shocks until the shock did nothing to me. They stopped all together and I passed out.

I awoke, cold, lying on a stone floor littered with too little straw. I could barely push myself over onto my side, I felt so depleted. I did finally push myself up on one elbow to look around. This cell made the jailhouse look like the Carlton-Ritz. No bed, a bucket in one corner and a plastic bowl near the door. I crawled the distance to the door. I found within the bowl water and a cold nasty lump or something that tasted like raw sweetened turnips. Somehow I got it down.

Laying there listening, all I heard was the moan and screams of others in pain. Mewling sounds echoing off the rock-lined corridors. The sound of a whip hitting a body, followed by a scream, and another voice begging it to stop. It didn't, nor did I care as I passed out.

The first two weeks were pure hell! The first days in the tough shoehide harness cut deep grooves into my skin and I was taken to the doctor. Unable to walk, they drug me by my feet; head bumping across the stone floor like a sack of flour. The doctor laughingly tended my cuts, applied some Vaseline on my harness and told my handler to place me in the turbo room till I softened up. Stupidly, I thought that meant I would have a rest. Wrong! I did have access to some much-needed grease for my harness, but I had to earn it the hard way.

As a kid, one of my uncles had horses. When they got overheated after a long run, they were hooked up to a wheel that they walked around in a tight circle. This cooled them. The turbo room was very much like the cooling rack for the horses with one major exception; we were not cooling off but heating up. The turbo looked from above like a huge spoked wheel. Each spoke held two slaves, locked in place by shackles on their wrists. Eight spokes radiated out from the central hub, so it took sixteen slaves to power one turbo generator, which gave the compound its electricity. The room in which the turbo engines were located was a huge domed cavern and it held three large turbo units.

My handler took me to a huge metal door; he banged on the outside till someone let us in. While I stayed outside the office, he transferred my number to their team. He departed and my time in this fresh hell began. The handler that lifted me from the chained location on the floor was a huge barrel-chested slave; he literally had muscles upon muscles and walked side to side instead of straight ahead, almost as if his legs did not work like normal men's legs due to the bulging muscles. Most of the men and women that I saw within this domed room were well muscled, I, who was no slouch on the outside, looked like a run down puny weakling besides these beasts.

This wall of a slave led me into a small blacksmith shop. Here I was fitted with hand shackles and I was released from the leg irons, with exception to the one on my right leg. He even commented that only Hunter's slaves wear that, and it was a sign of honor among the slaves. His number was 7-772; he was a mule as were most of the people within this domed room. Mule being a term used to describe a slave who was trained for hard labor, meaning plow mules, cart mules, logging mules, slaves that did heavy moving. 7-772 took me from the blacksmith to what he called the greasing room. He pulled from a 55 gallon drum a small mop that was filled with black axle grease, this he smeared all over me, hair, face, over all my harness and down my legs. His explanation was that it helps with the bugs and helps break down the harness faster. That was all that mattered for me to help with my greasing. Slipping out of that room, I was lead up to a turbo, they slowed but did not stop as I was locked into place and then the pace was quickened. My first mistake was to open my mouth and try to speak to my neighbor; I was silenced with a nasty tasting rag, which got locked around my head. Silence between slaves while at work was golden, afterwards - when not moaning - we could carry on conversations as long as they were done quietly. A month or more was spent working on the turbo engines. Within that noisy room I began to earn my bed and breakfast. Here, at least, the mules ate better than those slaves locked with in the cages. They may have eaten gruel but it was filled with chunks of meat, veggies, and even fruit. Plus weekly shots were given to all within the domed room, the slaves said they thought it was a vitamin booster. All I know is it made me very docile. My muscles seemed to take to this new regimen. With the constant pushing on that heavy mother of a turbine my legs seemed to grow faster, out growing my upper torso 2 to 1.

One day, two handlers came for me. I was taken from them, scraped of all the grease and taken out of the domed room. In route to my next station we made a side trip. I was lifted onto a long metal table, strapped down and left. Two men wearing black rubber body suits entered the room. They went about their tasks. All my hair was cut off; again, a white goop from a large container was rubbed all over my body and as it dried it began to burn lightly. That goop was hosed off, soap followed the hosing, bristle brushes were used to scrub my body till it shone a bright pink. Then I was flipped and the process was renewed. Soaped, scrubbed, shaved, then flipped. My legs were elevated, locked into doubled belts hanging from chains overhead. A hose was inserted up my ass and water turned on, halted and they backed off while the foul smelling fluid vacated my body. They repeated that process till the water ran clear. The shorter of the two ordered me to open my mouth and I obeyed. A metal device was fitted over my teeth he depressed a side trigger and my mouth was forced open to its widest extension.

Dental tools were used to check my teeth. A cavity was found and filled without so much as any numbing agent. My screams, like so many other times, were just ignored. While one did the dental check up, the other drew up vials of blood, placed a metal sleeve over my cock and started a motor. The sleeve actually began to pump my cock like someone was mouthing it; it felt great and helped me forget about the sadistic dentist who was mining his way to my belly button. I shot two loads before my cock was locked within a metal cage. I could no longer touch my cock, the metal encased it completely. I could piss by squatting only.

The handlers returned for me. Hands cuffed at my back, posture collar locked around my neck and they half walked/half ran me to my next station. While in the turbo room, my body had changed. It had grown more muscle due to the increased slave rations and better conditions that were allotted to the mules. We turned a corner and stepped into a room where we were greeted by craftsmen. I was placed on a raised dais, my hands relocated to cuffs hanging from the ceiling. These men took measurements of my body and harness. Some parts of the harness were increased mostly around my hips and thighs, my rib cage straps were tightened and they increased the size of my shoulder straps. Preparing me for what, I dared not ask.

Completed, we moved at a brisk pace down the corridor, turned into a side room and came face to face with Master Hunter who was sitting behind a desk. The handler saluted before turning on me with their batons - knocking my legs out from underneath me until I knelt in the presence of my owner.

Hunter, after saluting the handlers returned to his papers while the handlers assumed parade rest. He looked up at them and asked, "How is it handling?"

The one with more stripes on his shoulder spoke. "Sir, it seems to be better behaved. But as we all know, they change constantly at this stage of their training, Sir"

Hunter actually laughed. "On your feet slave, let me see what the turbo room did for you."

I stood and followed his directions; turn to the right, open your ass cheeks, make a muscle in your arm, etc, etc. I could have sworn the desk rose a few inches while he was looking at me. At least I hoped I was giving him a hardon. He pointed to the silver codpiece, "Ah, I see they milked you for your sperm deposit. Good, it is time you started earning your keep."

"Handler Josh, take this slave to the mines. Let him work on building his upper body to match his lower body. This one is known for being hard-headed, tell the overseer not to spare the rod if it needs it. He may wear my mark but he is to be treated like any other animal till I see improvement. Dismissed."

How I wanted to shout at him, but knew if I did I would find hell to be a pleasant vacation. I had learned one lesson well; speak when spoken to.

We ran to the deepest section of the underground caverns. Here the turbo engine did not light the passage, only flickering torches. I could hear the deep thuds of sledgehammers hitting the stone before I actually saw the men working. We rounded a stalagmite and found them working in a dusty dim corridor. One chain gang, by the looks of them, each lifting and slamming heavy sledge hammers onto steel pikes being driven into the ground by their labors. This way the limestone was broken into smaller pieces easily handled by yet another chain gang. Like the men around me, my right shackle was set to their chain by hammer and steel. A twelve pound hammer was placed into my hands and I entered yet another world of mules as my mind numbed.

If I slackened the steep pace, I was beaten till I picked up. If I went too fast; I was set upon for trying to damage the others. Food was plentiful and even better than that of the mules in the turbo room, plus we were given plenty of water. We slept, huddling like dogs to keep warm during the night. We worked hard and learned to take pleasure when we could. Sex was forbidden between slaves. True, some were handicapped as they were breeders - that meant their sperm was taken without their consent and sold to sperm banks. These slaves had their cocks locked away within a metal pod. They could not so much as touch their own cocks due to the device and to piss they had to squat like a woman. Life here was humiliation enough without having all aspects of being a male taken away. Even the basic distinction between sexes, the right to stand to piss, for some was removed. Oh, some did stand to piss even with the pods, it just gave them a private golden shower. Those that did not have bound cocks were the cock of the walk, so to speak. Using their cocks, they could manipulate other slaves into giving them a portion of their food rations for the simple pleasure of feeling alive again. Meaning to feel another man's cock slide into either their ever-hungry mouth or ass. If we were caught, they made certain we did not try that game again. Believe me, those sadistic bastards knew some evil ways to keep a cock, ass and mouth locked shut while making the body work. However, handlers could (and often did) use us as for sexual beasts or as they saw fit, that was one of the perks of their job.

I had been keeping track of my days here by marking my hammer handle with a stone, it was almost a month when the accident happened. We were working on a wall, trying to extend the corridor, when the wall began to split and crack open. We had been taught to pursue the cracking by hammering it as the rock cracked and laced apart. We had not been paying attention to the underside of the area where we were working when it buckled and a huge slab of limestone fell outward, pinning two of on my chain beneath the weight. It happened so fast, one moment we were singing and hammering in rhythm the next a huge plate of stone dropped, trapping 7-660 and 7-320. I dug with my hands, pulled and tossed small boulders out of the way, trying to reach them, all the while praying they were still alive. I could see the leg of 7-320, but it was not moving. I thought that just perhaps there was space under the slab for one of two men. My hammer handle had been broken, taking the blow that would have surely broken or done worse to my leg. We worked feverishly, breaking through the huge slab; I found a hammer used it to drive a split. When all the choking dust had been cleared we found what we feared, 7-320 had died from the weight of the stone and 7-660 was broken. They removed those damaged by the crushing rocks and carried away the two bodies. We were given extra water rations and put back to work as if nothing happened. My mind seemed to turn off while I was down in the underbelly hammering and moving fucking rock. It was horribly hard, dirty stinky work. Our bodies became caked with stone dust with only our sweat to wash it away. We were not given any showers during the time I was down there, our beards and hair grew unchecked, we looked like a mangy group of wild men. And for the most part, we were. We were driven constantly to do more work than the day before. When my friend 7-660 died, I channeled my anger into my hammer. They let me work unchecked. That slab broke into many chunks as I beat it to death. I worked feverishly hard till I passed out from sheer exhaustion.

When I woke the next day I should have realized something was odd. We were being fed en masse. Instead of my gruel and water being splattered in a plastic bowl, the slave in charge took a bowl from a tray, added water, then passed it to me. There were three other such bowls waiting to be doled out. I watched while I ate, both went to workers that, like me, had bust a gut trying to get friends out from the cave-in. Like always, we ate, returned the bowls to the kitchen slave and would pick up our tools and renew our attack on the never-ending mountain. I pushed myself upright, missed my footing and fell back a step. I went to grab my hammer and fell flat on my face. My head was too warm and moving was damn near impossible, every time I nearly got to my feet I would fall over. Whatever they had given me worked really fast. I dropped like a stone eventually. My friends watched as my shackle was broken from their chain. Handlers with a wheeled cart took me back to the cell.

Something alerted me to a presence outside in the corridor, the door creaked open and I did my damnedest to crawl in the opposite direction. A whip grabbed my back and flipped me and someone bellowed, "Get up, you lazy no good piece of shit! They want you!"

Turning my head, I knew if I so much as farted without permission I would be crushed by this monster of a handler. He could easily make the best muscle mules beg as he looked like a heavyweight powerlifter. Huge arms, thighs, chest, neck and he had a way with his whip. Most handlers only used a flogger or a quirt or some such nonsense, this bastard's choice of whip was a short single tail. That bastard knew how to use it too!

I crawled to where he stood, grabbed a hold of his boots and kissed them; he looked down and sneered, "Aww, that's nice." He jerked me up by my collar, spun me to face the wall and cuffed my hands at my back. He used the whip, cracking the popper like a gun, and flipping it on my back to move me down the corridor. The guard drove me into another interrogation room. Behind the desk was Hunter himself. I ran to him, he looked up and then over my shoulder.

"Did 9-745 give you any trouble?"

Hunter was talking to the handler who replied, "Sir, Yes, he tried to seduce me, Sir!"

Hunter was writing notes on this incident and without even looking up he ordered a punishment, "Bag him, guard!"

I screamed as they yanked me towards the back of room, "No, Please Sir!"

Two guards stepped in from the corridor and they simply drug me across the room. One opened a closet; hanging from a hook was what looked to be an open woven leather strap bag. Two guards took it out of the closet and worked the sides down upon itself. The same two guards lifted and placed my feet on a small wooden disk in the center of all those leather straps. Together they pulled the straps up and around me, so far, this was nothing I could not handle. My cuffs were removed while the bag was being lifted, worked over my body and a gag was fitted per request of Hunter. The third guard had been busy, he stepped forward pushed a button on hand-held panel dropping a large metal hook down from the ceiling. The tops of the bag were pulled over one central ring and hung over the large hook dangling from the ceiling. I rose and, as I did, the straps of the bag drew closer. As more of my body's weight drew down on the straps, the tighter the bag grew to my body. Breathing grew labored as the bag conformed to my body and stopped physical movement within the bag. This did not stop the guard from giving the bag a push that set me swinging back and forth like a pendulum from a clock.

Hunter ignored me while he worked on papers and answered phone calls, or spoke with his commanders and people of rank. Almost all that joined him in that office had bars and stripes that would indicate some kind of rank among the handlers. Some he met as equals without the need of a salute, still others saluted and waited patiently for his response before they spoke. The business of the Keep seemed to keep him constantly busy. Still, there were those times when he would stop work, put a pencil to his lips and watch me swinging back and forth, lost in thought. I learned of his plans for spring planting, how the upcoming slave auction would be held, which slaves would be primed and placed on the docket.

Eventually, I was lowered just enough to remove the gag. A chair was drawn up and a dyke took a seat near where I was rocking. I knew it was to be yet another interrogation, something to help me remain focused while I was in the compound. Their so-called rules of order. What a farce! While the interrogating officer got her papers in order, my handler took from his pocket a copper pot scrubber. This he opened and slipped over my cock down to the base, to which an alligator clip was attached with lead wires to that damn black box. Another handler caught my moving cage, placed a hook in the bottom panel and hit a button that made the straps tighten even more firmly around my body, then the interrogation began.

She touched the button to see if it worked - or just to see me jump. My response made her giggle. She cleared her throat, took a long drink of something from a cup, adjusted a microphone and began the questioning.

"What is its name?"

Oh, God, I thought. When will she ever get off this question? I replied, "Sir, 9-745, Sir!"

"What is the capital of Kentucky?"

"Sir, Frankfort, Sir!"

"What is slave number 9-745?"

"Sir, it's an inferior creature till trained, Sir!"

"What size boots does it wear?"

"Sir, 12D, Sir!"

"I have been told 9-745 that it is incapable of following simple orders, is this true, slave?"

"Sir, no, Sir!"

My nuts and cock caught on fire and she did not even have her hand near the button. That's when I looked over to Master Hunter's desk and he was depressing the button.

"Sir, please, I will do better, Sir!"

He released the button and spoke over her, "Damn right it will!"

"Is 9-745 stupid?"

"Sir, yes and no, Sir!"

Smoke rose from my flaming cock when she screamed, "If I were to look up at the sky and say the sky was orange what color would the sky be for you, eh, 9-745?"

"Sir, orange, Sir!"

Hunter was speaking at a quiet tone, "Slave 9-745, don't you want to get with the picture?"

I was almost in hysterics when I answered, "Sir, yes Master, yes, Sir!"

He walked over to where I was hanging in that damn bag, put out his hand and touched my leg gently, "The only way we can be together is for you to improve, and it is all up to you."

I was blubbering like a baby, "Sir, I am trying, really I am, Sir."

"You need to try extra hard for me, boy. Here, you have to prove yourself to be worthy enough to be my slave."

He turned then turned his back, "Answer all Commander Schmitt's questions truthfully and you will be home tonight." He left without saying goodbye.

Commander Schmitt continued drumming her questions into my brain. Over and over she questioned me about the accident in the mine. Whose fault was the accident? Who had been in charge of the detail? Why were we working a dangerous section of the mine? Who died in the accident? Had these slaves told me their names? What were there numbers? Who would I blame for the two slaves dying? Give her someone's number to blame!

Every unanswerable question I was shocked. Then there were times I got shocked cause she felt I needed that jolt to get my head working. At first the questioning seemed simple enough, as the questioning droned on and on I started loosing track of what she was saying. The jolt of electricity brought me back to an exasperated Commander screaming the question and finalizing the question with another jolt. I began to rock back and forth, which made my bag begin to rock. It actually gained momentum, then it happened. I could not answer the question because I did not hear her screaming it at me. She all but stood on that damn buzzer, which fried my cock and balls.

That vicious attack of electricity triggered a response that I would have never foreseen. My bladder began to empty itself upon the dyke. She had her head down as she was writing notes. I had just swung back to the left when the piss began to flow. It was like watching a laser out of control. My stream of piss arched out, hitting first the floor before it came in contact with the table, across her note, before returning the floor, then the bag carried me back the same path.

She hit the panic button; more handlers than I had ever seen ran into the room looking for a combative slave and found one very wet and pissed Commander. She pointed and they attacked. I was beaten senseless. When I awoke I was bound onto a dentist chair and a doctor was installing a catheter. A rubber tube was being slipped down inside my cock till piss shout out the end. He took a hypodermic syringe inserted it into a tube on the outside of the rubber hose and depressed the syringe. He looked up at me.

"We cannot have you pissing on people who are trying to help you, now can we? Do not try to remove this hose. If you pull on it, you will do yourself a lot of damage and make your cock nonfunctional again. Then a lot of your talents as a slave and sperm donor are lost and you will be sold for dog food." He bent the hose in upon itself, bound the folded sections with surgical tape followed by a tiny padlock. "Now, when you have to piss, you will have to beg a handler. Another freedom is taken from you, slave."

Once released from the chair, I found my legs unable to bare weight. Two handlers dragged my sorely battered body back to what I had hoped would be my cell and rest. I was taken into the guard's recreational room. My arms were cuffed at my back, legs strapped as one and I was forced to kneel. There my head was tilted back; a strap across my forehead locked my face looking at the ceiling. They forced my mouth open and a tube was inserted. The tube was pushed pass my tonsils and fed down till it hit the stomach. A funnel was added to the hose that ran into my stomach. I could see nothing but the ceiling and hear only the sounds of men moving around me. Using peripheral vision it seemed the handlers were opening a pathway around me. Hunter and Commander Schmidt entered from the outside corridor. Commander Schmidt stepped into a private room and returned with a plastic cup full of yellow liquid, her only statement before she started pouring was, "Piss on me slave? No! I piss in you!"

Hunter watched her quietly as she poured about a cup of piss down my throat and into my stomach. He unbuttoned his pants, pulled out his hog, placed that cock on the edge of the funnel and let the piss fly. His only words to me are that I had disappointed him and that I would have to prove my worthiness to be his slave. At that moment, I wanted nothing more than to be worthy enough to suck his cock or kiss his boots. Sadly, I knew I was not ready; I must improve to better serve him.

They filled my belly with piss. Removed the tube and made me beg, time and time again to relieve myself. When they finally did permit me to piss, the flow was recycled back into me and I knew I would have to give them the pleasure they needed. I would have to be sincere when I begged them to allow me to piss.

Word travels fast in the underground, every Handler there found out that I had pissed on Commander Schmidt. All took their turn filling my stomach with their full flavored piss and when I could hold no more, I learned to be sincere in my begging. After that training session, no matter where I was, if a Handler so much as needed to piss, I was the first they sought out to use. Another lesson learned. Never refuse anything given to a slave by a Handler.

I had been on a work detail, scrubbing the floors in the kitchen when the handler came for me. I stood there calmly as my hands were cuffed and leash was attached. Together we ran to the next lesson, after the pissing incident I became more eager to please. Perhaps, I realized, these people that had control over my well being had the right to help me improve. Hadn't they shown me time and time again that I lived wrong, behaved incorrectly when I was living as a free man? I was born a slave and I was lucky enough to have been found by Master Hunter; else wise, I would have died by now alone in an outsider prison.

We stopped before a metal door, the handler knocked, the door opened and we were admitted. My heart raced, not so much from the run to this location but cause I was here in this room. I remember being here before and that I have pleasant memories of being here but don't remember what I'd done. I was almost happy when they led me to a high backed wooden chair, backed into position, ordered to sit and even helped them as I was to sit on a large butt plug located near the back of the chair. Slowly, I lowered myself till the plug began to slip through my sphincter muscles then

Hand and Glove: The Path

I dropped my full weight and I was down. I liked how I felt with my ass plugged, it was good! Wooden boards locked my legs into place, locked my feet away and pinned me to the back of the chair. Straps over my chest helped increase the pressure, I loved this bondage and how it made me feel so secure. My arms were elevated, then bound to a board that was mounted just out front of my lap, each hand had its own glove and each finger was bound separately. My friend wanted me not to wiggle, so he made me extra secure and added many straps. My neck was locked as well, behind a wooden panel and my forehead frozen in location by a strap. My friend gave me a straw to drink from and I was told that when I was thirsty just to suck on it and I would find juices. Then something pinched my arm and I was wheeled into a dark little closet. The tiny room got warm and the lights started to flicker on the wall before me. Today I watch men marching in knee high boots while my friend's voice whispered in my ears.

After being released from my bondage chair it was as if blinders had been lifted off my eyes. Everywhere I looked as the Handler was leading me down the corridors I saw men wearing boots, boots I knew my job was to clean them when ordered. It was as if one day I had been blind and the next day I could see. My mouth actually salivated as I walked past men talking in the corridor. I did not see men, I saw four boots starring back at me in various states of unseemliness. If the Handler would have ordered, I would have not hesitated to drop down before all of them and tongue cleaned them to a spotless shine. It was my duty as a slave to make certain my Handler, owner, and Master's boots, foot gear to be spotless of any blemish. It was my job to maintain his foot gear.

We turned one way, then another; I was lost at the number of boots on parade. To the Handlers I must have looked to be a truly repentant slave with my head bowed in humility to those superior around me…when in fact I was suffering from boot lust. We exited the stone corridor, crossed a tile floor and entered a carpet area. My Handler stopped, my eyes crept forward and I saw the most beautiful boots I could ever hope to see. I dropped without being commanded to my knees.

I did not even hear the Handler's explanation to whoever had those boots as to why I was behaving so badly. He dropped my leash and backed away. I saw the movement of his boots but my eyes were focused on this pair that actually glowed as I looked at them, they shone as if they were the light themselves. I quivered like a slut in heat.

The owner of the boots stood. I lowered myself to my belly, staring as they walked across the carpet. They stopped, turned and another pair of boots entered the room. These were huge in comparison to the other pair and ran up to that owner's knee. I must have moaned or done something to call their attention to me. I heard laughter trickle down from above me. Normally I would have looked to see who and why they were laughing, but today my eyes were frozen on that massive pair of boots. I wanted them, I needed to taste them, feel them on me. With my belly to the ground I crawled to where those huge boots were. I put out my hand as if to touch them and got my hand trapped under the sole of the big boot. God, it felt so good when the boot did that to me.

Those massive boots turned, grinding my hand underneath them as if my hand was nothing. They moved a short distance and the owner sat. This time I heard his voice, demanding, "Who are you?"

At first I whispered out of reverence, "Sir, slave 9-745, Sir!"

"What lessons has 9-745 learned?"

I began reciting the lessons, just slightly louder than a whisper at first, till the out burst became loud and almost boastful, "Sir, this slave, must when addressing a superior always start and finish each statement with Sir, Sir! Sir, this slave, must maintain silence unless asked a direct question, Sir. Sir, this slave, when answering must reply simply as a long winded reply from this slave is not tolerated, Sir! Sir, this slave, owns nothing, Sir! Sir, this slave, does not even own the air it breaths, all is on loan to me by my Owner until that Owner wishes to with hold that air, Sir!"

"Slave 9-745, does it wish to say anything about itself?"

"Sir, yes, this slave would like to speak on its behalf, Sir. Sir, this slave needs to be punished severely, this slave, has had wrongful thoughts when it came here. This slave tried to use the only person that has ever shown it kindness to affect its own wealth and standing, Sir!"

Another voice spoke to me from above, "Master Hunter does not believe that slave 9-745 can be trusted, it has lied and cheated others before it came here. All that 9-745 has said is true, but we need proof that it has changed its old ways. 9-745 will be put to a test."

"Slave 9-745 you will be working in the kitchen. It will be really tempting for it to steal food from the floor, tables or bins and eat it but that is strictly forbidden. 9-745 will eat only the food that it is given every morning and night, nothing more. It will watch all slaves in the kitchen; anyone it sees stealing or eating food other than its rations it will report to us their number. If so much as a crumb is stolen while it is on duty or working it is your duty to report the wrongful act or it will not eat that night. However, should it catch a thief it will be given that much more food. If it lies like it did outside it will not be fed for two days and it will go hungry. Does slave 9-745 understand its order?"

"Sir, Yes, Sir!"

"Repeat the order slave."

"Sir, this slave is to catch any thieves within the kitchen. Should this slave fail, its meals will be reduced. If it is successful, increased, and if it lies it will go hungry for two days, Sir.

"A Handler will bring it here daily for its report. Remember it must report the number of the offending slaves. Do not fail me at this slave!" His voice was commanding, I knew that voice, it was my Owner's. "Handler, take this slave to the kitchen and place him on their detail. You will return him to me daily for his report. Dismissed!"

My handler caught up my leash, gave a tug and I turned, leaving those marvelous boots behind me. Secretly, I held my hand where the boot had ground it into the floor. It had been over five months or more since Hunter had touched me. That boot grinding my hand under it told me he still loved me. As I departed the room, another slave was being brought in. As I ran beside my Handler, I wondered if that slave would be given the same lesson to spy on the kitchen and me. We entered the kitchen about the time that thought had wandered into my mind, and it was lost on the size of the kitchen. It was huge!

Men in white suits watched or supervised slaves as they stirred huge kettles of bubbling white goop, slave fare. Ovens lined one wall, grills down the middle. All over the place there was activity. I stood calmly waiting, while my handler found a work detail. When he returned, my chains were modified. Once trained as a mule, always a mule, and I was to join a labor division of the kitchen with the heavy grunt laborers. Everywhere I seemed to look, people were eating, how would I remember all their numbers? True, every slave had a tag with their number, but just the volume of numbers would fry my brain. Damn near everyone I saw eating wore collars. What a task was before me!

That day, I suffered under the whip of one vicious bastard, another slave! He had us lifting bags of grain, carrying them down the hallway and taking them into a freshly cleaned room. We were kept in constant motion, lifting, shifting, dropping and moving back to the original site for more bags of grain. When one storage room was emptied, we were set about sweeping up the lost grains, mopping the whole floor first with water then with nearly pure bleach. If I was seeing the whip-wielding slave correctly, he periodically ate grains like they were peanuts that he kept hidden in his palm. He was the first that I reported. That night I got double rations.

The next day I reported two slaves who were stealing food. The third day I failed to report (like another slave had done before me) a major theft. I was beaten and roughly bound with no food, only water. The following day, I was put on my knees scrubbing huge kettles until they would shine. While in that location, I saw three slaves eating openly from bread loaves cooling on a rack. Those I reported and even supplied their proper numbers. I was taken into a side room while these slaves were brought before the board and accused of theft. I had to watch as they were beaten, not like most slaves on their backs, these slaves were beaten on the soles of their feet. That night I ate in dispassionate silence. Next morning, I saw those that had their feet beaten, they could barely walk and were being beaten harshly by the head cook for their constant fuck ups.

I heard how cold it was topside and gave thanks that my owner saw to it that I should be below working, instead of above in the ice and snow. I actually prospered within those kitchens. I worked hard and found it pleasant. Once the cooks found out that I enjoyed scrubbing the pans I was taken from the labor chain and transferred into the dish washing area. It was a different form of dirty work and hard labor. Here I lifted huge kettles onto carts that would be taken out to the many-caged animals within our underground. Each cart was drawn by two mules and driven by one handler. Five carts went out each meal. Before and between the meals there was always constant activity as the kitchens not only prepared goop for the slaves but hearty meals for the Handlers, Command Staff and Owners/Buyers that would visit.

Nightly I would make my report and either be fed or do without food till I could find someone who was wrongfully stealing food. I was not a saint - the temptation was just too strong and I, too, got reported, taken before the judges and punished for my theft. Twenty to fifty lashes helped us realize our crimes against the state. The time I was reported, I received fifty plus twenty, as I was there to report, not steal, from the state. When I got back to my cage, even though there was food, I refused to eat it as my own way of punishing myself.

I was there within the kitchens till they came for me. I knew I had not broken the covenant; I had not eaten anything but my rations so I was not going before the judges, so then where? I was taken into a cleaning room. My hands bound before me, placed within a hook and lifted till I stood on my toes. The Handlers departed and those rubber freaks entered. I was shaved from head to toe; they applied hot wax and ripped out any residue. None too gently did they scrub every part of my body. A round bulb was inserted into my ass and I was milked of sperm. My cock never even hardened while I was milked. Clean both inside and out, the Handlers returned. My hands were cuffed at my back, I was gagged and they escorted me down the corridor and past a guard.

With hands secured at the small of my back and two guards, one at the front and one at the rear, I was escorted up that same long winding flight of steps that Cappy and J.D. had dragged me down many months ago. I walked them easier this time, knowing the limitations of my chains and the renewed strength of my body. I was being taken topside. Was Hunter forgiving me? My mind kicked back into the wait and see of a slave and we continued our climbing from out of the darkness into the light.

Having ascended those curving mossy steps yet another time, I was thankful for someone's detailed mind. At the landing just before the door, a sign hung from the back of that door, *Sunglasses may be required.* Simply stated but very well meaning, especially for any slave that had been underground in limited lighting for at least three months. My Handlers grabbed a pair for each of them before placing a pair of elastic banded goggles over my head. Almost cautiously, they opened the door and we stepped out into morning light. Spring was upon the mighty land. By the looks of the trees and their budding, it was just past that fated time when I had left Portsmouth in route to Hunter. Had a year passed so rapidly? So much had changed, so much!

A new building had been born while I had been underground learning how to improve myself. Mannerisms changed as we stepped into the outside world. Below, a standard leash of chain was used when I was taken from one room to another. Up here, one held that same chain while the second held a cattle prod that would easily take me down should I attempt to run or strike out. Together, the three musketeers struck out and across the short distance towards Hunter's estate. It was an incredible morning, the sky was bright with filtered sunlight, the trees showing promise of a glorious spring and the green grass beneath my feet was softer than any carpet. I had survived the rigors of slave training and changed in more ways and even I dare imagine.

Part of the change was present in how I walked with the handlers. I had learned the proper mind set while I was inside the caverns. I had learned that, like everyone in the world, each of us had our jobs. The handlers were there to see to it that I did not hurt myself and to help me see the error of my backward thinking. I had the most treasured job known to man as a slave. Hadn't I been cut from the herd of dumb animals that run wild across the surface? Hadn't I been trained physically to handle the rigors of my breed? True, I had been whipped, kept bound, forced to do hard labor till I saw the error in my negative thinking; until I had cast off the negative programming that had been drilled into me for twenty nine years by a negative thinking society.

Now, I stood once again on topsider soil. Above the ground, I knew I would be tested to see if I had learned proper thought. My handlers walked me across the divide from the entrance to my underworld towards that big log cabin and around the side on the gravel covered pathway. Along with the scents of spring, , I could smell coffee brewing in the house and heard men's voices speaking of crop rotation. I wanted to lift my head to see but kept my head lowered out of respect to those superior. In this fashion, head lowered, my handlers guided me up a dozen wooden step and across a wooden deck to stand before those huge handsome black knee high boots that I had once seen in a vision. It was he, my owner. Without being told, or ordered, I dropped to my knees, lowered my head to the floor and held my breath.

It was their right to see me or not. They chose, as is the custom of superiors, to ignore my presence. So I settled in for a long wait, head pressed against the wood. Whatever they were doing when I rudely interrupted them by being escorted into their presence was more to their liking. My handlers were told to leave it and go about their business. My leash was dropped; the chain hitting the wooden planking and gave off too much noise for my comfort. It brought too much attention to my presence. It was as if I was under the lens of a microscope every detail was under scrutiny as I knelt, waiting acknowledgement of existence.

The fresh air or something in bloom started the tickle in my nose. I tried stifling what I knew was about to happen by holding a finger under my nose while trying to limit my movement before them. My lungs expanded and I sneezed into my knees. That sneeze triggered my fear of rejection, and that triggered a body response of quivering. Their conversation halted as they watched my body shake uncontrollably. I was in his presence, I wanted this meeting to go so well and to be betrayed by my own body! I did not know what to do, which only triggered more shivering. Luckily, I held my place and someone tossed me a lifeline.

I heard an overly loud snap that was repeated, "Slave 9-745, without looking up, follow my voice." He snapped his fingers repeatedly till I crawled nearer to his boots, then ordered, "Halt." He was sitting by the way his boots were at rest, "Kiss the soles of my boots, slave."

His boots were resting on their heels. Hesitantly, I slipped my head forward, tentatively like a turtle and kissed the soles of both boots. He seemed to like what he saw or felt when my lips came into contact with those boot soles. Another order was issued, "Clean off my boot soles, let no dirt remain when it is finished."

My trainers had helped me understand my improper thinking. The superior boot does not move, the slave moves with limited non-threatening movements when serving a superior's boot. I found my best positions for serving while down below, sucking on handler's boot leather. I kept my turtle like position, hands folded neatly before me, my neck and head extended with my torso balanced over my folded legs. In the turtle position, I could serve one boot while the other was invited to occupy my back or shoulders as did this superior today. His boot touch sent my body into waves of little quakes, that ran through my body it was as if I was on drugs, high as a kite from only licking this superior's boot sole. Rationalization left me numb as I gave myself over to the pleasure I was giving him at seeing me and feeling my tongue work every square inch of his boot sole. He must have been to the stable as I found flakes of green matter caked between the sole and heel. Whatever it was did not matter, only the fact that I served my owner well.

Their conversation was not halted by my presence nor did they speak to me while I was on my assigned task. I half heard what they said, placing my total concentration on licking the underside of the sole, the boot heel and even working my tongue around the upper welting without getting my tongue on the smooth leather of the upper boot. When he was satisfied by my labors on one boot, it was dislodged from my lips and relocated to my back, with the other lowered in place. This way I served both his boots to the best of my abilities and gave to my owner what was his due after too long a wait.

A slave approached, it did not even falter when it saw me on the floor before him. They gave it orders and sent it on an errand; it ran off down the steps and out across the gravel, returning a few minutes later with a Handler by the ring of his boots on the planking. Was I to be taken away and this boot sole not finished?

The slave brought a chair, the handler sat and the three men began a conversation about the upcoming slave sale. Was I to be part of this sale? No clues were given to tell me if I was or wasn't to be a part of the spring auction. Would it have mattered to me? I was unable to control anything anymore. I lived only to serve.

Once the boot sole was done to his level of perfection, I was granted permission to clean the balance of his boots with my tongue and lips. If I could have gotten a hardon, I would have; instead, my body went into quivering overdrive which made them laugh. It was good to know I pleased them enough to make them laugh. I was being a good servant to my Lord and Master. My tongue danced across that incredibly smooth leather as I wove a pattern that gave me complete and total coverage of his boot. Slowly, I crept up his boot shaft and stole a glimpse of my owner far above me. It felt so damn good to be there on my knees licking the leather covered leg of my god, Hunter. He did not notice my ingression, and out of fear I turned my eyes downward and refocused my attention to the proper place, his boot. Time never mattered when one's serving one's Master. It was as if the act of serving made time halt for those that were serving and those that were being served.

He rose, kicked me back a step. I wanted to scream that I wasn't finished but remained silent. He walked away, leaving me where I was kneeling. The slave ran up, grabbed my leash, ordered me to stand and follow. I was led to the back-screened door, the leash dropped; I was to remain in place till the leash was lifted again. The slave withdrew but returned a few minutes later with a bowl. I had missed my ration when they had come for me. I ate in silence till the slave lifted my leash and I was led into the house. The kitchen was filled with wonderful smells, passing as we walked down a short hallway, turned and stepped into my owner's office. He was present; I dropped at command and crawled into a hole beneath his desk. While he worked I attended to his boots, finishing a job that I had just begun, worshipping my God with tongue and lips.

His cock hardened while I worked my tongue deep into his boot. I wanted him to feel my presence, willed him to feel my tongue on his cock and I was amazed when his cock grew within his pants and he had to adjust himself.

He pushed back his chair; pulled my head up between his legs, looked down upon me from his height and chuckled, "Look what it has done to me. What is it going to do about this, slave 9-745?"

I knew it was a trick question. I knew it was a question I was not to answer. He would direct how I was to next service his rising needs. He unbuttoned his fly, lifted his weight in the chair put his hand into his pants and pulled out his cock and balls. I was ordered to open my mouth. Into my mouth his cock was placed followed by an order, "Keep your mouth around my cock, and do not work your tongue as I do not wish to shoot a load. Your mouth will serve only as a cock warmer, nothing more."

He reset his chair, my mouth was sealed around his hardening cock and he went to work. Yes, my mouth began to ache from the constant forced position but I dared not let it close. That was when I realized this was a test of wills. He wanted me to fail, to do what I had been taught and to suck his cock till it came down my throat. This way I would fail and be sent back to the caverns below. I had to constantly keep refocusing my attention on just being a cock warmer, he did catch me by surprise when his cock began to trickle piss. Without thought I swallowed his sweet nectar. The battle raged in silence, on occasion he would crack a fart. I enjoyed each one. The test of wills continued as his cock would harden creeping slowly down my throat, it leaked pre-cum, forcing me to swallow constantly which only made his cock harder. Then it would soften as if he took hold of it mentally and changed the subject line. Back and forth we see-sawed till, in a fit of exasperation, he reached under the desk and grabbed my collar and forced his cock deep down into my throat. A deep guttural voice commanded that I suck till he came. Amazingly, he laid back and allowed me to fuck my face on his wonderful cock. When he neared his climax, he grabbed a hold of my collar forced his cock deep within my throat and shot his load.

There was a knock to the door, he bellowed for whomever to enter. I remained between his legs cleaning up his overly soggy cock while he chatted with the man standing before the desk. When they stopped speaking, my leash was lifted and I was told to go with the trainer.

The trainer wore a brown jump suit, one I had not seen before. He was a slave, but one who had risen through the ranks and served best by training slaves to serve better. He led me towards a large barn that had fenced in rings on either side of the barn. This area smelled rich with animal smells. I was lead into a stall. The trainer ordered me to stand in one position while he added another chain to my collar. In this way I was locked between two wooden beams supporting a wooden ceiling that ran the length of the building.

He walked away and returned carrying an armload of straps and things that jingled as he dropped them. He measured my feet, my hands and walked away again and returned to drop more stuff at my feet.

I must have looked puzzled by what he was doing. His way of relieving the stress that I was having right then was to run his hand over my torso and scratch behind my ears. That felt so good, I could have cried out for more. But I maintained silence.

Into my hands he placed a small rolled paper tube and ordered me to wrap my fingers around it. Ace bandage were loosely bound over my fingers. Each hand was inserted into a leather bag that was laced around my wrists, effectively taking away my hands. Over the hands were placed another bag of heavy leather, this too was laced in place and reminded me of a horses hoof. The trainer placed leather shackles above my elbows and connected them across my back, thus keeping my hands at a certain height. Once my hands were covered, he grabbed up a handful of straps and began placing them around my head. One set wrapped around my forehead, another from my chin to the back of my head and still a final set was to be locked near my mouth. The trainer ordered my mouth open, into which he set a metal and black rubber device. He held it up for me to see. It had a core of metal but the center part was hinged so the metal bar moved. Over the center hinge was a small black rubber ball that would sit on my tongue and the balance of the metal was wrapped in more rubber till it exited my mouth. On both sides of my mouth corner were two metal cheek plates and a large D ring. It was to that D ring that the straps at the side of my face were attached, thus holding my mouth open and my tongue locked down to the floor of my mouth. It took some getting use to and, while he worked else where on my body, I almost constantly shook my head.

A heavy leather belt was bound around my lower back. The trainer grabbed my cock and balls, bound my balls deep into their nutsack and pulled the sack between my legs before securing them to something at my rear. My cock was left to dangle midair. A finger found its way in-between my ass cheeks and into my asshole. It stayed there long enough to get the hole spit slick and ready for whatever was to come my way.

A gruff looking trainer wearing a split leather apron came into to check my feet. He stood at one side, his head facing behind me, then touched my left ankle and lifted it off the floor. My foot was pulled between his legs and held in place while he worked with something that he placed underneath my foot. It felt like a piece of steel that he molded to match my under sole. He did this to both feet, then walked outside the barn and began beating on some metal. While he was busy outside, my trainer went about adding more harness straps to the metal in my mouth and helped me understand when he pulled one way that I was to turn that way.

The old, gruff, no-nonsense trainer returned and fitted my feet with metal braces that lifted me up on my toes and held me in place. It was as if I had been placed in cowboy boots without the boot, only the high arch that would come from wearing really tall heels. Below the toes were thick circles of leather, which gave me an extra inch in height. The blacksmith added leather around the bottom of the soles, sewing and cinching my feet into these new boots till my feet were encased up to mid-calf. Satisfied with the look he withdrew. I stood there shifting my feet back and forth trying to get use to these new boots when my trainer returned. He walked behind me, pried open my ass cheeks and inserted what felt like a little larger than normal butt plug to which two straps were attached that lifted the plug within my hole. Oddly enough when it was in, that plug felt really good and something kept brushing the back of my legs.

He released the chains holding me in place moved behind me and said, "Giddy Up!" I moved forward one cautious step at a time. He pulled on the left trace and said, "Gee Ha," and I slowly turned to the left. He said, "Gee!" and pulled me to the right. In this fashion I was walked outside the barn and into the first circle to my right.

In the center of the circle was a log that had been buried till about four feet stuck out of the ground. On the top of the log was a huge pin that held a long rod extending out into the circle. Together the trainer and I walked the whole circle without the rod. Upon completion of the first circuit, he attached me to the rod, pulling all my traces back and attaching them to the rod. At this point, he took up his buggy whip and started me moving with the call to, "Giddy Up!" His whip tapped me lightly and I moved forward.

The boots on my feet were awkward. At first I had to literally lift them slowly and set them down slowly, as I could not get a feel for my foot within the boots. My trainer seemed to understand the slow movement at first and allow me time to acquaint myself with the new foot gear. After two turns around the circle, he was ready for me to earn my keep. His whip, when it touched my back, had a little more fire to it. I moved forward at a brisk walk but stumbled. He called a halt by pulling back on the trace that was locked within my mouth. The bit in my mouth dug back and forced my mouth widely open, from that day forward I knew what it meant to halt.

He stepped up close, lifted one foot about a foot off the ground, and told me to put it down then do the same with the other. Slowly, we made a circle, with my feet being lifted high into the air then being placed down. We increased speed and I finally got the hang of what he wanted. I pranced as I walked; each time I did it right my 'tail' sent goose bumps up my spine as the plug worked its magic on my hole. I found that I was gaining speed within the ring. Pleasing the trainer gave me enhanced pleasure. He worked me all day, just keeping my feet beneath me. I had not an ounce of a clue as to what this was preparing me for, nor did it matter. I was outside in the fresh air and not below ground.

The sky was darkening when I was returned the barn. I was returned to slave security, that being my right shackle was connected to an extremely long chain via a padlock. Even with the extra footgear, my hoop of steel shackle was present and easily available should they see the need for extra security. My trainer released my extra straps, after which he unbound my nuts and released the plug in my ass. He changed my mouth bit for a lighter version; this one held a ball within the cup of my mouth - inhibiting speech and allowing me to close my jaw. I was given a brisk rub down with a rag that made my body tingle and my cock hard. Interestingly enough, the trainer did not remove my boots or hand pieces, nor remove the shackle that maintained their placement. Lead by his hand on my bridle, I pranced to my new home, a small wooden stall. Wood ran over ¾ of the way up and the balance of the distance held iron bars that went into the wooden ceiling. In one corner, a bucket hung from the wall; this held water. I thought I had to have died and gone to heaven; having this much water present was at least a sign of good fortune. I was still fed the same goop as all the other animals, but had to stand to eat from a wooden trough like any other horse might. I was luckier than most slaves to be lying on a fresh bed of straw, sleeping topside, with the fresh air and sunlight. That night I dreamed of running in these new boots. Running on all fours like a horse or a mule, behind me was a carriage, holding the reins was my owner. One hand held my reins, the other, a whip that he used to spur me onwards, driving me to run faster. The carriage was squeaking as it hit bumps in the road.

I awoke with a start. My trainer stood in the doorway, I rose to meet him and had a shortened leather bag placed over my mouth and chin. I found my food within. While I ate, he worked on preparing me for the new day's work, others were being likewise prepared.

It was odd to hear the whinny of a horse coming from a handsome black mane stallion, which was fitted in a different harness than I had. He had a saddle that hung from his shoulders. They added a very secure looking harness that bound his lower back and gave him much needed support for his rider. Stirrups were added and hung down the front of his torso. He did have a heavy bit in his mouth, which looked to be much like mine. He had handsome hair, pulled into a long ponytail down his back, and his head hair had been groomed to curve around his face. The tail that was plugged into his ass looked huge as it arched up his back and dragged the ground as he was led outside to await his rider. He literally hopped from one foot to the other. He was so graceful and such a show horse. How I envied him that day.

My harness straps were being fitted as I stood there, munching quietly on my breakfast. By the time my balls were bound out of the way and my tail installed, I had finished my feed. Trainer, with his hand full of reins, led me to a common water fountain. I was given chance to drink my fill before we went to work and was not alone at the watering hole. Other beasts of burden were being led out by ones and twos to go to work on the farm.

I was led back into the circle. There I ran till I warmed up, then taken from the circle, allowed to drink again and rest while my trainer spoke with another. I could have shit when Commander Schmidt walked down the dusty road in full riding gear and boots to claim her mount, the big stallion. She saw me drinking and approached to speak to my trainer about my characteristics. She actually laid her gloved hand on my quiver and patted me as she spoke. To her I was only a manimal. She claimed her mount, climbed in the saddle, set her spurs to his tender side and rode off on back of that hot looking manimal. He carried her proudly, too.

I was taught how to pull a cart over the following weeks and began to seriously earn my keep as a manimal within the barn. I actually liked pulling the small carts around the farm. My first training cart was a water cart. Empty, it weighted about 35 pounds, but once full it weighted several hundred. It took all my strength to get the cart moving once the tanker on back was filled. With patience, my trainer drove me forward with his whip while we climbed small hillsides to get to where the slaves were laboring. My job was to make certain water was taken to all the slaves within the fields while they were out and working. Each chain gang we passed lessened the burden that I had to pull till, at a gallop, I was run back to the water tower for the second load. Normally two loads would be taken to the fields per day. Except when the temperature began to rise, then I was pressed to take up to four a day.

While at the barn, my hair was kept upon my head but taken from my face. They wanted the manimals; the plow mules, cart mules and horses to maintain a certain image. Our work keeps us building and maintaining muscle, our diet rarely changed with the exception when a trainer rewarded his pet with an apple for above and beyond good behavior. The first time I earned an apple - even a slice at a time - made me roll my eyes and snap my lips. The taste was like nothing I ever remembered. Oh, how I worked harder to get another.

They began training me to work side by side with another mule; later we were paired and worked in unison to pull larger and heavier carts. We were used to pull in felled logs from the forest. The same logs that would be transformed into lumber for furniture or small cottages that were being built in the deep forest. It was our job to haul in the large logs; my trainer saw that we moved them with speed as his whip kept us moving forward. Nightly we would most often drop in our stalls, too exhausted to do much more than sleep till the next day. We were punished if we used human speech and rewarded when we used horse or mule noises, a honey dipped carrot chip went a long way on a manimal that had not had a sweet in over a year.

We were awakened really early one morning, fed and prepared as usual. We walked as a pair, side-by-side, harnessed to the long wooden post that would attach us to the cart, log, or whatever we were to pull. We met others walking with their trainers traveling the same road; all were heavy labor mules just like my companion and me. Our trainer dropped our reins and stepped aside to speak with the foreman in charge of this field, to my stunned disbelief it was Sir Cappy. He did not even notice when I shook my head to frighten off a fly that had been buzzing around my ear. Nor did he look when I neighed a greeting to the other manimals I had worked with in the field. We all just stood there, waiting our trainers like the dumb animals we had been trained to be.

They lead us up to a stump that had been partially cut from the earth; it was our job to pull it the balance of the way from the earth so we could plow the field for first planting. Initially two mules were put to work on the stump. We worked till our lungs were hurting and it felt like our hearts were about to burst in our chests before our trainer called a halt. While we got our wind, a second team was connected to our chain. Together the four of us got the stump moving, but it was not budging more that a touch. Again we waited, sides heaving, sweat dripping, while another team was added to the four-manimal team that was already set to the stump. Sir Cappy came over, snapped his bullwhip over our heads while our trainers pulled on our leads screaming us to pull. The six manimal team not only pulled the damn stump from the ground, we ripped it apart as it broke free of the surface. We spent the greater part of two weeks within that field as a six-manimal team turning one stump after another. Once the field was cleared, a four-manimal team went to work breaking up the soil and doing what the trainers called the first rotation. This first rotation was almost as hard as the stump removal had been. We broke the soil three ways, side to side, lengthwise then widthwise, making certain that we got up all the stump arms and large stones before a two manimal team were put to work finalizing the soil.

When I entered the world of the mules, it had been spring. When I was lead away to another world, spring had given away to the summer heat. No man had used me sexually while I was a mule. Our trainers had to have added something to our food that kept us from achieving an erection. I was taken from my stall and, as usual, fitted with my harness then led outside to be hooked before a small carriage. There I waited till either my trainer would come or whoever would take the reins. I was somewhat dumbfounded when I saw Master Hunter approach. He was wearing those boots that I remembered so vividly. He stopped to speak to my trainer, together they both climbed into the carriage. Hunter took the reins, snapped them against my hide and said, "Giddy up, mule."

I moved forward, taking him towards the house till he pulled on my reins and turned me to the right. While they rode in comfort, I pulled the carriage, eager to be of service to my owner and happy to please. Just the sight of him had a strange affect on me. I would shake and quiver as if he was a God and I too far down to be even noticed, in awe of his control. He had changed a little while I was away learning my true calling. He had a touch more gray around his temples and he seemed to have just a little paunch growing around his midwaist. Still, he was a very handsome Master.

I carried them wherever he wanted to go that day. First to check on the logging, there he spoke at length to the foreman while I fidgeted in my harness. I was anxious to feel the wind in my face. That job completed, he picked up my pace and let me run to the next area, slaves were hard at work planting the new field with wheat. He made me stop so he could stand and survey the planting from the height of the carriage. I jerked forward a couple of steps when a horsefly stung my back and damn near made him fall, he used my reins to catch himself and grind the bit into the corners of my mouth. I halted, he cursed till the trainer pointed out the black fly. His whip killed it and bit into my back but I held my place. We moved like this from field to field - through creeks and over the hillside until he had seen all that he needed to survey on this trip. That was the last night I had in the stable.

The following morning I was taken from the stall by my trainer later than most working manimals. I was fed as usual but I could sense change was coming my way. I was almost terrified of what my Master had decided, but chose to wait and see what transpired before I went into an all out panic. My trainer removed my hand hoofs, removed the hand mittens and bandages. My hands were brilliant white compared to the balance of my tanned body. The extra harness parts were removed, taking me back down to that of a standard slave harness. Then came the blacksmith. He made quick work of removing my foot hooves and setting my feet back upon earth. My feet had grown tender while within those leathered boots, now they would have to redevelop the hardened skin of a barefooted slave. The head harness with night bit was left intact and I was led by my trainer towards the great house and an uncertain future.

My trainer led me up to a post, where he tied my reins. He walked up the steps, knocked and was admitted to the log cabin. I could have run away if I had the mind to do so -which I did not. Here I had found through hard labor that I was appreciated and treated with respect. Here, I served best when I served in silence and humility. The door opened as my trainer and Master Hunter exited the dark interior. Together they walked down the steps in my direction, I grew excited to see them both and neighed a greeting to them. Master Hunter's face broke open with an incredible smile that radiated his pleasure in seeing me standing there waiting his pleasure. It was he that took my reins and led me away, while my trainer returned the barn and perhaps another mule.

I tried to prance as I had been taught as a mule but found it extremely uncomfortable without my hoofs and had to settle down and walk like a slave beside his Master. He led me down a pathway into the forest and beyond earshot of those at the cabin. We walked into a clearing, he stopped, grabbed my bridle, released the straps and pulled it off my head, taking the bit from my mouth and dropping it to the ground. Then he walked across the clearing. He turned to look at me and spoke, "9-745 crawl to your Master."

Without any doubt in my mind, I dropped to my hands and paws. I crawled the short distance to where he stood, watching and appraising me, till I was at his boots. He picked up a thick collar from the ground, placed it around my neck, buckled it tight, added a leash and spoke again, "Heel, dog slave, heel."

Together a man and his manimal walked to the creek near the back of the cabin. There, as he ordered, I removed his boots and clothes. I followed him into the creek, he laughed while I played in the water and as he bathed me of all the grime that had accumulated from the barn. Exiting the creek, he had me tongue his whole body. I did it gladly as this man had become my God. I wanted nothing more than to serve him, so if licking was what he wanted, licking is what he got. I started at his feet and licked my way to his head. Special attention was given to his armpits, his ears and what lay hidden between his butt cheeks. He seemed to enjoy holding me by his iron collar and directing my head, this way I did get to lick his heavily laden balls and his well-risen mast of a cock. He rolled over, climbed to his knees and grabbed me around the waist, pulling me to him. Spitting on his hand was all the lube I needed and his cock was buried to his balls. He took his time fucking my ass. He loved to fuck, then slap, my ass, or to reach under and grab my tits and roll them while his weight was on my back. I was growling while he worked his cock in and out of my manimal hole and when he came, I howled like a wild dog. Spent, he pushed me to the ground with his weight, his panting breath blowing into my ear.

I helped him back into his boots. He forsook his clothes, preferring to carry them over his arm. Together, we made our way back to the cabin, Master and his dog slave. It had taken a year and over three months for him to take me back to the cabin. Now I knew my place, so I thought. Now we could pick up where things had been left off, but it would never be the same. I knew that - or should have known – when, as we walked towards the back door, a trainer in a green jumpsuit was there to take me to my next station. I actually clung to his booted legs when the trainer tried to pry me off him. It was he that sent me away with an order and a barked command, "I do not own you, slave! This trainer is the very best, 9-745, go with him. 9-745 must be ready by fall! Go!"

My Master walked up the steps, wearing nothing but his dignity, opened the back door and stepped inside. I actually howled and groaned, as I was led away by this new trainer. I was taken to the logging site. Into my hands was placed a twelve pound axe. I and other slaves were taught how to fell trees safely. The air, new diet and hard labor helped my body change and grow. He wanted me to be balanced by the way my muscles developed. I worked to clear the land and my upper body took shape. When I was not working in logging, I was out in the fields lifting and moving boulders, clearing the land for yet other projects that were not important to me. I grew in strength and muscle tone over the summer months. No work was too hard for me to do. I would have busted my gut to serve my God again in any capacity he so desired. Here at the logger's camp, I was stripped of all hair, kept shaved by my own or another slave's hand.

I was taken from the logger's camp with others. One trainer and many handlers led our chain gang down the dusty road to whatever they wanted us to be used next. We were taken into a small barn. The chains at our ankles were removed and another was attached to our collars, these were connected to a steel 'O' ring that ran over a pipe in the ceiling. We were docile, to say the least. Too little sleep combined with too much work and not enough food kept us in an altered space.

As a team, we walked single file through the small barn, each step dragged the chain and hoop along the ceiling bar. A wooden barn door was pulled down its track and we marched into a white tile room. Handlers - ten in all - stood around the walls waiting our approach. Each handler was naked to the waist and wearing rubber bib overalls with boots and large black and red rubber elbow-length gloves. The first five slaves were called forward; we walked to the center of the room. Warm water was sprayed over our dirty bodies, then soapy water was sprayed from another hose. The handlers waded in and began scrubbing our bodies, making certain that they got every surface washed at least once. Another jolt of water hit us and we were sprayed clean. The first five slaves were directed beyond the scrub room. As we stepped from one room to the next, a blast of air dried us. Other slaves came to us, one per mule, and we were led into separate chutes, then attached to a chain while other handlers walked around us. As the handlers approached, they could be heard discussing the physical tone of the last mule, its qualities and its rank within their system.

When standing before me, they ran fingers inside my mouth, checked my eyes, stuck a probe up my nose, looked into my ears, grabbed my nuts, fingered my cock and shoved a finger into my asshole. My handler went over my body looking for blemishes, made a note about my back and checked the soles of my feet. A slave replaced him as we moved down the line. The slave stuck metal numbers on my right bicep with tape, told me to turn my head and sprayed something over the numbers. He blew on them, as if to make them dry faster, then peeled off the tape. I saw my number painted on my right bicep. Whatever for, I thought?

Once completed at that station, mike, of all slaves, led me down my chute and into a small room. Slave mike gave me four shots, checked my vitals and shoved a bulb up inside my ass. A sleeve, much like a condom, was slipped down over my cock. The bulb was connected to wires that ran to another of those damn boxes. I flinched and tried to pull back till his hand pulled me and he said so not to be heard, "It's ok, 9-745, this slave has no intentions of hurting it." Slave mike used electricity to milk my prostrate of every drop of sperm I had been holding for the past three or more months.

Slave mike broke the connection, the chain that mounted me to the ceiling rail, he opened the door and I stepped out and was met by none other than J.D. He led me out of the small outbuilding, down a path and into a large blacksmith shop. Someone has seen fit to send J.D. on this errand. Seeing as he was the one who fitted my first harness, it was his job to remove it. What had molded me more than the harshness of the underground training was to be removed; it was a catachresis, a rebirth.

To this day, I do not know why I cried when he cut the thigh straps and the shoulder straps till the damn harness fell from me. I felt more naked right then than at any other time in my life.

One full body harness gone, I was fitted with a much abbreviated version. A belt was cinched and riveted around my waist, two straps ran down on either side of my genitals and those were riveted just below my nutsack to a single strap. This single strap was pulled between my ass cheeks and belted in place at the back. Once those straps were in place, a blacksmith approached and made measurements for what turned out to be a codpiece of steel. This slave looked awkward; huge heavy muscled arms and chest with almost small legs in comparison. I was fitted with a cock and ball cage. It held spikes inside the cage to help me forget about getting a hardon or attempting to play with my cock. Before I left the smithy, my ass was filled with a plug, the belt strapped over the waist belt and that padlocked it in place.

Another station then removed us of all body hair and gave us each a shot in the hip as we were led away to our new assignments. I was placed on a small chain gang that was used daily for planting or tilling the soil around our crops. In the morning, our padlocks were opened, our plugs were pulled and we were granted time to take a much needed shit, then hosed out, cleaned, and reinstalled with the plug. Pissing we could do damn near anywhere; shitting was done according to schedule, mornings and evenings. Our chain gang reported biweekly to a milking station. The only time our cocks were released from their cock cages and our plugs removed was when it was time for them to take our sperm. We learned to look forward to our milking sessions, as it was a pleasant change from the standard routine of the week. This way we earned our keep in two ways and a slave must constantly look for ways to assist his owner.

Underneath those full body harnesses was snow white skin, but after a month or more working at tilling the soil, planting trees, doing hundreds of odd jobs our bodies began to color in and regain the healthy look of a happy docile slave. Yes, the work was hard, yes the days were horribly long; but we prospered, we learned and we grew to expect certain things. We learned that if we slacked our pace, a whip would help us return to speed. We learned if we grew sick we would be taken, treated and returned to work. We learned that no matter what we thought of our opinions it was incorrect, their way was the best, tried and true, way.

Our diet changed as we did, depending on the amount of labor we were performing. When I worked in the turbo room, I was fed large bowls of slave goop, it filled our stomachs and was chocked full of essential nutrients a body needs to survive. When I served as a miner, our slave goop was more watery and sweeter than that we had in the turbo rooms. I do remember being constantly hungry with those hammer gangs, but I prospered and moved onwards.

Even now, when one of us was singled out, cut from the chain gang and placed on a private detail, it was for our own good. Like the time I was taken. A handler took me off the chain gang, bound my arms and walked me in through a different route to the mouth of the caverns. I did not want to go, thinking I had done something wrong, his whip drove me forward. I stopped struggling once we entered the cavern, the weight of the world above seemed to depress my need to fight. That and when the guard standing at his post asked if the handler needed assistance.

I was taken down an unfamiliar corridor into an office. Sir Cappy was behind this desk. He looked up, grinned a toothy smile asked for my number, which was given by my handler. Sir Cappy walked around his desk, ordered me to pose, flex muscles, and fingered my teeth. He turned and spoke to the handler, "Show 9-745 where it will be placed when the time comes, and show it how it is to behave while on the stage."

I was led across the corridor and up a small flight of steps, then out on a wooden circle in what looked like an amphitheater. He dropped the chain to my neck, moved me into position and secured my leg shackle to a ring in the floor before releasing my bound arms. He showed me what I was expected to do when I was next brought here. He showed me instead of telling me. I was to flex all my muscles, arms, thighs, stomach, and chest, open my mouth wide and stick out my tongue, bend over spreading my legs and open my ass cheeks. He made me repeat the processes three times before I was given an ok. We left that place, walked down the corridor and back to my chain gang. I thought nothing of it till a couple of weeks passed and all the slaves were in an uproar. Guests were arriving and I was taken off the chain gang, down into the caverns, where I was to be prepped for the show.

Chapter 5

"True believers are not intent on bolstering and advancing a cherished self, but are those craving to be rid of unwanted self"

Hoofer: "The Battle for Your Mind" By Dick Sutphen

That day started earlier than normal for us that were to be part of the big show. We were taken out for a long run around the farm. Some of the handlers joined us in our jog around the estate and a trainer riding a bicycle guided us. We started just before daybreak with a slow running walk that picked up speed till we were in an endorphin pumping full run. We ran for the sake of running; to feel the wind in our faces. He directed our run so that we joyously ran by the main house, guests were outside having coffee and being served breakfast when twenty happy slaves ran into view. We were halted just before the steps of the house. Some of the guests came down to eye the panting manimals who were leaning over, sucking in air and flexing our legs, having enjoyed our run.

The guests were an odd crowd. Some seemed to be distant, hold-offish, others men and women, alike stepped within our ranks. One even caught my sweat on her delicate handkerchief and put it to her nose to smell. Another, a handsome man, slapped my butt, grabbing a handful. I flinched, turned to eye him, said nothing. Only watched to see what he was going to do with what he caught. Seeing no resistance, he dropped my cheek and returned to the porch.

Hunter stepped off the porch to walk among us and called back to those enjoying breakfast. "How do you like my manimals, folks? Aren't they the finest pieces of meat you have ever seen?" They applauded. He motioned the trainer to come forward. "Call them one at a time and have them stand here before this group, so they may see their assets before the show this evening."

So we were introduced to the guests on the porch, "Slave 3-691, front and center! Female, childbearing hips, housebroken and trained to guard the owner. Slave 3-775, female, mule, designed for hard labor; slave 3-420, female, guard animal; slave 4-772, male, educator, speaks 5 languages; slave 4-831, male, business, speaks 3 Latin languages; 4-922, male, educator, speaks Chinese/Russian. Slave 5-100, male, pre disposition towards pre-med; slave 5-101, male, pre disposition towards pre-med, slave 7-331, male, breeder, sperm count +7; 7-332, male, breeder, sperm count +8; slave 7-333, male, breeder, sperm count +7. Slave 8-101, male, bi sexual, breeder; 8-103, female, bi sexual; 8-104, female, lesbian. Slave 9-664, male, castrated mule-hard labor; slave 9-745, male, breeder, sperm count +9, mule-hard labor; slave 9-667, male, breeder, sperm count +9, mule-hard labor; slave 9-770, male, castrated mule-hard labor; slave 9-781, male, breeder, sperm count +8, mule-hard labor; slave10-080, male, show horse, breeder, sperm count +9; slave 10-081, female, show horse, breeder and there you have the whole line for tonight's show!"

Hunter stepped back into the limelight, "Ladies and gentlemen, for those of you who wish to view these manimals one more time, they go from here to be washed down. Those of you who wish to watch may follow them to the barn. After they are washed down, you will not see them till the show begins this evening." Hunter turned to the trainer, "Take them and make certain they put on a good show for these folks. Feed them well when they are taken down into the caverns. Make certain all are prepped and primed for tonight's performance."

We walked down to the barn and were greeted by a handful of slaves, waiting with buckets of soapy water. They made it a great show for the tourists and even we joined in on the fun, spraying our visitors when we shook off too much soap into the peering audience. You would have thought these people had never seen slaves bathed, as it seemed like they studied our every move. Once washed, we were dried briskly with soft towels and taken one by one down into the caverns to be fed and prepared for this evening's show. I felt like a prized manimal by the way I was being treated today.

We were fed our rations and put to work once out of sight of the tourists. We cleaned and prepared the area where the show would be held that night. We scrubbed the floors till they could be eaten from, cleaned, swept and even perfumed the air so the stink of the other animals would not confuse those attending the show. Handlers, like us slaves, were busy checking electronics attached to each chair arm to make certain each guest could vote for who was best of the show.

They kept us busy the balance of the day. Four of us were taken into a private room that was stacked with dirty boots. All of us must have had our boot fetishes enhanced while we were undergoing training for no sooner than the door shut we were upon those boots. We licked our way around the room before we sat down on the floor and began spit polishing each to a high shine. Hell, days could have passed and we would have been happy there cleaning, licking, and sucking on our superior's boots. Nevertheless, we were taken from that room, guided down the corridor, cleaned up again, placed on tables, given full body massages and oiled. Stepping out into the corridor, we walked with a spring to our steps. None of us had been treated this well before and probably would not again. We were fed a very filling meal. Not just slave goop, but each of us were given an apple. It was a reward for making the handler's boots shine, we were told when we looked puzzled.

Our chain of four comprised of three mules and one female, we were singled out and led down the passage into a private room. An awaiting slave, who had his mouth gagged into silence, removed our plugs and hosed our asses till they ran clean. An enema of olive oil was given to each of us just in case a guest wished to insert a finger or an object. Ours is not to reason why, ours is but to obey or die.

Freshly oiled, holes cleaned and oiled, we were taken to the staging area. Each of us was removed from the single chain, placed on leashes that were connected to an overhead beam and allowed to kneel till our numbers were called. When called, we were to stand, walk to the handler who would unlock our cages, lead us up the steps and out on the platform where we would be connected to the ring in the floor and we would kneel. Once the spotlights were upon us and our number announced, we were to rise and show off our bodies to the best of our abilities. We were told a bell would ring when our part of the show was over. A handler would come for us and take us down another flight of steps and into a private room. Once in the room, we would be rewarded for our good behavior. So, nothing was amiss in our books. We were just showing off our bodies to guests who were here to see how our training styles varied from other training compounds. Right?

My number was called after eleven others had gone before me. We were different than those outside, we had patience and strength trained into us that gave us peace of mind. We were doing what we were told without question. There isn't a greater gift that a slave may give its owner than total obedience.

I rose to my feet, marched the short distance to my handler, who removed the padlock and cock cage. He rubbed some oil onto my cock and balls so they would glisten in the lights. Taking my chain from the ceiling bar, he led me up the steps and across the hollow sounding floor to the platform that was outlined in tiny lights. He bent over, attaching my right leg shackle to a chain already present and unsnapped the leash at my neck. With his hand he motioned me to kneel and my show began.

"Slave 9-745, male, mule, hard labor. I fell forward onto my stomach pressed my head to the floor and walked my ass into the air, spread my legs wide, grabbed both sides of my ass cheeks and spread them to show my puckering rosette. I lifted my torso into the air, stood straight back, turned rapidly to make muscles in both arms, leaned forward for showing off my pecs, grabbed both sides of my rib cage and flexed my six pack. I leaned back till my body was in an arch and flashed my hardening cock at the audience that was lost behind the brightness of the lights. I had fun teasing them with my body, showing off my strong white teeth, opening my mouth and sticking out my tongue. I wanted them to admire what Hunter and his slave camp had given to me; a perfectly flawless body that was stronger than I had ever imagined. I felt like I was fluid motion while I moved about on the platform and I was enjoying myself till I heard the bell.

A handler came, removed my leg from the chain attached to the ring. He snapped a leash to my collar and led me down to a large room. I was looking around for my reward when a doctor arrived. He tossed me an apple and, while I was eating it, he gave me a big shot into my hip. The apple in my face held my attention until I began to notice the room was overly hot. I tried to get to my feet without much success. The handler helped me stand and half carried me while I tried to walk a short distance to a table in the middle of the room. They gently lay me down and while the doctor took my blood pressure, the room seemed to fill with other slaves.

Everything seemed to have a dreamlike quality as the room became distorted and faces became elongated. The shackle on my right ankle was cut and removed. Slaves helped slide me into a leather bag, my arms were slipped into sleeves and those were tucked in next to my body. The garment was gathered, pulled over my shoulders and chest. Many hands were adjusting the garment while I lay there watching, not moving, and just trying to focus on what was happening. One held the two sides together while another laced the two halves of the suit tight. They took their own sweet time as they smoothed out the leather while they laced me securely into this garment that was encasing my whole body from feet to neck in soft black leather. Straps were laid over my calves, thighs, and lower torso, another just below my nipples, before each of these was buckled securely in place. Each one was securely placed and tightened properly and locked with a golden padlock. As if I was going to escape! I felt so snug in this wonderful suit. The apple was a good reward at the time, but this garment was pleasure beyond anything I had known since I had been here.

An order was given and I complied, "Open your mouth 9-745."

A bite guard was inserted between my teeth and I was ordered to close my mouth. My tongue told me why I could only partially close my mouth. A tube had been inserted along with the rubber bite guard. They used tape to hold the tube within my mouth and a chinstrap to make certain it did not come out by accident. They forced me to breathe through the damn tube when they stuffed cotton into my nose, sealing it from its intended job. They seemed to work quicker, my eyes were taped closed and my ears stuffed with wax that stopped anything but the loudest sounds. My head was gently lifted from the table and a leather hood was pulled down over my face, the tube in my mouth was adjusted, as was the hood. It was snugly laced down on the right side just over my ear. A thick collar was worked under my neck, pulled around to the front and buckled in place. I felt the click of yet another padlock.

I was rolled onto my right side; something was slipped in below me. I was rolled back to my left and adjusted by hands that pulled me back and forth until I was squared upon whatever was at my back. Straps fused me to the board. I felt my world shift as I was lifted off the table and carried a short distance. Then I bounced a short distance before being lifted again and set down. Thankfully the shot helped me loose consciousness and I traveled to wherever my new Master had chosen to have me delivered.

Awareness came suddenly. I was no longer bound within the leather sleep-sack, however my head was still encased within the hood. My arms were bound below a table of some sort upon which my body did lay. I was face up. My legs were bound spread to the edges of the table and it was impossible to lift my torso from the table-top.

I was startled when a pair of silky hands glided over my chest, laid claim to my nipples and worked them slowly till they were hard. Those silky hands coasted slowly over my six-pack, outlining them as they made their way down to my rising cock and hard, firm, balls. I loved the way those hands made me feel. I felt my legs released one at a time from their bondage; each was lifted and hooked into something overhead, allowing them to float. The hands pulled me down to the edge of the table, I knew what was coming, and his cock punched though my butt muscle. Odd how it did not feel like Hunter's big cock, I thought, but decided to go with the flow as that cock seemed to know how to awaken my ass. Whoever was riding me, like to slam fuck. Pulling almost out of my butt muscle before putting his weight and strength behind his entrance. If the cock had been much larger I would have thought the Sheriff had gotten a hold of my ass again. Each time he slammed into me, the table actually rocked. I would have been pushed off the table if I had not be bound in place, thankfully I was. As quickly as he mounted, he shot his load in quick jabs and pulled out. He walked around to my head, placed something into the tube within my mouth. Piss began to flow, cutting off my only airway, I had no other choice than to drink fast or be without oxygen. I was lucky because, like his fuck, the piss ran out fast and he was finished. He climbed back into my saddle and rode me yet another time, this time was for his pleasure, and he seemed to fuck me for days before he shot his second load. He withdrew his cock, patted my chest and left the room.

A few minutes later, I heard the door open. I felt my hood being unlaced and pulled off. The tape on my eyes was pulled off with not so much any care as to what lay beneath and the tube in my mouth was removed. The creature that was standing near my table, removing my bondage had the markings of a slave; that is, it had a collar (though the collar was leather and the buckle variety not heavy steel like mine). His master must like him portly because this slave was fat to the notch of being obese.

Huge breasts hung over his ample tummy, his right nipple was pierced and he was wearing a leather jockstrap and boots. When he turned, there was a tattoo of an eagle spread across his shoulders.

The slave was constantly trying to get me to speak, I knew it was a test and, when I didn't he got angry and stormed out of the room. A very small room it was, too. Cramped quarters like I had been in at the farm.

Oh, God! That's when everything hit home and I realized I was no longer on the farm! That the big show had been the fall auction! I had been on the block and sold to pay for my upkeep as was the rights of Buena Vista and Hunter got outbid. Oh, God, I thought now what do I do?

Looking around, trying to take my mind off of my recent sale to an unknown owner, I found nothing that said I was still hopefully on the farm. The room was tiny, one door of metal was the exit, and a single bulb burned overhead, the room was painted white with white ceiling. There was a bucket with a lid in one corner and a bondage table in the middle of this closet!

I used the bucket to relieve the growing pressure in my ass, shit blew and piss did too. I worked off my bondage by doing pushups, exercises that keep my blood pumping and waited to be taken to the new owner. No one came; I was growing hungry and thirsty when a panel in the door opened and a plastic bowl was pushed within, followed by a big plastic bottle of water. The food was not to what I was accustomed; not our standard slave goop, the tasteless mess that stuck to your fingers and stomach. This was rice, chunks of fruit, nuts, an ivory colored paste with no taste and bits of meat. It went down easily enough and filled my void and, with the water, all was good.

I slept that night in a tight fetal position, worried that somehow I had failed to please my owner. Or else I would have been in his presence. Then I rationalized - perhaps the owner was still at the farm and I had arrived before him. I slept well once I had drawn that conclusion.

In the morning, the fat slave entered, ordered me onto the table. My eyes were covered with tape and pads. The hood was drawn over my head and laced tightly in place. He placed my legs in the stirrups that hung from the ceiling, bound my hands and withdrew. I heard the door slam as he departed. A few minutes later the door opened in came those silky hands. Master Hands is what I began to call my owner. Today he worked on my nipples, got them nice and erect before adding alligator clamps and rolling them between his fingers, making me hiss and suck air. He bound my balls deep into their sack, took a paddle to them, the pain was good for this slave. While holding my nuts deep in their sack, he began to close his hand, grinding my nuts into nut dust. While I was moaning in pleasure his - or his slave's - mouth closed over my cock. Whoever it was turned out to be one mean cocksucker, because he used his teeth to grate along every soft nerve my cock had exposed, which was all of my cock. One hand pulling on the chain that bound my tits, the other crushing my nuts, I tried to deny what I knew I could not. I blew a mind altering climax that almost took my breath away. The greedy cock sucking pig sucked it down and just kept sucking even beyond the comfort zone. Before my cock could come back for seconds the owner bound my cock by wrapping thin cord from the base to just below the head. I could feel my heart beating just within my cock head alone.

Somehow he connected my nuts to my aching tits, added a weight that pulled down on both, grabbed my hips and jabbed his cock into my hole. He came almost as quickly as I had, paused a few minutes and began to piss my butt full. Damn if his cock did not get harder when my ass was filled with his piss. The second cumming was long over due. He fucked my ass like a rabbit, using rapid fire jabs of his cock. Slamming his balls and crotch into my open hole, the force of our union made slapping sounds that I could hear clearly even with a hood. He came in silence, withdrew his cock and put his slave to tonguing out my wet runny asshole. That bastard of a slave loved it and my ass loved his attention, for it seemed my hole opened wide to his prying, sucking, tongue. A wet fart that held probably more than I would have wanted took us both by surprise, his only response was a girlish giggle and an order for more. When he was finished having his pleasure with my open - and now clean – ass, he withdrew, leaving me hooded and bound.

I stayed that way for what seemed like days till the door opened and Master Hands was back home. He took his time playing with my ass, using a rubber cock to fuck open my asshole, then his cock replaced his toy. Leaning into me, he removed the bondage that had bound my nuts, they ached, and they hurt when he began slapping them with a leather strap. I would have climbed off the table if I could, instead I clamped my ass muscles around his cock and began working them to milk his embedded cock. Such was the training that we had been taught within the caverns, how to use our bodies to affect change in our owners. I worked my ass muscles, using them to pull on his short spud of a cock. When he was not busy torturing my nipples or forcing his fingers into my mouth, he was jab fucking my hole, slowly, drawing out the pleasure he was having with my body. My job was to lie there and endure, but I should enjoy it, make it more pleasurable for the owner, with subtle slave tricks like milking his cock with well-trained butt muscles.

I screamed when he pulled the tit clamps off, writhed to his pleasure when he worked the circulation back into each of them, and coasted on the endorphins that my body provided when he took a whip to my six-pack and chest. His slave was put to work on my brutally painful cock, it having been bound tight for hours. It had to be blackish purple by this time. That bastard of a slave had a very talented mouth. He worked only the unbound cock head using his teeth to nip around the edge before impaling his whole mouth on my hard meat. My nuts were pulled back down into their nut sack, bound deep and paddled as the slave worked to make my cock desire, more than anything, another climax like before. His mouth was pulled off and the Master jabbed back into home plate and drove himself home. I thought while I lay there that only one worked on me at a time, they never seemed to be in unison working to make me suffer more at the same time. Of course, his slave could have his tongue buried into his owner's ass while I was being fucked or some such ordeal, the thought came and went just as quickly. Just like the owner, he came and departed leaving the slave to attend to my needs.

I was released from all the bondage except the hood. To that the slave added the collar and the padlock, making any attempts by my hands to free my head impossible. As if I would attempt to remove my own hood. Anything placed on a slave by a Master remained on the slave till removed by either an order or by the Master's own hand. To do something as silly as to remove a correctional device without an order meant that the slave was attempting to mimic an owner, handler or trainer. The punishment was severe for a slave to display anything that eked of free will. There were worse punishments in the caverns than even I ever wanted to consider. Even for us there are horror stories of the pit and what happens to a slave who is not on the right path. It is one thing to be a mule, breeder, and educator slave and there is the dark side of slavery; to be reduced to a ghost slave. A slave, who fears to leave the shadow of his owner, is a ghost slave, and should they depart from the shadow all hell will be turned upon that slave, again. Having seen one who had been reduced to that low a slave, I did not wish to see another.

The door panel slid open, food and water was placed inside and my days drew past slowly. Twice a day, the owner visited to use my body for his needs. Two or more times the slave would enter my closet; once to take and clean my slop jar, another time to gather up the bowls and empty jugs of water. No one came to take me for a run, or to work out, that I did as best I could within the confines of my room.

I almost broke the rules when I found myself fiddling with the lace that held my hood intact and locked around my head. I punished myself by not permitting myself to piss for a day. The pain was a good focus. If I had dared that move at the farm, my hands would have been bound at my back and a more intense hood would have been locked in place of this light one. This I could endure, it was the boredom that would make me nuts.

I, who had been trained for hard labor, longed for a hammer to work in the mines, or an axe to be cutting wood for the winter, or time at the turbo walking constantly around in a tight circle pushing with every leg muscle that heavy ass machine that created electricity for the compound. I became depressed as the days crawled into weeks, and stopped eating. Still the owner came in daily to use me. I could have been an inflatable doll for all he cared, and it would have suited his needs the better. I found some rope that the slave had left behind I had tied it around my neck and was trying to snuff myself when the fat bastard entered the room. He fought me to get the rope unwound and succeeded in taking that - and almost everything that I could have used to damage myself - away. I had hoped the Master would have beaten me that night but he did not show up for his usual fuck.

Men entered my hellhole, slaves from Buena Vista by the look of their jump suits. I cried as they entered, praying they would take me home. Instead they lifted me onto the table, bound me securely and started IV's. If I would not eat one way, I would another. Master Silky Hands returned that night to fuck my ass, yet again. Again I did not see him. What was he so fucking afraid of, that I must be blindfolded before he used me?

That night, in a fit of total desperation I prayed to my God, Hunter. He must have heard my pleas for rescue, because on the following morning, the door to my closet opened and there stood a handler I actually knew! I must have looked like shit by his reaction. As he stepped in and shut the door, he commented, "Damn slave, you look like you have been put through hell and not a good one at that!" He began removing the needles in my arm, adding a bandage and removing my bondage. From a satchel at his side he took a jump suit, pulled out boots and laid them on the table. "I will be back in a minute be dressed and ready or do you need help?" My silence told him I could handle this, so he departed.

He returned with the fat slave, "Your owner here has invoked a ruling within the contract. He claims you are faulty material and wants a 100% refund." The handler turned to me, winked and said, "You are to be returned, hospitalized, reconditioned and resold. Let's hope who ever buys you next time will help this Sir reclaim that which he paid for you. That is after your medical bills have been paid and your reconditioning fees."

Master Silky Hands turned beet red and went off, demanding his money back ASAP due to that slave (pointing to me) being not what he wanted. The door was left open while my handler escorted the fat man back into another room and they began a heated argument.

"Sir, if you would read the contract, here and here. It simply states that should a slave be returned as faulty merchandise, it is the owner's responsibility to the slave to pay for any medical expenses required to return the slave back to the state of prime health at the time of purchase. It is also your job to pay any fees for reconditioning and, by the looks of this slave, he will need both reassurances and self-esteem modifications. Sir, may I ask a question?" My handler was trying to find out why I had become faulty. Was it the owner's stupidity or mine? "Why did you purchase one of the highest priced slaves on our market? A mule is designed and trained for hard labor, by the looks of your apartment you do not need a mule but a standard slave that is trained for house duties."

I was wearing the jump suit and boots when my handler returned with a wheelchair. He put me into an oversized sweat jacket with a hood; it must have been cold outside, zipped it up, cuffed my hands in front and pulled the sleeves over to cover the metal. I was seated, straps bound my legs to bars on either side, and another strap like a seat belt locked me within the chair and with a pat on my shoulder. I was wheeled down the hallway and into a disgusting pigsty of a living room/kitchen. Trash littered every flat surface, magazines were stacked knee high and greater in places in the room, newspapers were scattered all over the rooms and open cans of half eaten food were almost everywhere. I was amazed that my room was so tidy; but then, I was the maniac who policed the floor for any trash. A clean and spotless house is the sign of a good and happy slave.

My handler picked up the paper work and had Master Hands sign and initial two spots he missed. The papers were placed into a briefcase that was dumped into my lap, and we departed. Outside in the corridor, my handler asked if I was going to be nice or did he have to gag me. He gave me no choice, adding a gag and drawing the hood over my head. I wanted to be nice. Anything to get away from the psychotic troll!

I was wheeled into an elevator. We went down, exiting into a beautiful lobby of an apartment complex. No one seemed to notice me as my handler took us out the front door and into the crisp sunshine of a winter's day. Snow was drifting down from the sky above; it was an absolutely wonderful day. We walked about two blocks, turned a corner and stepped up to a white van. My rescuer stepped beyond, keyed a lock on the backside of the van and a ramp began to extend itself out to me. He pushed me into the van, flipped a button on a console and adjusted my chair till it was locked in place between two wheel braces on the floor. With a thud, the ramp and back door closed. My handler climbed into the driver's seat and started the engine, allowing it to warm the inside of the van while he made adjustments to my bondage.

He pulled something that looked like a tube of toothpaste from his brief case. He turned to me with care in his eyes for my well being; never had I felt as weak as I did that day. Still, I was excited, having escaped what would have been my death if Hunter had not heard my prayers and sent help.

He opened the tube and extracted the gag, "You have to be hungry. Our doctors worked on this for those we rescue from bad owners. It will give you some much needed energy and help you relax on our trip home. And it's actually good for you."

Hand and Glove: The Path

To prove to me that it was not something dangerous he squeezed a little of the tube into his mouth, smacked his lips and showed me it was gone. He put the tube to my lips, squeezed in half the tube and let my tongue do the rest. It tasted like fresh strawberries; I squeezed in the balance of the tube while we drove off.

The windows on the van were blacked out. Perhaps so people would not be shocked at what may have gone on inside the van, perhaps for my safety should I gain freedom and want to come back and teach Master Hands a lesson, who knows! It was just good to be going home again. Interestingly, as the van warmed, music played and I found myself nodding off within the wheelchair. I knew I was weak, but thought the excitement I would have kept me awake.

When I came to, I found myself in a bed with linens and a blanket pulled up and over my chest. One arm was bound to a cloth-covered plank and I was receiving an IV while the other was bound to the side of the bed in leather hospital restraints. The bed was surrounded by curtains, still someone must have been paying attention. The curtains were drawn open, and in stepped my handler dressed in a white lab coat. He sat down on my bedside, "You were too weak to be taken directly back to Buena Vista, so I made a pit stop. We are, at present, within a rescue mission of ours. Other slaves and a few owners are here. You lost a lot of fluids, so we are replacing them, and we will begin to help you reclaim your body with some of our more modern techniques."

He leaned forward and pulled a hypodermic from a tray, filled it from a small vial in his pocket and dropped the fluid into the IV line. "Now you will sleep. When you awaken, 9-745, you will feel much like your old self and we can begin the journey home."

I don't know how long I stayed bedfast before I was permitted to work out in their gym. It was slow going and they made certain that I did not overdo. They also knew that, once I got back to Buena Vista, I would have to endure some serious hardships. The slave medical staff made certain I was ready before I was permitted to leave. All knew, including me, any slave that is returned to Buena Vista would have to be physically able to handle the hardships of standard slavery. A slave returned for any reason meant there had been a breakdown within the system, it may not have been the fault of the slave for its return, but it would be the slave that would get the worse end of the deal. It would be singled out for all the hardest labors and be taught the error of its way. In my case, as a mule, I should have been able to stick out the situation. I opted out by starving myself, using freewill. That free will must now be taken from me.

I had become more and more restless as I recovered, until one day after the doctors gave me yet another examination, clearance was given for me to go home. I was given a bag of civilian clothes, got my butt plugged and was ready when the handler showed up with my foot gear and something extra. Short lace up boots went over bare feet and I was ordered to stand, hands clasped at the back of my neck. He put around my waist a leather and steel belt that held two separate metal leg braces, both of which had metal covered leather straps. Straps went around my upper thigh, lower thigh just above my knee cap, below my kneecap, around my ankle and a boot strap went under my boot and got locked in place by a suitcase snap. Having these braces on my legs, the handler could literally lock my legs out stretched or bent. Once locked into the position he wanted, there wasn't a way to break them of the position till he keyed the change. Running was not an option.

Just as I had entered, I left by way of a wheelchair. Bound into it of course, the straps at my ankles were very visible, as were the leg braces, and he had made certain that if I so much as wiggled out of line, the butt plug was attached to one of the compound's own black boxes. With the push of a button, he could fry my insides and my screams would only seem like a patient having a fit. Ingenious and twisted way to travel the friendly skies but somewhat expected. The doctor gave me a clean bill of health late that afternoon, BV, Buena Vista's command recommended that I be brought on home before all the profits from my next sale were blown in the hospital.

UA allowed the handicapped man and his doctor/handler to board the plane early, Buena Vista had booked our flights home on first class. It is a wonder I had not been placed in cargo and the handler taken first class. This was their way to insure that I arrived in good working condition. He took the aisle seat, I the window. He made certain that his medical bag was near by, just like that damn black box, should I get uppity. He even went ahead and bound my legs together, explaining to the stewardess that he didn't want me kicking the poor lady in front of us. My medical condition made me jump and flinch on occasion, especially when he was nervous. To help the steward-ess understand he put one hand lovingly on my leg while the other hit the controls of that box. The message was driven home and we were left alone for the most part of the trip.

I got to watch the beautiful city lights below us before my handler closed the blinds. He called for pillows and blankets and made a fuss about getting me comfort-able when I knew he had something else planned. Handlers are tricky bastards! He unbuttoned my shirt on the pretense of listening to my heart, lungs and attached a set of alligator clamps to my chest. I hissed as the teeth ground into my hardened nipples and he helped by patting my chest. Ever the loving and attentive handler, not! Dinner was served, I was given a vegetarian dinner while he had this big juicy steak, pota-toes, green beans and dessert. I wanted his meal and was about to ask for it when he stepped out of the bathroom, returning too quickly. He was so polite in explaining that I had a special diet. Yeah, slave goop that I had to maintain or else get deathly ill. Which just might be the case, but I would love to find out for myself. He helped me forget the nice dinner he had by placing the box on a regular beat; blast, blast, blast, pause, Blast! I was a regular Nervous Nelly by the way the stewardess had to have seen me twitching away in my seat. The plane landed near midnight and the passen-gers disembarked, I had to wait till last when a chair could be brought to me.

Once off the plane, we walked casually up the ramps, caught an elevator down to luggage and exited. A standard handicapped van was awaiting my return along with four handsome handlers just in case I became anxious or combative in route home. It wasn't as before that the wheelchair and I were loaded into the van. This time I was taken from the chair, lifted by two very burly men, carried into the back of the van and dropped. The wheelchair was returned to a porter and my guys climbed into the van with me. While the van drove forward, the braces - along with all my clothes - were removed. My hands were bound and drawn widely outspread, as were my legs. A gag was forced between my teeth and a blindfold was put over my eyes. Once done, I knew I was back home and the boys were happy I had returned.

My handler was the first to start the funny business. He made a comment to the others that this slave had been giving him a hard time all the way back; meaning his cock had been hard the whole trip, not that I was being a pain in his ass. They suggested that he do something about this problem he had. He said, ok and climbed in back where I lay all bound and helpless. My butt plug was pulled. His butt plug was centered and forced into my handsome bubble butt and he rode me hard. I loved it!

That began their private party. Three handlers made use of my holes and when they stopped for gas the driver slid in for his share of the all American pie, me. I was fucked this way to Sunday and back again. A cock in my mouth one in my butt if I had more holes those too would have been occupied. I swear they should have hung the bumper sticker "If this van's rocking don't come knocking." Still, it did make the trip home a lot more pleasant.

When next the van stopped we would be at home. Their final way of saying thanks was to place a thick leather hood over my head, zip and lace it up the back and add straps across my mouth and eyes. When the van door opened and closed I knew they were gone and I was left for the next team. The back of the van opened, I felt someone climb up by the way the van shifted. Both my hands and feet were released while a toe to my ribs indicated in a no nonsense fashion that I should roll over onto my back. A pair of hands grabbed my hands, rope was bound around my wrists, cinched and more rope was bound just above my elbows. This, too, was cinched tight. They repeated the steps on my legs, bound my ankles, then above my knees. Something long and hard was slipped between my ankles, and then forced between my thighs as it was pushed higher and forced between my upper arms and my cinched wrists. I was lifted and moved to the end of the van so the men in the van could jump down. Together they lifted me and I had the distinct impression I was in a Tarzan flick, like I was an animal being carried in by the great white hunter on a wooden pole. It was a brutal way to bring me back to the caverns but one of the best ways to say to me, the party is over, it has work to do. All my joints hurt from this forced position as all my weight was focused on my elbows and knees, weak joints to begin with. Luckily it was a short walk for them to carry me back into the caverns and set me down on the hard stone floor while a guard marked my number on my right arm. 9-745 returned home in shame.

Once checked in, the pole and I were lifted. We went about 100 yards before the pole was removed and I was physically carried into a room and dropped unceremoniously on the floor. A female voice was talking to a subordinate male; he took his orders and departed. Her boots rang out clearly on the floor as she approached; one boot lifted my chin and looked down my body, "Remove its hood." The hood was jerked off my head, the lights momentarily blinding me and while I blinked to adjust to the bright lights, her boot lifted my chin and she laughed, "Oh, it's you again!"

Two men twice her size were looking down at her. It could not be helped as she was a petite woman, yet carried herself as if she was ten feet tall with balls to match. I could have shit when I realized who it was I was lying before. The same Commander Schmidt that I had mistakenly pissed upon during a brutal interrogation. There she stood, in the middle of her command room, black jump suit, black military combat boots, blonde hair tied into a bun on top of her head, delicate like a flower. But I knew from past experience, that delicate flower had thorns. Lots of thorns and she loved to use them on anyone that got in her way.

Her hand cupped her chin as she looked down on me, she was thinking, quickly making up her mind and began to bark orders, "We go by the book with this one, use the Standard Operational Procedures for returning slaves. Help it to realize we do not tolerate any slave returning to us, especially one that tried to take its own life." I saw a twinkle form in the corner of her eyes and knew I was about to be either brutally beaten or taught a very serious lesson that I just might not survive, "Harry, send a slave to bring you a real horse with riding gear and call in two mules. By the looks of it, make them brutes. Take this piece of slave scum to every field. Let them see what happens to a slave who does not obey. Go! You have orders and get this piece of shit out of my office before it attracts flies."

I sung praises to my Hunter God while I was being carried by pole to two fields, so the slaves who were doing final harvest could see what a no account slave I was to have been returned. I had left the caverns being carried by two brute mules, slaves who had been transformed into nothing but a wall of muscle. Dumb but handsome, if you liked that kind of thing. Harry was on horseback carrying his favorite of whips, a braided cat. He used it on me instead of the brutes while the brutes carried me from one field to the other, three fields should be all that needed a final harvest this late in the year. Luckily I was right, they only had to run to two adjoining fields before returning to the warmth of the caverns. Harry kept me warm with his whip as it cut any hide it hit into bloody red ribbons. That was the point, to make the field slaves see a bloody slave hanging like dead meat on a pole. Once Harry's whip started striking my body, I began to wail a cry that could have equaled any fire engine. It must have been a sight to hear and see; two heavy brutes carrying a bloody slave on a stick followed by a handler on a black stallion who was cutting the slave into ribbons. Somewhere on the way back I passed out and my cracking voice became silent.

Dumb from pain in all my joints, I was jarred to semi-consciousness by a wealth of new pain. I do not know which is worse, being first bound or having the ropes removed after being bound a long time. I think it's the latter! My shoulders felt like they had been torn from their sockets, I heard and felt a heavy soft thump and passed out. Cloy and nasty smelling perfume brought me back to consciousness. The pain was renewed as they removed yet another cord from my body. Every time I passed out they waited, then popped a snap capsule under my nose that brought me back to consciousness and another bound limb was released. They wanted me to remember every aspect of this lesson and the ones that would be following my return to base.

When I did finally fully awaken, I was seated in a metal chair, my arms, legs, torso bound tightly to the chair by heavy straps, even my forehead was locked to a headrest. The only thing that moved was my jaw. I must have been in the chair for quite some time, as my stomach was growling from lack of food. I could only look forward at a wall length mirror to see a slave devoid of hair, strapped into a heavy metal chair, bound and waiting his fate.

The door opened and a man stepped beyond the arch. He was dressed from head to toe in black leather. There wasn't a patch of skin showing, he even wore a leather hood. This was the Master of my most jaded dreams and, as he turned to look at me, his cold blue eyes actually hurt. It had to be Hunter.

He walked over to a tray that was before me, pulled back a cloth to reveal two of those black boxes with four cords running in my direction. I could only imagine where they led. He spoke, his voice was not Hunter's, but there could be a way to disguise his voice. "Why did it fail its owner?" He flipped on both boxes and adjusted four knobs. All I could do was stammer in my nervousness. His finger went towards a button and, before he could press it, I screamed! He looked at me and inquired again, "Why did it fail its last owner?"

My voice cracked in my nervousness to tell him, "I don't know why Sir."

Two buttons were depressed; I jumped within my bonds as all my nerves screamed in unison. He released the buttons; I slumped down into the chair, sweat dripping from all my pores.

He spoke again, " why did it fail its owner?" He watched me watch him, his fingers crept towards the dials, and made a change to the level of pain I would feel when he next hit the buttons.

I began stammering, stuttering my words, "S-s-sir! This slave thought Sir!"

"Oh!" he said. "It thought. By what rights does a slave have to think? Was it ordered to think?"

"Sir, no Sir. This slave was wrong to think Sir. Sir, this slave, had too much time on its hands Sir." The buttons were hit; I rose into the chair as I screamed this god awful sound that had to come from the depths of my soul, the voice cracked. The buttons were released and I slammed back into the chair thankful the straps help me in place.

The man in the black leather unbuttoned his fly, pulled out a very hard, aching cock and began pulling on it. His cock oozed a river of pre cum. I could not take my eyes off of his cock, Hunter's cock. I knew this was my Lord, my owner and my God Hunter, here torturing me for his pleasure.

"So, this slave 9-745 is faulted because it thinks? Is that correct slave 9-745?"

"Sir, yes, Sir, this slave thought too much, Sir!"

"Does slave 9-745 realize it has gone against the way, our chosen path?"

"Sir, this slave knows it has wronged all those of the way, Sir."

He touched one button just to watch me squirm in my seat as my ass caught the brunt of the electric shock. The button was released; his cock seemed to swell as he watched me squirming to avoid what I could not.

"Slave 9-745, it must make amends, it must correct its wrongful thinking! Is it ready to step on the path of redemption?" He paused, flipped some of the buttons, turned some of the dials on the black boxes and when he looked up his eyes had gone cold and cruel. "Answer me, slave!"

I swallowed hard, again swallowed, trying to get up my nerve for what he wanted me to say. He looked at me, boring a hole through my head mentally, commanding me to give the go ahead. I swallowed one more time, opened my mouth and screamed at the top of my lungs, "SIR, YES SIR!"

He hit all the buttons, my body arced up in the chair as every nerve was hit by a pounding of electricity, then I passed out and was no more.

When I could finally move any part of my body without loud moans, I rolled my head to one side and was shocked at what I saw. A handler was lying beside me. One of his big meaty arms was laid over my body and he was snoring into my ear. I was dying for a drink of water and needed to piss like a fucking racehorse. He moved, rolling to his side and taking his arm with him. My fear of this unknown handler was tangible, like a fly hanging in a spider's web and waiting for the spider to come calling.

I saw my chance to find what I desired more than anything - a drink of water and a much needed piss. Cautiously, I rolled to the edge of the bed, dropped my feet to the floor was lifting myself up with my legs when they gave out and I fell back. He woke with a start; grabbed at the place I should have been, sat up in bed, flipped on the light and found me collapsed on the floor besides his bed.

"What the fuck are you doing down there, 9-745?"

"Sir, I stammered, this slave wanted a drink and a piss, Sir." I crouched down, head to the floor, afraid that he was going to hit me. I trembled like a leaf, fearing he would hit me or worse while he leaned over looking down on me. "Sir, forgive me, I tried to be quiet but when I stood up my legs gave out and I fell. All I wanted was a drink and a chance to piss, Sir."

"Of all the stupid tricks, slave. The doctor said your legs and arms would not hold your body weight yet! Since I am the one that basically broke them, I have to put up with it, in my quarters, till it's mended. Then, slave, I can get you back on track." He rolled out of bed and returned a couple of minutes later with a chilled glass in his hands he passed it to me. "Here drink it all down. Doc said it would make it more comfortable while its body healed."

"Now, beg me to let you piss, slave."

"Sir, please, Sir. Let me piss Sir. I will do anything you desire if you will only let me piss, kind Sir."

He actually laughed in my face, "First lesson, slave, I am in no way kind. Go ahead cut loose, you may piss, slave." I must have gotten a perplexed look on my face; he looked down at me puzzled as if asking silently, what's wrong now?

"Sir, I am trying but nothing is coming out, Sir."

"Whoops, my fault, slave." Leaning forward he found the tube exiting my cock, released the cock stop and my piss flowed freely into a collections bag near the foot of my bed. He scooped me up like I was a little child and got me back into bed and under his covers. "Need anything else before the lights are turned out, slave?"

I yawned hugely, saying, "Sir, no Sir."

He crawled back in bed, pulled me in beside him and reached for the light. "One thing, slave. From here on out, no matter how badly you feel, you will not refuse me anything. The word 'no' is stricken from your lips and actions." He rolled on to his side and pulled me to him. One of his hands worked on my left nipple as he drifted off into sleepland and I joined him not soon after.

I awoke, ravenous with the smell of bacon all around me. Rising, I half limped into the kitchenette and found my muscles less sore than last night. He looked up at me and actually smiled. Training began immediately. I was ordered to my knees with my hands tucked beneath my thighs, palms up and to wait silently for breakfast.

He sat at the table above me eating bacon, eggs, toast, drinking fresh orange juice and hot coffee with cream. When he was finished he rose from the table washed the plate and fork then turned to the stove to fix my breakfast. A few table scraps were there in the bowl but so was the ever-present meal of all slaves within the compound, our beloved slave goop. Still, it hit the spot and staved off starvation. Just barely.

Kneeling beside the made bed, he made me watch his morning routine and remember it for when I would be responsible for such details. A uniform was pulled out of his closet, standard issue black jumpsuit, combat boots were checked before a quick polish and shine. He went to shower, shave, and returned from drying himself to find me licking a spot off his boot. He laughed but corrected me for moving from the spot he had indicated. He dressed himself, as I made an interesting mental sidenote; he was very much like my Hunter, even to the same aspect of placing his cock and balls into a black leather jewel case before sliding them into his jump suit. Odd how two people could have the same traits.

He turned to me, placed a plug in my ass, and then placed that ass in a wheelchair. Straps secured the slave so it would not fall out should we hit a bump or two, he explained with a laugh. Door opened, I pushed through and into Handler Central, all the housing for handlers was underground in one of the better areas with, for some, rumor has it, access to the outdoors. This traveling route took me to see the most twisted doctor on the whole campground. Doctor Dick, or as they called him behind his back, Twisted Dick was awaiting my return almost too eagerly.

Today the doctor was in a good mood, at least it looked that way. He was wearing a vibrant blue and yellow diving suit under his lab coat. Tricky Dicky loved rubber, loved how it felt and loved in his spare time transforming his slaves into rubber objects that served him like no other Master on the base. Full encasement, no skin exposed and they had multiples of tubing running from their nostrils or mouths or just a collection of tubes extending from out of where there should have been eyes, nose and mouth.

I was trapped in the wheelchair with my handler Dan watching as doc applied creams to my abraded rope burns, checked to see how my leg tension was developing and just seeming to pick and probe our time away. He drew blood to run some tests, checked the weight of my balls then scheduled me for a milking and gave me three more shots. For what, who knows, we slaves seem to get shots pretty regularly, like our drawn blood and for those of us who are sperm donors, we seemed to get it twice as often.

I was to have two more days of recovery time before I would return to light duty. My handler had to prepare for his shift and he had to figure out where to stow me. He took me back to his apartment, released me long enough to remove my plug, fill my butt with a huge enema and make me squat over an open drain till all the fluids were drained out. I cleaned up any mess, had washed my hands when he returned to fill my hole with a standard slave plug. He rode me back to the bed, dropped me on it. Beside the bed was a large glass of juice when he ordered me to drink completely. I was ordered to lie down, get comfortable. He wrapped leather shackles around my swollen wrists and ankles; those got bound together, hands in the rear. A leather hood was pulled over my head, laced tight and into my mouth he fit a penis gag with a hole in the end. At first I thought it was to give me more breathing room until I felt him moving my penis. Two tubes became one, I would be recycling my own piss all day or till he returned to change things. A blanket was pulled over my body, the juice did its job and I was out like a light. I slept fitfully most of the day, and heard him - or someone - enter midday and returned to sleep till he came home after his shift. That night, after another big dose of juice, I slept again, more comfortable than I had since I was with Hunter. Plus, I loved it when he took what was his, my ass, in the middle of the night.

On the third day I was taken back another way from having visited Tricky Dicky and been placed on light duty. In a wheelchair no less, I was taken up a long ramp and outside the caverns to the central blacksmith. I was to have that which was taken from me, my right shackle, replaced. This time, I was not horrified by the prospect nor was it applied to my ankle while hot. The black smith must have kept these rings of steel always made up. All he did was size my ankle, find one on the wall, pop it open, place it over my ankle and hammer it closed. Now I was a slave of Buena Vista again, the shackle was that which connected us to all chains.

Handler Dan picked up some special gear he had ordered; steel spreaders that locked midway and arm spreaders. He was clothed, I was naked and bound into the wheelchair and he decided to take a quick walk around. I nearly turned blue before he realized I was freezing to death. We stepped into a new outbuilding, found a hidden elevator and descended into the depths. So much building was going on topside. Change was afoot, even the main house was having expansion. A great room was being added to host more efficiently Hunter's events. It would seem that Hunter and Cappy believed in returning a major portion of the slave sale profits to improve the surrounding area.

Light duty began light, but as the days moved forward they changed as more burdens were placed on me and I got back into the slave groove. I had learned Handler Dan's morning routine, he still cooked his breakfast not wishing to provide me with more temptation than I could handle. But while he was doing that, I made the bed, laid out his uniform of the day, licked and buffed his boots to a high shine, even tidied the apartment. While he ate, I knelt at his side, head bowed just incase he should want something that I could fetch for him. While I ate he showered. The first day that I met him with a warm towel just about blew his mind. He stood there not knowing what to do as I patted and rubbed him dry. I dressed him afterwards and was rewarded those first few days of light duty by being taken to a private room, chained in place and left with a whole room of boots to spit shine before he returned. When he returned to fetch me home, he found me in the floor, eyes glazed in high boot lust, cock hard and unable to touch it. He took me home ordered me to kneel at the door as he walked across the room and sat down. "Crawl to my boots, little pig," he said.

Brother did I crawl and did he give my tongue and body a work out with his boots. It was one thing to kiss the soles of his boots or to run my tongue over his com-bat boots, but something different totally to hold out my nuts and beg him to stomp them, which he gladly did! I opened his boots with the aid of my teeth, used my chin to pull the laces and tongue out of his boots and used my thighs as a bootjack for him to pull them off. Then he shoved my head into that wet rich moist leather and made me drink in his boot, I felt I had died and gone to heaven right then and there. Once finished with these boots, I helped him out of his uniform and into something more comfortable - a pair of long leather shorts that gave him a killer basket and buns like no tomorrow.

He ordered me to fix dinner. Handlers had it lucky within our compound. The kitchen prepared meals for the handlers that could be eaten in their cafeteria or could be picked up and taken out. Or a list could be provided to the main chef and the meal would be sent into the home. Our cupboard was bare, so Master Dan called in an order and sent me to bring it home while he rested. The jog did me good but I failed to realize, as did Master Dan that while a slave could be seen leaving Handlers Central, returning was to be the hard part. Normally no unattended slaves were permitted within a handler's private domain. Returning from the kitchen, I was stopped and questioned by two handlers and, when I could not provide a name or number for my handler, I was about to be taken elsewhere. As luck would have it, Dan second guessed me and appeared as if out of nowhere to rescue my ass again. Either that, or his hunger got the best of him and he wanted to see if I was chowing down on his steak in some side corner.

He actually fed me some of his steak while I knelt beside him. Damn, that bloody red meat tasted good! After dinner Master Dan became restless had me pull out his thigh high engineer boots put on his socks, and I got the pleasure of helping him into them. He looked fucking hot! Thigh high boots, leather shorts with a bulging basket, big handsome tight chest, big chewable nipples and two no nonsense arms filled with muscle. He picked up the phone, called someone and told him that he would be along. My elbows were bound; he placed my hands in the new spreader bar and locked it before me. He added his leash to my neck and we were away.

We seemed to walk a long time. He kept getting catcalls from other handlers that admired his looks; he was a very handsome man. We rode up on an elevator, stepped outside into the cold night and he ran me to the blacksmith's shed. Thank god it was hot in there because it wasn't outside. He had failed to get me a marker that was supposed to be placed on my steel neck collar. A blue painted tag that had his number hammered into the surface was slipped over the steel and riveted in place. The blacksmith commented about the arm spreaders and Master Dan ordered some other device while looking in my direction. Quickly he ran me back to the elevator and down. I was shivering with the cold till we stepped around a crudely cut entrance and stood within something from Dante's vision of hell.

Stupidly I had stepped forward into the room when a jerk on my leash turned me around to face him. "Anxious to get started, is it?"

I must have paled because he laughed and led me deeper into the depths of the dungeon. It wasn't a huge room, about a 30 x 30 cut from hard limestone rock, opened by slaves by the look of the walls. The floor was compressed dirt, easy to walk on and helped dull the sounds of whips hitting flesh, men and women screaming, others fucking with all manner of sex going on. He led me out into the center; he was looking for someone, then found him and made a beeline for the man. The man we were stalking was a handsome big Afro-American who rippled with sexuality, at the time he was using a white male mule. By the looks of the mule's back it had taken quiet a flogging.

Master Dan greeted this blue-black man as he was fucking the mule over a bench. The other handler's name was Tony and I was surprised to hear my Master calling this man Sir. Ok, I thought. Perhaps my mind was playing tricks or this man held higher rank, which would explain the exchange. I never gave it much thought as I was unbound and tied over an upright fuck bench. Once bound, Master Dan went in search of something interesting to use on my ass, he returned with a few things and began broadening my horizons.

I was positioned so my legs were spread and bound open. My torso was pushed over something that resembled a sawhorse but my torso ran over a long plank before my arms dropped and were bound on the underside. In this position, I could easily be used as a sandwich between two Masters. It did not take too long before Master Dan had me crying out as he laid one razor strop after another into my butt cheeks. He switched to a heavy frat paddle to raise me onto my toes for a while, before switching back to the strop. My ass had to have been at least cherry when he stopped for a breather and to talk to Tony, who was still fucking that mule's ass.

When he returned, he seemed to have a renewed vigor for my blood. Or at least for my ass to have blisters for the next week. He was using his empty utility belt to raise the level of appreciation he wanted out of me. Each blast of his arm and belt seemed to raise me up on my toes, he would pause till I settled and blast into my ass again. This belting went on till he saw the blisters forming. Then he laid into me rapid fire! He wanted me to scream out, loud and clear! Believe me, he got it in spades. When he stopped I was sobbing hard. He waited till I stopped and ran his hand over my glowing ass, just his light touch hurt really bad. He released me from my bound position, said good night to Tony and he led me home.

Once home, he pushed me to my knees, his boot pried open my legs and it settled over my cock and balls. Slowly his weight came down on them, crushing them under Vibram soles. His boot turned once, my hands encircled his leg and my head bowed to his Mastery. His boot crushing my cock and balls made me want to please him so badly, yes, it fucking hurt. But it hurt so damn good! He literally stepped over my body, plunging me in writhing pain from the pressure of his boots on my nut sack. I did not care, and I crawled after him till he told me to stop.

"On your back, 9-745, legs apart, wider! Grab its fucking worthless slave nuts and hold them up to me! Beg me to make them hurt!"

Such an evil bastard, I was in full-blown boot lust and he knew it. I laid back, opened my legs wide, grabbed my nuts and held them up to him in my fist, pulling them as far as I could from my body. "Good Sir, please, please hurt them, Sir!"

He made me watch as his right thigh high black engineer boot rose slowly to my nuts to check the distance. I watched and moaned as the boot descended to the floor. He made a tentative run just to my nuts and let his boot settle to the floor again. I was moaning like a bitch in heat, holding my nuts out to him. His boot swung up in a massive arc that collided with my nuts and kicked my hand away. I screamed as the boot swung past. I saw stars and his boot in them, and I writhed on the floor. My balls were beyond pain, taken into pleasure. Like a sick fool I took up my balls again and begged him to kick them again! "Sir, hadn't I been wrong in my thinking, Sir?" I reminded him.

His deep chuckle told me all I needed to know. He was enjoying making me beg for this pain. The area between the boot sole and the heel connected with my carefully gathered nuts, I howled and shot a load of cum that had to have covered my whole chest and realized. Again I had failed! His boots kicked me every way but Sunday, he went stomping mad when I, a breeder slave, lost my precious fluid. He was ranting as he stomped, kicking my body. When he stopped, my head was pinned to the floor, my lips were bloody and I felt like I had been through hell!

He walked away from me and sat down. I crawled to him, begged his forgiveness. He put me to work tonguing my blood off his boots. I did it graciously. While I worked on his boots he was brooding. His hand rested under his chin and he watched me with an evil grin slipping like sinister dreams across his face. He wanted to really hurt me for another fuck up on my part and I knew it. Any time now, I could be dead meat and no one would care. After all, I was only a worthless fuck up slave who had been recently rejected and returned to base camp for retraining.

I had worked the dust off the bottoms of his boots and was working up the insides when he caught my collar, pulled me up into the 'v' of his legs, and closed his boots around me, trapping me. He had to see the terror in my eyes at that moment. He coughed up a wad of snot, spit it at me and it landed near my mouth. "Eat it, fuck up!" he snarled.

Almost afraid not to put out my tongue, I scooped the glob into my mouth and swallowed. His gloved hand slammed into my cheek, "9-745, why is it such a Goddamn fuck up?" His legs opened, his hand pushed me away as if he were ashamed of me. I held my distance a few minutes and crawled back to his boots and returned to tonguing them clean of my blood. I lapped his boots in silence, his stony eyes watching my every move. I knew nothing I could do at this time would please him, but to follow his existing orders till orders changed.

Once the boots were all cleaned of my blood per his orders, he had me mount his right boot, placing my balls under and touching the boots. Using only my balls, I buffed his boots, knowing well-oiled boots don't buff to a high shine. It didn't matter, he wanted me there. That was good enough for me. When I did not do what he felt he wanted, his leg would slam my nuts into my body. I worked up a sweat working my balls into his huge leather boots.

He stood, dropping me to the floor, and walked across the room, pulling a cigar from a humidor. Walking back, he sat and made me watch him as he clipped the cigar, that tip was dropped into my mouth and he lighted the cigar from a cedar match. He motioned for me to crawl between his legs again. He tilted my head, ordered my mouth open and he exhaled his smoke into my lungs. I choked on the smoke. He ordered me back to the ends of his outstretched boots; they were placed into my lap. He smoked his cigar slowly, eyeing me over every exhalation. His boots lifted, the cigar held about an inch of ash. I was summoned to his side, mouth open, the ash dropped sizzling into my mouth and ordered to swallow.

"Hands behind its back!" came the order. He glided the hot end of the cigar over my lips and down my chest before he halted at my right nipple. There he held it while I moaned; I flinched due to the heat and got slapped for my mistake. He moved over to the left nipple, that was toasted as well. He pulled my head back, rolling it upwards towards the ceiling and held it there with one hand. He took a long draw on the cigar. I watched him out of the corner of my eye. "As your Handler, slave 9-745, I have the right to burn the tip of your cock head for cumming without permission!"

His cigar touched my chest and began a fiery dance down my stomach. The really sick thing about all this was how my cock got hard and he noticed. My cock was feeding on the terror and fear he was projecting towards me and that cock had a mind of its own. His cigar crept down lower, burning me here and there. My terror grew, as he got closer to my cock. The tip touched the base of my cock and I cried out. "Shut the fuck up, slave or I will give you something to cry about!" he threatened.

Fear tinged my voice when I began begging him, "Sir, oh please Sir, no Sir!"

He got really angry and screamed at me, "What was that word you just used faggot?!"

Now I was scared, I could not remember which word he wanted me to say, so I repeated myself, "Sir, oh please Sir don't burn me there Sir!" His cigar brushed me on my cock and I screamed.

He bellowed, "Slave 9-745, you used the word, no. Didn't you, cock sucker?" He had lowered his face to mine when he shouted that at me, his cigar no less than a half an inch from my face.

My body started shaking from fear of what he was going to do to me for saying that one word and I knew that he had the rights.

He withdrew his cigar from his mouth, spit from the cigar drooled on to my lips and I actually licked it up before being told. He made me watch him as he blew on the ash till it got white-hot. The shaking began as tremor after tremor rolled over my body. His cigar strolled slowly down my body, bypassing the nipples, ignoring my belly and dropping into my lap.

Like a fool my cock was waving at him. The hand that had been holding my head lifted and grabbed my cock. His other hand connected with the underside of my cockhead, and he ground his cigar out!

My scream was blood curling to say the least.

Then he pushed me away and walked out of the room. Leaving me crying on the floor from pain and understanding that not only had I failed Buena Vista but I had failed my God Hunter and now Master Dan. I was damned as a slave.

When he returned, he walked into the room, stepped over my body and began removing his boots by himself. I crawled to him put my hand to his boots and you would have thought I had shocked him. He turned, placed one boot on my forehead and kicked me away. A bootjack on the floor helped him remove the boots, those he left where they dropped. His socks he tossed on the floor besides them, turned to me and whispered, "Don't even think you that you deserve them now, slave."

He reached into his closet pulled out a hank of rope and approached me. He hogtied and gagged me before he went about getting the rest of the way undressed. He went to his desk, turned on his computer and began typing. When he finished, he walked across the room, put an envelope outside on his door. Not even looking at me, he walked to the bathroom to take a piss and then went to bed.

I did not sleep a wink that night for worrying about what was going to happen to me when I was returned to full active duty.

He slept though his normal waking time. Rising late, he put on sweats and left me still bound from the night before.

I knew better than to piss on the floor. I waited, praying he would return.

When he did return I was released and ordered to tongue bathe him. I did my damnedest to please him. When done, he forced my mouth open and fed me his piss. He pulled rubber straps from out of his closet, tossed them in my direction, pulled out other items and walked towards me with a shit-eating grin plastered across his face. I knew I was in for a world of hurt. One strap went under my knees, encircling my back and pulling the legs into my chest before being cinched closed. He had positioned two other straps within the bend of my waist while he strapped my thighs to my chest; those were locked around each ankle and drawn up tight. He bound my hands simply with a strap around the wrists, placed his arms around me and lifted me as if I was nothing. A cabinet that I assumed was a bar was opened and I was slipped onto a waiting dildo that locked me in place more completely than if I was bound. He closed the sides of the box, bound my hands to opposite walls by individual shackles, dropped the neck plate into position and sealed the front panel. He was obviously still pissed from last night's performance. I had broken the sacred covenant by using the word no.

It was his right to punish me in hopes that the word and lesson would be driven home. Movement within the box was not permitted, the dildo in my ass and the tight padded walls pushed in upon me. He stayed within the room for awhile, dressed in civilian clothes. Just before he departed, he approached and ordered me to open my mouth. He installed a spurred ball into the cavity within my mouth, speech was not necessary, the sharp pins in the ball helped me realize any tongue movement created unaccustomed pain to the roof of my mouth and tongue. The lace was bound tightly at the back of my head. Earplugs were inserted, wires were fed through holes drilled to the outside of the box and I watched as they were connected to a CD player. Standing there, he opened the disc panel; removed and reinserted a series of CD's flipped the switch and watched me for signs. Seeing none, he removed an earplug, adjusted the volume and reinserted the earplug into my ear, those he taped into my ears as a way of confirming their location. A soft symphony began to play in my ears and I watched him move about the room.

A heavy down parka was dropped near my box. He pulled from somewhere below my view heavily padded leather and wood panels. Two were slipped into grooves on either side of my head, another was located at the back and a strap locked my head to it, the fourth panel was seated before my face, all those got locked into place by something that snapped. My final view of him was as he placed the top lid over my head, four snaps locked in place and I entered total darkness. The music gave away to words. Locked into a box, I had no clue when he departed. I was alone. Each tightly bound limb struggled to move and found no movement was possible; the box was a brutal reality. Alive, totally restrained, incapable of any movement, joints aching, body numbing to a dull ache as the program ran its course. This one knew I had wronged him by using the one forbidden word to a slave's lips. This punishment was the worse of them all, to be locked away, unable to move, to assist, to earn my rations as the words continued to drum into my psyche how much this one had failed. I knew I was a failure, this box only confirmed what I knew.

I had not been fed this morning, hadn't earned it by rights. I had failed in the outside world before my Hunter had cut me from the herd. Had failed as a newly purchased slave because I thought too well of myself, and had failed Master Dan when I used the word, no. My balls were badly bruised and swollen when I had finally seen them, and my poor cock still hurt from his cigar. Even my ass and anywhere his boot hit hurt none of that mattered. What really concerned me while he was away is how badly I had fucked up! I dared say the 'n' word to him after he strictly forbade me to use it by mouth or action. I knew better than he that he had to burn my cock as punishment for saying the 'n' word.

Yes, I was a total failure. I confessed openly without shame. I mouthed the words within my confessional. The pain in my mouth helped me shout them into my box and the words played on. Confession complete, I cried, let myself pity my inability to get right with the bigger picture. I dug deep into my mind and found all those negative thoughts and shouted them out, hoping he would hear and understand my fears. While he was gone I ran through every scenario twice or more. Worked myself into a deep self-hatred, a pure loathing for myself and how I had become while away from Buena Vista. He has all the rights in the world to beat me to death and I knew it! He told me he was not a kind man! Hadn't he?

The CD changed and my mind followed its newly directed path. I saw myself working in the caves, rooting out other negative bullshit that was hidden deep in the depths of my soul. Each were spoken out loud, named and dismissed as I no longer wanted them to hold me back from what I knew was my intended destiny. Hadn't I, as a freeman, dreamed of this box and jerked off over the thought of this purge, hadn't I? I gnawed on myself mentally as the CD worked its way deep into my soul and showed me where I was holding back and why. Hadn't daddy taught me to be a good cocksucker? Was it wrong that I enjoyed rough treatment by men? I was an inferior being designed to serve others. I had known since birth that I was nothing till someone told me what I was. I was nothing but property till I was trained to serve completely. I was the fuck up, I was wrong. How dare I even breathe his air or eat his food? I had to get with the big picture if I was going to please this handler and ever be fit to serve my Hunter.

The click caught me by surprise, another CD helped change my thinking to see how I had dared hold back. This one was wrong, had wrongful thinking, this one worked hard to purge itself of all negative thinking. It was better to serve, to give totally and not think of its needs but of its superior's needs. Locked within the box, body cramping, this one no longer cared; it was set on a mission to destroy if not harness its ego and win. Since the latest sabotage by its own ego, it knew its ego had to die if it was to survive its own transgressions against the sacred Covenant that we slaves lived by; "Give of itself completely. Serve totally, protect and it will live another day."

Silence filled my void, the CD's had halted, how many had there been? How long had this slave been locked into confinement? Did it matter to this slave? Not in the least, this is where its handler had placed it and this is where it would stay till its handler released it. Straining, I could hear nothing beyond the box. Still, I realized he was outside, as a new CD began worming its message deep into my psyche and it was taught how to use its body to please, the words implanted its new teachings deep into my subconscious mind while my mind played out each scenario behind closed eyes. Yes, this one could milk a Sir's cock using only its ass muscles. It practiced on the cock buried within its hole; tighten, squeeze, relax. Work that muscle like your arm muscles to please by milking his cock, by accepting his cock or fist, it's an honor to serve completely. Work your tongue deep into his butt, dig deeper, find pleasure in serving totally. A slave's gift to his owner is to be a total service animal. All bodily secretions from the owner are to be viewed as a gift from a God. Drink, eat, suck, worship...it's a slave's duty to be useful.

He opened the box and peered down inside. The box top panels were removed, the pin gag removed and he presented me with a black rubber cock attached to a bucket with an order, "Suck it dry, 9-745."

He withdrew while I sucked on the rubber penis, allowing the warm fluid trickle down my raw throat to fill my empty belly with rich nutrients. He muttered under his breath that I had been in the box now for two days. Was it necessary that he give me more time to rethink my position?

My response seemed to take him by surprise. "Sir, that is your choice, Sir," and I returned to sucking the bucket dry.

He released me from the box, even helped me rub back into my stiff body some necessary circulation before he applied his boot. His boot toe between my ass-crack got me moving in the direction I was suppose to take. I crawled till I bumped into his boots. Tentatively, hands shaking, I found his boot and rested my head on it, ass upraised as I had been taught.

His boot shifted and came to rest on my head. The meaning was not lost on either of us. His weight was added; it was his right to crush me here for all my stupidity. I did not cry out, as much as it hurt. That had to have pleased him because the boot left my head, the boot toe toed my chin.

I rose slowly just in case that was not his intention. My hands drew back to my ankles and there I knelt, head bowed.

His treatment, the box and reapplied programming had made me very aware of my own stupidity and foolishness. I had met my match, I was defeated or tried to give him that impression.

I was ordered to the kitchen to pickup his dinner and to return.

He ate in silence with some music playing in the background. I knelt at his side, my bowl of slave goop sitting before me. As hungry as I was, I dared not eat it till permission was granted. He watched, knowing that something had changed while he was gone.

His dinner finished and mine cold, he gave me the order to eat.

I all but devoured the bowl.

He put a toothbrush into my hands, drove me with his boots to a side of the room he was not near and put me to work scrubbing the floor. I was to use the tooth-brush, a can of powdered soda and a glass of water to clean the whole floor before bedtime. When he went to bed, I was not even a quarter of the room finished. I worked throughout the night. When he awoke he found me slumped over almost asleep, his belt to my ass got me fired back up and focused.

He showered, had breakfast and was dressed and almost ready to go to work when he came for me. He studied my work. It failed. I would repeat the task tonight.

He attached his leash to my collar and we went to work. I was still on light duty so I had no clue where I would be placed today. Was shocked when he dropped me off in the kitchen and placed on scrubbing duty. He knew, like I did, that if I was caught sneaking any food from the kitchen how severely I would be punished.

I was whipped a lot that day for being a slacker.

He took me home, fed me, as he had already eaten, gave me a moment to piss or shit then placed me back on the floor cleaning. His belt helped to keep me focused whenever I got lax in my duties. He stayed up later than normal, driving me to do better work, making me do a section over as he was using his belt to help me remain focused. He was in another part of his suite. I must have stopped due to exhaustion when his belt caught me totally by surprise.

I screamed as he slammed that damn belt into me. Instead of returning to work, I bowed over offering him my ass to beat. He did a few swings before his boot connected with my ass in a head banging awakening, "Up, slave. Rise!"

I struggled to crawl to my feet, wavering like a flag being tossed by a breeze.

"Turn and look at your Master!"

I turned too quickly and almost fell. He would have let me but I struggled to keep my feet under me.

His hand wrapped itself around my throat, lifted and forced me to look at him, again he was angry, "I heard complaints about your work today and tonight I see you are not doing one of your duties as a slave, house cleaning. It's a total fuck up, slave!" His open palm slammed into my face, "I will not tolerate this shit from 9-745!" He dropped me and walked off in total disgust, before turning, demanding, "Crawl here!" He pointed to the floor at his boots.

I dropped to my knees and crawled, I had no more options than to obey.

When I arrived, he looked down; I felt his disgust, "Kiss my boots faggot!"

I kissed them out of respect and out of need to make him happier with me.

He walked a short distance and sat down, "Here, come!" He made me tongue clean the soles of his boots. Afterwards, he placed the toe of one boot under my balls and on the male gee spot, and then forced me to tongue clean the other boot. Any movement on my part made my body jerk and spasm, as my balls were worked with his boot toe. The pain helped clear my head and keep me focused on making his boot shine. One boot completed to his satisfaction, I was ordered upon the other. When they both met his eye of approval, I was ordered to kneel up.

He drew me closer to where he sat, ordered my mouth to open and began feeding me his gloved fingers one at a time. Each had to be sucked slowly into my mouth, my mouth opened and another entered for their washing. Once all five were done, he began inserting twos or threes till he had my mouth filled with his fingers and I was gagging. He wanted to work his whole hand into my mouth and proclaimed one day he would fist my mouth like my ass. I helped him undress for bed. He dressed me for bed; rope bondage tightly cinched around my legs, arms and my mouth gagged with rope wound around my head. He slept in his nice big bed, I on the floor.

When he awoke in the morning, my gag was removed. I drank his piss then ate his ass and was unbound. While we showered and his breakfast cooked slowly, I dried him and used his wet towel to dry myself. He ate his breakfast and I eventually was ordered to eat mine. No more table scraps came my way, only slave goop. He went to work, taking me at least as far as chain gang. I was attached and went with them. He gave no indication if I would return that night to him as I was marched away.

We were escorted down into an older corridor where we were given buckets, heavy industrial rubber gloves, short rubber boots. At one conjunction the handlers picked up old kerosene lanterns as we continued into the depths of the mountain. The lanterns were lighted as we stepped from electronically lighted pathways into a dark, dank, smelly corridor and continued our descent. The air around us grew moist, the rocks felt damp and our footing was slippery even with the rubber boots. Our handlers stopped the forward march, placed a lantern in one wall, opened the other and lighted an old fashioned torch. That torch ignited others as the handler first walked down the corridor, touching torches till they burst into flame and moved onwards.

We were paired up; two slaves at a time were removed from the chains. There just wasn't any place to run if we had chosen to. The handlers moved us till we stood before a series of gratings in the floor, took off two slaves then moved deeper down the corridor removing two more. This was repeated till all eight were settled before these grates. The handler walked up among us, "Ok, slaves, it will take two of you to lift the grates. Positions lift!"

The stench of this room was rising from what ever was hidden below these grates. Drawing closer to grab hold of the rusty iron metal damn near made me sick. I held my breath and lifted the steel. One edge rose, but the other was fused to the ground; old hinges creaked as the trapdoors swung up and over to lean against a wall. We stood aside till a handler with torch in hand could look within the opening. There, looking up at us, were glassy eyed slaves almost starved to death and light blind by their reactions to the torches.

It would seem this lesson was meant for all of us to learn. There are things on this compound worse than death, this rotting in a cage known as the pit. Medics were called by way of a hand held unit while we helped the poor bastards out of their own pits and tried cleaning them of their dried feces. Ours looked horrible, like something out of a WWII concentration camp, nothing but skin, bones and the hollow eyes.

Medics with wheeled carts and wheelchairs took them all away, most of them would survive, however, ours was questionable. He had been here the longest, about four months according to his tag date. The balance of the day was spent cleaning and disinfecting those hellacious holes. We all knew they would be used sooner than later to help some poor slave get his head wrapped around his training. It was harsh, the pit, but some slaves, some men needed it to break down their will. Elsewise they would just not be suitable for our training or our lifestyle. Hell if I did not start getting with the picture - I could just as well end up here as any of these men.

We returned by way of a communal shower, total debugging and disinfections before we would be permitted anywhere near living quarters. We may be slaves and there are times slaves should be allowed to wallow in their own filth, but if one is serving a handler or top or Master it is wise that this slave be clean and freshly prepared.

That night I was returned earlier than my Master. I awaited his presence, kneeling at the door and when he entered my head hit the floor. He actually stepped back outside to check the number on his door to see if he was home before he stepped back inside, crossed the short distance and placed his boots within range. My head moved forward and I kissed each boot with intense respect. When he ordered my head rose as did I to assist him with wind down.

I had learned a lesson in that box and with the pit cleaning party. Returning early, I had taken the time to season and prepare his steak, potatoes were cooking in the oven, other veggies were laid out and waiting. Hesitantly, I cleared my throat; he turned looking at me puzzled as I asked, "Sir, by your leave. Your dinner can be ready within 15 minutes but may I suggest a shower and a massage before, Sir?"

He allowed me to disrobe him, place him into a nice hot bath instead of a shower. While he soaked, I polished his boots, making them ready for the next day's wear and put them away with his uniform. When I returned, I was permitted to scrub his back, soap and scrub his body. As he rose from the bath I toweled him dry and guided him towards his bed. Warm oil went to work loosening his tight muscles. He actually feel asleep as I was working the knots out of his shoulders and back. I continued the massage to his feet; he flipped over and allowed me to work my way up his front, slowly kneading him all over till he melted. While he rested I finished up his dinner, as it was way past his normal eating schedule when done. I woke him for his dinner and knelt at his side should he have need. His way of rewarding me for my efforts was to give me food and a pat on the head in route to watch TV. Once the kitchen and bathroom were tidied, I joined him there. I was sent to fetch his thin gloves.

While he sat watching TV, he used those gloves to trace patterns lightly across my body, around and around my lips. He loved to force a finger into my mouth for sucking and licking. I enjoyed tasting the cigars on his gloves while I sucked each digit into my oral hole. That evening, he began a game of sorts. My face was impaled on his cock. I had to keep it warm. Then it dawned on me; this was my God Hunter's game. Yes, I knew this one well. Keep his cock in my mouth, not shutting my mouth; just remain focused on pleasing him without making him cum. He sat for hours with my face impaled on his cock while my jaws ached to be closed. That night I got my just reward; his cum down my throat.

Other nights I got it elsewhere.

Chapter 6

We will now discuss in a little more detail the Struggle for Existence.

Darwin

For the most part everything ran smoothly. I learned his schedule and learned to please my master in all ways. I was his toilet in the morning and evenings, taking his piss. I learned to accept his way as the only way. Like him, we both left for work at the same time. He had the freedom to move as he desired, I was placed on a chain gang and used till I was done with my job. Many days he was home before I returned, but those few days that I got home before he, I made certain they were special just for him.

We slaves were driven to perfect our way of thinking, to purge ourselves of negative emotions and to confess our crimes against the way. Master Dan loved to make me confess and try to be a good slave, so I did. I found that confessions were really good for this slave's mindset. Too often I questioned myself about things I did, by the simple act of confessing, my confusion cleared. Some confessions were good, others, the ones that were done before a board of handlers, made me nervous. Still, all were necessary for me to continue to grow. I had mistakenly tried to take my life by thinking for myself and not my owner; that digression had to be purged, driven out of me, if I was ever to crawl up out of the cesspool and walk the open air in chains as a trusted slave. I worked hardest to purge myself of my failings and my superiors helped me daily to see the errors of my ways.

Hard labor was one of the better ways to help me purge the negative thinking. During hard labor all I had to do was work and think positive thoughts about how I would better myself. I found myself reporting slaves that were slackening off the handler's preset pace, I found myself confessing to others crimes and got caught in my attempt to cover up for another. Every step forward seemed to take me two steps back. Eventually someone got tired of my bullshit games and Master Dan was penalized for my failure, and I was taken one morning from him. By his reaction this was not to his liking, but it was an order from the board of handlers and out of his hands. Two heavily muscled handlers walked me down the corridors, one holding my leash, the other the chain to my leg shackle. I was taken out to a field, the sun was slightly warm, but the ground still held some cold. Once we were out of the cavern, they ran me to the field where a huge mountain of rocks in all sizes had been piled. I was shown the pile. One handler walked out a great distance and drove a stake into the ground, a measuring stick was dropped near it. That location was for smaller stones. He walked closer to where I stood, drove another stake into the ground, dropped another measure and told me this is where the large rocks go, then walked to where his partner stood pointing the stake and told me "This is where the medium rocks go."

I worked all day on that pile of rocks and didn't even clear half of the pile before nightfall. I made a big mistake and thought we would be going in for the evening. Stopping, I approached one handler as if to say let's go home. I was dumb-founded when he set upon me with his leathered baton and beat me back to the rocks. They lighted a fire to keep warm, food was brought to them and I got none. They drove me when I slacked off, using their fists, whips, voices or boots until I returned to the mountain of rocks. When I begged for water they opened their flies, gladly I dropped and drunk their piss. It actually helped my aching stomach. I worked throughout the night. A shift change came for the handlers but not for me. I really must have pissed off someone with that last confession for this to be happening to me. Another meal missed while I worked on the rubble, moving even the smallest stones until all were located as my handlers had ordered. Near exhaustion, I wavered towards the fire and dropped to my knees, panting the job was all done as ordered. One handler rose, walked down the line of rocks, came back and said that I had the rocks placed incorrectly.

I had not watched, but I believe he moved the measuring sticks. Or I had just totally fucked myself over again. I was given warm water to drink in the form of their piss, helped to my feet with a paddle slamming my ass and taken by my collar down the rows of rocks. I was to move the medium rocks beyond the small rocks and when I was finished I could eat and rest. It was slow going, but with the help of the handlers riding my ass every step of the way I got that pile, almost chest high, moved. And then they had a shift change.

I knew I was damned. Someone had found out that I still thought, not just fol-lowed orders but thought. Assumed the blame for others, thought. Reported slaves that were slackers, thought. Reported people just to have something to confess, thought.

The handlers that were changing out gave me a bowl of hard slave goop and a small measure of water. I stuffed it all in my mouth before they changed their minds and chokingly got it all down with the aid of that little water. I moved one pile and almost got finished before my body betrayed me and I became a lump on the ground.

I haven't a clue how I got home, or how I got back to Master Dan's place, but when I awoke I was home. He kicked me awake and sent me to make him breakfast and watched as I did. We showered together, I dried him, he watched me as I squat-ted over the open drain to shit, wiping my ass with newspaper. He ate his breakfast and I mine. He made me focus by slapping my face until I continued dressing him. He walked over, picked up the telephone and made an angry call, then slammed the receiver down. Quickly he walked past me, reached into his closet and brought out his knee high engineers, demanding "Drop to your knees, fuck up. Let's see just how much you respect me! Arms straight out, palms up! Do it, fuck up!" Onto my right palm went his left boot and on my left palm his right. "Keep your arms up and my boots off the floor, slave!"

Each boot forced my hands downward, till his screams to lift my arms brought them back up into alignment. My arms and body started shaking, he shouted at me again to focus. The weight seemed extreme, one boot would drop then the other till his commanding shouts made me correct them, put them in check and lift them back up. My knees hurt; I told myself I had endured worse. But my arms kept drooping. He walked from behind me to a vase in which he kept birch canes. In passing, he slapped the back of my head. Each time I pushed my arms up it felt as if the boots grew heavi-er; I could have sworn I was holding some invisible spirit as he stood within Master Dan's boots. He chose a cane, walked behind me. I knew if his boots fell I would feel the rod cut across my shoulders. When the rod hit, it literally took me by surprise. I wasn't expecting the blow. True the boots had slipped down as my arms struggled to hold them upright but I had not dropped them. The pain gave me reason and strength to push them back up and hold them out from my body.

My arms started shaking. He yelled in my ear, "Raise those arms, you stupid fuck! Keep my boots in the air, slave!" The past few days of heavy labor were really getting to me. Moving a ton or more of boulders by myself and then having to constantly relocate them to suit first one handler than another. Oh God! The cane struck my back viciously. My arms began to quiver uncontrollably. Another stripe was cut into this lazy slave's hide, followed by another! One boot dropped to the floor.

Master Dan was screaming about how much of a fuck up I was and hitting me with that damn cane when the next boot dropped to the floor. A rain of fire ran all over my back, suddenly it stopped. He became silent. The cane dropped too loudly on the stone floor. The only other sounds were my panting and my mournful plea of, "Sir?"

Pissed, he attached my leash and all but drug me out and down the corridor. My leash was passed into the hands of the handler of the day. With a short two word burst, "Keep him!" and he was gone.

That day I was driven to fill a water tanker by pedaling a bicycle-like device. As I pedaled, cups dipped into the water, ran up a line and spilled over into a huge funnel. The water then ran into the water tanker. Other slaves were working the same way, but for some reason my bicycle seemed to move slower than theirs. Only later did I find out why, the handlers had a way of tightening the tension so I was basically riding my bicycle uphill all day while everyone else was riding on smooth ground. I failed to complete my quota for the day and slept in a tight steel barred cage for my troubles. I was fed and watered, that was the only good thing about the day. I was the only slave in a cage.

I awoke to a dull ache in my back and legs. A handler had opened my cage door and was ordering me out. By luck of rotation it was Master Dan. Cold food and water was placed before me. I ate, not tasting the stuff, only knowing I needed it to continue. He pulled me to the bicycle and stood by while I tried to get my quota finished for yesterday as well as my new one for today. If I slowed he was on me like a fly on shit! When I missed my footing his leather strop nailed my back. He was a fucking lunatic, yelling at me, hitting me, driving me to do better. I slept another night in that tight cage; worked for what seemed like a week on filling that tanker. Nothing I did was good enough. Everyone pressed me to do better, to improve. If their screams in my ears did not do it, their strops did help me increase me speed.

I had failed to please Master Dan. I had shown him disrespect and was being ordered to crawl on my knees up and down the corridor outside his door with his boots in my hand. I crawled, brother did I crawl; till my knees left blood did I crawl. My arms gave up their precious cargo, his boots hit the ground and he stomped me bad. I knew I deserved it but one blow knocked me out. I awoke to my worst nightmare.

I found myself bound to a metal cot, legs bound down the foot and my arms bound to the opposite end. I was in the jailhouse and Jack was in the room with me as was Carl, both wearing shit eating grins. They blistered my backside with their belts because I had become a stupid fuck up of a slave.

When I came around again, I knew I was in hell. I was still bound to the metal cot and Master Dan was there looking down on me, arms crossed and beside him stood Master Dan or was that Master Hunter, I was confused. I tried shaking my head to clear it, but that only made the room spin.

I heard Master Dan speaking, "He is a rebel this one."

Another voice, "Break him, you are being unfair to him this way."

Still another voice, Hunter's I thought, "Leave a little fire, you know how I like them, boy."

Something pinched my butt and stung. When I came too again I was back in Master Dan's suite, bound in upon myself in a tight very restrictive ball of aches, chains literally wrapped around my whole body and any attempt to move made me hurt all the harder. The door opened, Master Dan stepped in home from the day. He looked my way, I knew that look, the *I had fucked up bad* look. I wanted to speak, even opened my mouth which only brought his anger to me. He crossed the room in a flash, stuffed something off the floor into my mouth and dared me to speak. He had dinner; his actions when out of eyesight told me he was furious with me. Pots crashed, he tossed things aside finally drew a chair over near me, opened the humidor and brought out a cigar. He stomped me down into a position that suited him. Dropped his boot onto my bound body ignoring my low moans and went about lighting his cigar. Ashes fell on me where I lay. I was nothing beneath his feet, was the message that was being transmitted to me.

He released me so that he could use me. I was helpless as he held up my chin and slammed his fist into my face, repeated the blow and tossed me to the floor like a dishrag. He walked away, sat down in his wingback, opened his legs, took a long draw on his cigar, inhaled, shut his eyes and slowly exhaled the smoke. Like a fool I crawled in his direction. My reasoning was he was like daddy, daddy knew how to keep his boy in line. My hand made contact with his boot. I could have been fire by the way that boot pulled back so fast, but he kept his seat.

I tried another approach, aimed my head between his open boots, and crawled between. A hot ash caressed my body. While I waited I licked the blood from my lips good. Slowly, I raised myself upwards. He paid me no heed, starring into space, smoking as if I was not there. I raised myself higher to crotch level, but again his fist caught me by surprise. My head reeled back as I tumbled to the floor, lay there, moaning softly. Daddy was in a dark mood, I thought.

Still I persisted, crawling back to the openings between his legs. I was shaking from exhaustion, fear, and terror and knew all this was my fault, that only I could fix daddy's mood. I lay there for the longest time, him sitting above me, both of us ignoring the other, both of us wanting the other each on our own terms. One more time, I thought to myself, steeled myself for another fist in my face and rose slowly up between his legs. He grabbed the back of my head, holding it firm and slammed his open palm on one cheek, then backhanded me by the other. Instead of falling away, I dared fate and held my place. He looked down on me and saw me for the first time. He took a long hard drag on his cigar, the end going from a dull red into a bright cherry orange. He inhaled, sucking the rich smoke into his lungs, leaned forward. My mouth opened and he blew the smoke directly into my lungs. He sat back watching to see if I would hold it till given a sign for release. Once given, I exhaled and rapidly inhaled a mouthful of fresh air.

His cigar went between his lips as one hand unbuttoned his fly and pulled out his rapidly hardening cock. He pulled my bloody lips over his cock and held my face down on his shaft. His hand departed the back of my head, allowing me the chance to rise up his shaft before his hand pushed me back down. Once started, the piston continued its cycle of down then up then down. Once on his cock, he tuned me out while he smoked his cigar. It was as if he was elsewhere dreaming a dream and I was only a tool to be used for his satisfaction of the moment. If I had not been there his fist would have done the same job without as much hassle.

He made me work for his jism that night. While I worked his cock he played with his nipples, rolling them hard and smoking his stogie. He was drawing close to shooting his load when he did something that surprised the hell out of me. His cock was swelling and preparing to burst a nut when he placed the cherry of his cigar to his right nipple. He flinched as he ground the cigar into his nipple, humped his hips forward, grabbing the back of my head, forcing his cock deep and shooting not one load but two. I was pushed off his cock with no ceremony and as a means to cover up his own embarrassment he bound me to the foot of the bed and went to sleep. By his actions, I knew that his nipple burning was to remain a secret or something really bad would come my way.

The previous week's events followed by that night's helped me crawl over the line into righteousness. Yes, when it awoke it was in a different frame of mind. It knew its place; it harbored no ill will towards its Master for how it was used. It was, after all, only a slave and its master was a well-respected handler.

Sir noticed my changes probably faster than it did. That first morning as it prepared Sir's breakfast, it made reference to itself in the third person, Sir rolled his eyebrows at it as if to say are these changes real or just a game. Their lessons had finally reached the depths of my core being. It knew that they had all the right in the world to keep working it till there was nothing more to it but a dried up husk. All that they had been saying, all the lectures, the forced programming clicked and this slave became one with the way of the slave. It was reborn, so to speak. Yet it had a nagging concern, was this only its way to preserve itself or is there a darkness lying just below the surface? Only time could tell.

They kept after me for a month or more, forcing me to improve upon myself; until, they too trusted that it had made the best possible choice and had found righteousness. When it was grilled in an interrogation it broke down and cried, begging forgiveness and was genuinely concerned not for itself but for the handlers who had given me their trust and it had betrayed that trust. Now its training took on a more personal level. It was trained how it could please its master better. It was trained using hypnosis, deep programming and a form called hyper-empheria, super consciousness, and memorization. All the master had to do was speak a key word, tell me what he wanted stored, and it absorbed the material and could give back total recall. Its physical prowess was enhanced as it was taught how to get comfortable with a cock deep inside its throat. It was taught tantric sexual practices so that it would supply its owner with supreme pleasure. It received a tongue piercing so that it would give its master greater pleasure while giving its Sir a blowjob. A guiche was inserted below its balls. It may not be owned at present but in the future it would be. As a sperm donor, its cock was not its own. A Prince Albert piercing was installed; as well as deep programming so that it would no longer touch its cock sexually, for its cock no longer gave it pleasure. Other lessons in massage, house cleaning, general sewing, leather cleaning and care were included into its lessons. Best of all Master Dan began to use it more regularly to serve his needs and not caring for its needs or wants.

It found serving its Sir more pleasurable. It would awake early, prepare coffee and awake its Sir with coffee in bed, his morning blowjob and his first piss when it was not left in bondage the night before. It took pride in having its Sir stepping out of the house with spit shined boots, ironed uniform and it took more pride in its duties as it worked within the compound. Then there was the time that 'they' decided that I needed sensitivity training handler style.

Master Dan arrived home whistling and in an overly good mood. Under his arm was a cloth bag which normally meant that he had picked up something from the leather craftsmen within the hold. Perhaps it was due to him having the following day off. He did not explain and it was not my job to ask. Normally Master Dan had a schedule of events that it assumed would occur when he arrived at home, as a rule there wasn't any deviation from his schedule. Tonight was not the norm.

It greeted him at the door on my knees, kissed his boots; his cocktail awaited him on the table near where it would remove his boots. He sat, opened the bag and pulled into view a handsomely crafted black leather hood. It was busy tonguing his boots but it could see up his leg and the package's contents. It was surprised by feelings when it beheld this object's presence in its life, overjoyed that Sir would have fun using it on me. Once his boots were removed, he stood, it stripped him of his uniform while Sir was sipping his drink. Sir soaked while it prepared his dinner and dinner was awaiting the Sir's pleasure when he exited the bathroom in his robe. It waited at his side, standing, hands folded neatly at my back, head bowed. Should the Sir need more wine or gravy, without orders it fetched what it thought Sir needed. Dessert served, Master rose, placed table scraps into its bowl and gave it its normal rations of slave chow.

He took his leisure on the computer while it cleaned up and made coffee for Sir's pleasure. When it brought the coffee into the den it was ordered to kneel between Sir's open legs. The hood was pulled over my head. Sir took his time fitting the hood, pulling it into place, checking if it had good breathing, eye clearance before the hood was laced around its head.

The hood was interesting because there were grommets over each ear allowing for this slave to hear his Master's commands and the hood was lined so the smooth surface connected with my skin.

"Open your mouth, meat!" He installed a penis gag that had to be woven through straps in the hood before it was buckled in place. This seemed to satisfy him, that it would be able to suck cock even while in the hood. Eye patches were placed over its eyes, those, too, got buckled behind its head, no light came from beyond those patches, and it was locked into darkness. He added a chin support that was buckled at the top of my head, my moan told him that the straps held my mouth tightly sealed around the penis gag. By his hand running over my enclosed head, it knew Sir liked his slave this way. The zipper was closed down the back, giving me no access to the laces. It felt the tell-tale click of a padlock, telling me it would be within this hood for a time. It found it interesting that, without eyes, my body seemed more sensitive and more alive than when it had fully functioning eyes. He moved me till he was pleased with my position, rose and dressed without my help.

Not unlike a child with a new play toy, Master Dan had to take me out to play with , it was after all his option, and this slave was there to please. Once dressed as he desired, he stepped around me and placed my hands onto his boots. He was wearing thigh high lace up boots that he wanted me to lace without sight. In many ways it is grateful that it got a very understanding, patient Master. Tonight, he was extremely patient as it laced him into his boots. He loved tall boots just as much as it loved to service tall boots. In that capacity we were a match. He graciously allowed this slave to reach higher so that my fingers could tell me what he was wearing with these boots.

Hand and Glove: The Path

His leather codpiece shorts told all it need know.

Times were a-changing. After it had finished his boots, my hands were placed into fingerless gloves that laced and got locked into place; a leather strap bound them together. A thick leather collar that forced my head downward was buckled around my neck, to which a leash was attached and it was lifted. With his hand near my neck it was led up the two steps and out the door. It knew the area to which we were walking. His hand gave me confidence and he did not betray that trust, as do some slave handlers who lead their slaves into walls for the humor of the moment, not realizing how easily our trust can be shattered.

Inside the play arena, Sir bound me to an upright cross, my legs spread-eagle, my arms supported by a chain overhead and my nuts bound before weighted. He made me anticipate him and his first stroke. He had to be walking around the room chatting with friends as it waited helplessly anticipating his return. He began with a light pat of his gloved hand to my shoulder; he massaged my back helping its muscles loosen from the weeks of long hard labor. It was as if he wanted me to melt into him. My head rolled back and was caught by his chest and he nibbled on my flesh before biting it hard, pushing his teeth deep and making me moan. How he made this slave feel when he was happy and it deserved these good times. His hands traveled all over my body, lightly touching, possessing what he already owned. All of this making my body hum like a high tension line in a storm. His hands coaxed my fire to burn for him as they traveled their route down from my hands, over my shoulders, down my ribs, along my hips and down to my ankles and feet. Then up within the 'v' of my legs and to finger the edges of my asscrack. All of me burned to feel him inside of me, gladly would it have begged to have him fuck me, but we both knew it was not quite the time, as my fire had to be brighter.

Master had great pleasure working on my body, and it believes it took his foreplay very well. Sir started with a nice thick flogger of doeskin. Using this mop, he helped loosen the deeper knots within my muscles. It was all but purring when Sir began alternating his deerskin flogger with a flogger that stung. Interesting effect to have a man working with two hands flogging one's back, especially if one hand has a kitten and the other a tiger. Sir knew how to awaken the pain and pleasure centers in this slave till all fused into one big massive pleasure. Master's style of flogging was very artistic; much like a fan dancer, as he seemed to dance with his floggers. Whereas some tops are lumberjacks, chopping wood instead of flogging. He kept up the flogging till this slave shone like the only light bulb in a darkened cavern. Both sides of my body glowed with his talents.

Like Sir, this slave was tired from a long week. He lowered me to the ground and guided me to a quiet zone. There, kneeling, my arms outstretched on a cold boulder, he used his thigh high laced boots to fuck with this slave's head. Like saws the laces cut into my brutally tender back. Each time he applied them, it shuddered, almost surrendering my position. Only his commands held me in place. When he tired of that game, he sandwiched me within his boots. There it found comfort of sorts, as it was neither comfortable nor uncomfortable - it just was. Its head was placed into Sir's lap and it was ordered to lick Sir's leathers till his pet got excited. The codpiece removed, it entertained his cock, giving him pleasure as much as servicing gave me pleasure.

This slave was lifted, placed over a boulder and Sir's cock split its ass cheeks while another's cock filled its mouth. Used as a sandwich, both Sirs had great fun using this slave to find their own pleasure. The cock in my mouth was not as large as my

Sir's, and its style of fucking was swift jabs, followed by a pause, then more swift chin-slamming jabs. The cock in my mouth belonged to my Sir's best friend Anthony. It was his voice that rang in my ears as they fucked me from both sides. Master fucked like a machine, steady and constantly working his piston to reach greater depths, to him it gave its all. The cock in its mouth shot a load and withdrew quickly, but Sir (always the generous one!) allowed another to step up to home plate and batter up. Four cocks later, Master finally had his fill of slave butt and shot his load deep within this slave's guts, it was never so thankful!

Sir saw to it that this slave was kept within the hood for a week, complete with its hands in bondage as well. It was confused as to why the Sir would want to dress himself and prepare his own breakfast, but it was not for this slave to question the powers that be. When he left in the morning for work, this slave was taken to one of the learning labs. There it was restrained, locked into an immobile position with ear clips placed within its hood. It had to listen to a program being played over and over and over till Sir reclaimed it and took it home.

When home, Sir took perverse pleasure in tormenting this slave. He would bind it on its hands and knees, install a posture collar, making its head face forward and remove its gag. While Sir watched TV, it was fed bits of food. But only after Sir had slowly traced lines around and around this slave's lips. When he placed the food into its mouth, it had to suck Sir's fingers tenderly before he would drop the food so it could swallow. He spent hours making it focus only on its lips and mouth. During this lip training, Sir made a change to this slave's diet. Every morning and evening slaves were fed white gooey stuff that resembled grits or cream of wheat with chunks of meat, veggies and cooked fruit. This was the basic slave diet.

Sir chose to make the slave focus even more on its lips and mouth by making its breakfast liquid and, to add to its humiliation, this slave had to suck it from a bucket with a hollow rubber cock attached. The bucket was hung in a place that Sir could watch while he ate and to that liquid he often added his piss, just to keep this slave aware he was in charge. As much as it hated the damn bucket it loved the humiliation - especially when Sir would have me do simple pet tricks by emptying the bucket in the mess hall as other handlers watched with glee. It simply did not matter to this slave; all that mattered is that it had given him pleasure and served well. It should have known the hood was preparing me for something, but it just never dawned on me.

While in the hood without eyes my ears increased in intensity. This slave could hear a fart a block away and tell you who let the blast. So why was this slave so surprised when it overheard a conversation that occurred after a rapid knocking at the suite door? Master Dan excitedly blurted, "Oh shit, you aren't even dressed! Come on, the Commander is on her way! Never mind, you dress and I will take the slave to processing. Meet her there!"

It was taken that day to the doctor's lab where blood was drawn, it was milked and its now healed cock was locked between its legs. It went with a guide to be shaved and it was in that room the hood was removed for the first time in over eight days. It had to keep its eyes closed while they shaved its head and body of all accumulated hair.

No pleasant goodbyes, no hug, no kiss, nothing that would hint that it was not going to return to Master Dan's suite, but was locked into a tiny steel cage within a room of other cages. These cages gave us no comfort nor was there room for us to lay flat or sit upright. Our only comfort was sitting hunched over, legs curled around and underneath. In cold silence we waited our fates.

Handler Anthony came to this one's cage, it was pulled out, lifted to its feet and basically drug to the staging room. It kept thinking to itself, how could it be sold without it having been on the auction block? Was it sold or was it being shipped off to a breeding farm or traded for another farm animal? Both slave rumors designed to make us work to stay on our home soil, I told myself. Nevertheless, it was still being marched down the corridor, through the door to stand at an appointed place as handler Anthony made final preparations.

A heavy chain and hook were hanging from the ceiling; there, my steel collar was attached. With a click, this slave found itself on its tip-toes struggling to stand without strangling. Sir Anthony was moving about the room, pulling out items and tossing them on a central table as it watched in silence; rubber diver's suit, open face mask, heavy gloves, modified gas mask, posture collar, catheter and hoses. Sir Anthony approached with a wicked smile on his face, he chatted with me about having had great time fucking my face while watching my Sir fuck its butt. As he chatted he wrapped and buckled restraints around each limb.

My legs were first to be connected to the chains, followed by each arm. Before it realized - as it has slunk into a black funk - Sir Anthony had it bound and its limbs spread open. It knew by this point that if it so much as voiced a complaint, it would be treated to a severe attitude adjustment prior to shipment. Sir Anthony must have read my mindset correctly and, as an added precaution, he gagged my face with a chinstrap and an inflatable gag.

It heard voices outside the doorway, the door opened and in stepped the Commander of the Compound and my Sir. My whole body seemed to lean forward as it to show him that it was here. He looked my way but it was as if it no longer existed. His eyes did not register its presence. The Commander was speaking, "Dan, you have done an excellent job with 9-745. I honestly thought when it was returned that we had a lost one on our hands and it would have to be sold to the glue factory. You are just as good as Hunter proclaimed you would be. Thank God you two resemble each other."

Did this slave hear her words correctly? Were Master Dan and Hunter alike? No, this could not be; but that would explain some things! That old saying all of us has a twin somewhere on this planet; maybe Hunter had found his and used him on me. Bastard, I inwardly cursed. Hunter, you are a Bastard!

The bitch just could not leave things alone, nor could she allow me something to hold on to for the next fucking owner this slave would be lucky enough to have. Who in their right mind would buy this slave without first seeing it on an auction block? Who but Master Hunter had the resources to keep tabs on my training and previous owner, could he be just that sneaky to...

Commander Schmidt was just milking my Sir for all it was worth and his head was swelling with each stroke, "What was your secret on breaking this mule-headed slave?"

Damn if Master Dan didn't laugh. "First I pushed it towards total exhaustion, forced it into the programming chamber and had others help drive it till it dropped; then, I became the good cop making everyone else be the bad cop. The boy fell for it hook, line and sinker! Hell, I bet it loves me as much as it fears me. I used its love for me like any other weakness till it finally broke. Once it broke, the programming took its ability to rise beyond my bootstrap and away forever. Now it obeys - without question - any handler's orders as if they come from God!"

The commander was studying Master Dan's face as he talked. She would smile on occasion then look back at him perplexed. Finally she asked him the big question, "Dan, answer me honestly. Do you love that slave? Do you think you own 9-745?"

Dan seemed to stop, his head dropped onto his chest, he thought a moment while studying his boot. Then looked at her, cleared his throat as if he had gotten cotton mouth, "It was all a game to me, Sir. I wanted to see how far it would go if it thought it was loved and to be honest, I never told it that I loved it. It was only a thing to serve my needs. No Sir, I do not love that creature." Her head was turned away as Dan looked over in Anthony's direction and continued, "Sir, I love another who does not even know I exist and is way above my rank. Maybe one day I can tell that person how much I adore him, but not now. My career is far too important, Sir."

"Glad to know this Dan. Stay here and see to its packing. Make it understand that it has only one choice for it to survive and that is to please its new owner at all costs. Because if it is returned to us, it will never leave here again. No more options are open for it at this compound." She put her hand as if to open the door when it opened inward. As she was stepping towards the exit, she remembered something in her pocket, stopped and pulled it out then handed it to Dan. "Almost forgot, its new owner sent some special instructions and very unique equipment for its packaging. Please take the time to read these instructions before you package it for shipment."

After she departed and before the door closed, three slaves were ushered into the room by another friend of Dan's who greeted him and set the slaves to doing their duty, preparing me for shipment. Dan was studying the papers, he looked up then pointed at this slave, "Get it ready. Double shave 9-745; douche his ass till it's clear. Richard, will you supervise while I read these instructions?"

"Not a problem," replied Richard, who was a handsome man in his own right. That is if you like beefy muscle bears, like this slave does. They began by cutting off the metal tag on my slave collar. That was no longer needed since it would no longer be down within this compound. One slave dry scraped my scalp and places where hair usually grew on me. Another inserted a hose into my ass and filled it with cold water. Sir Anthony stepped to higher ground while this slave's ass was dumped and filled again. The three slaves worked with silent efficiency doing what they had to have done many times before. One catheterized my cock, another dried my body, and still another greased my hole. On command, they all powdered my body, head to toes while Master Dan and one slave went to retrieve whatever my new owner had sent for my packaging.

My ass was filled with a rubber cock "the size of my new owner's cock," laughed Master Dan as it was inserted and a strap harness locked it within my bowels. Foam rubber booties were pulled over my feet, over which padding was taped to brace the area between calves and ankles. Sir Anthony took up a control box, and turning a dial my arms rose over my head till they became centered above me. I was lifted off the floor by the chains attached to my wrists and a slave steadied me as it encircled my legs with its arm. Two slaves approached where it hung with something between them that looked much like a huge black rubber condom. Masters Anthony and Dan had to lend their muscles to pull the ring open while the other slave lowered my legs into the tight confines of the rubber until my feet came in contact with the ground. It took three men to work at unrolling the rubber condom up my legs, over my thighs and over my butt until the material ran out just below my nipples. This rubber condom was tight but not uncomfortable and restricted any movement of my legs or feet; escape would be damn near impossible. I was securely bound from the waist down.

Each hand, in turn, was removed from its upright position, lowered, the restraints removed, circulation massaged back into them before they progressed with their bondage. My fingers were rolled over a tube, bound lightly and placed within fingerless balled mittens, each of these laced into place. Each arm was inserted into what could best be described as a rubber overcoat. One slave inserted his hands up and into the arms of the garment, took my hands and, with the aid of others, pulled the sleeves over my arms. The overcoat was zipped tightly across my heaving chest, extending below my waist.

Sir Anthony was working the dials on the control while the slaves held me upright. The mirror before me allowed me to watch a table tilting one edge to the floor. The flooring of my packing crate was located on the tabletop and, almost gently, the slaves lifted me to the edge and held me in place as the table righted itself. Rubber restraints crossed my chest, locking my arms to my sides. It found it interesting watching the care and concentration of the slaves and the handlers as they went about preparing this slave to meet its new owner. A slave adjusted my head, placing blocks of foam to cushion it and, while the head was elevated, a thick rubber posture collar was buckled into place.

The table lowered as the sides to my packing box were lifted. Plastic bags were inserted on the outsides of my legs; those were filled with an expanding foam this would safeguard the cargo from breakage. They repeated that procedure till all but my head was locked within the hardening foam. My beloved Handler, Master Dan, peered over the edge of the box. His hand descended to cup my chin and lay his hand on my cheek, which was wet with tears. He actually caught up a handful, carried them to his mouth, licked them off his fingers and smiled. Must this slave always be used and betrayed by love? I felt totally betrayed, as it had been my love for him that helped me become one with the way of the slave.

The box in which this slave was lying was shifted, it clicked and the upper portions around my head were lowered while a slave held onto my head. They placed a roll of red tubing on my chest were it could see and remember what was about to be done to it. Stupidly it began moving its head back and forth in a way of avoiding what it knew was coming. Master Dan put a halt to that simple act of defiance by grabbing my chin and applying pressure. He drew real close to its ear and began whispering, "Stop it slave! Stop being such a God damned fool!" He turned to the room, "Give me a few minutes with this slave. Leave me, please." Master Dan pulled up a rolling stool and sat beside me. "Listen to me, slave. I do not have to tell you jackshit, but I have had the honor of working with it, preparing it for the ultimate challenge in its worthless life. It has been chosen to serve the Master of Masters, it is going to him as our present to the Lord."

He called for them to return. One slave took my head from Master Dan as he stepped back and allowed those trained in the next steps to take their places. Three uncaring bastard slaves went to work. The red tubing was dipped into sterile KY jelly and inserted in my right nostril and down the back of my coughing sneezing throat. It was an invasion like no other and then the other nostril got the same treatment. Tape wrapped carefully around the tube locked them in my nostrils and each inhalation had the smell of a Goodyear tire store.

Memories flooded my mind of being fucked over a row of tires by a hot grease monkey. He was an older man and I was a kid with a bad attitude who thought the world owed me. He caught me stealing from his place and gave me an option of either him calling the police or him correcting the situation. I chose him, he took me into the backroom, made me strip out of my clothes and tossed me one of his dirty jump suits. It was impossible to hide my hardon when I stepped out of the backroom, his rich daddy spunk was written all over the jump suit. I worked for him, pumping gas as he continued working under the hoods of cars and I found I enjoyed working with him. When he closed, he fed me greasy hamburgers from a greasy joint next door and took me into the grease pit for my 'head adjustment,' as he called it.

It opened its mouth to scream in protest of the nasal tubes and should not have done so. A bite guard was inserted that held a flat tube between my front teeth, it was removed, adjusted and reinserted, and this time glue sealed it to my teeth and gums. A slave's finger traveled over the bite guard, making certain all edges were sealed and pulling my lips forward. My lips were smeared heavily with grease and the excess was wiped away. It sighed knowing and accepting that it was resigned to its fate.

One slave held my head as the others pulled the open facemask over my head, pulling it down into place, removing the posture collar and sealing it around my neck. It knew by the looks in the eyes of those working over me that the final phase of my encasement was upon me; soon, it would enter the darkness. In less than a half an hour it had been sealed within a suit of rubber from which it could not escape without help from the outside world. It was truly helpless.

Master Dan refused to place my head into whatever had been sent. Instead he pulled over my head the hood that it had occupied for over eight days. Gingerly, they worked the tubes through existing holes and, while they worked, my mind switched gears back to the garage in Norfolk. What was that grease monkey's name? It was, ah yes, Greg. Greg had handsome black hair was fading to gray, pulled back into a ponytail that earmarked him for a rebel and a leather headband made him look totally out of place. He was still a handsome man at 50, well defined body once you looked beyond the jumpsuit and grease. Which was something I learned to do in the following months. Still, that first night was memorable once we were able to close the doors of the bay. He took me into the back and ordered me to strip, bound my hands lifted them overhead to a nail in the wall, then he bound my legs spread. He returned with a fan belt in his hands and used it to teach me a lesson about stealing from hard working men. Afterwards he laid me down on his cot in the back room and fucked me into silence. I worked for him for about four months till my old man found me. He had stopped in to gas up his Harley, along with some of his buddies. Greg was a lump on the ground after they finished with him and I returned to hell and home.

The lacing of the hood complete, the zipper closed, padlock set and the posture collar was pulled back in place and buckled. The sides slipped back in place, plastic bags were fitted and filled so that my head would not be banged in shipment. A fan was directed towards the box so the plastic could cure and Master Dan filled my eyes one more time. He checked the tubes in my nostrils, checked the air passage through my mouth and looked with deep concern into my eyes. A small silver oxygen bottle was slipped in beside me and fitted to the tube running into my mouth. His hands dropped nearer to my head, something was pushed into the grommets opposite each ear and he whispered into a small microphone as he worked.

"Once we seal the box begin breathing in from the tube in your mouth and exhale through your nostrils. Your new owner sent it along so its passage is not too stressful. Believe me, slave, it will help with the trip. Try it now so that I may see that it works. Inhale, hold, hold, hold, and exhale. Good, it feels a light buzz doesn't it? Blink its eyes to say yes. Good slave, it will love its new owner as I do!"

He snapped the blindfold in place and it felt them securing the lid. Music very quietly began playing in my ears; it inhaled on the gas, held and exhaled. The music occupied its mind as the crate was moved and its journey began to its new owner. Inhale, hold, exhale...what was that music saying as my body melted into the rubber suit? The rubber suit was all that contained this liquid slave as it inhaled again, exhaled with the music whispering an intoxicating voice. Subtly, teasingly it spoke quietly in my ears in whispered undertones.

Master only knows where it was in its journey when his voice began to fill its head with visions of servitude. The voice summoned up visions of this slave lying before a throne; it locked in chains of its own desire, serving for the sake of pleasing the One. Thus it learned it would be one of many, it would be a team player, all for the One. It is to take pride in serving its Lord, as the Lord will take pride in its service. To have respect it must first give respect. A slave is seen and not heard. My Lord's voice drummed its message into my subconscious and conscious minds till it accepted his words as gospel.

The music faded, it did not notice; his voice rang clearly in its mind. The gas no longer had its effect, it did not matter, and the tubes were being slowly removed from its nostrils. Fingers invaded its mouth, peeled out the bite guard. A moist finger followed the removal of the bite guard; it sucked it like a child would suckle its mother's tit. More wet fingers entered its mouth hole, giving it more reasons to suck on those fingers and taking in their offered moisture. This way the rawness of its throat found enough moisture to swallow. A small ice chip was dropped into its mouth. Slowly, as if it had been in surgery, they nursed it back to consciousness, yet the owner's voice cycled within its head.

It was told to close its eyes; the snaps on its blindfold were ripped off. Hesitantly, its eyes cleared and it looked up to see strangers looking down upon it. The crate sides were lowered. Its strapped arms were released, lifted and bent while someone held its arms. Helping his limbs to regain circulation, they cautiously moved and shifted the arms before they were replaced at its side. They removed the collar around its neck, freed its head from the confines of the leather hood, then the rubber hood, and the air around them smelled different. Clearer perhaps? It was just an odd observation to have while it lay there. Hands busied themselves by peeling it out of its rubber confinement. How long had it traveled this way? Where was it?

Its torso was elevated as two slaves peeled off the coat, pulling its bound fingerless hands from the sleeves. One slave held me, allowing it to lie back upon the supporting slave while another washed it gently with a sweet smelling solution that reminded it of lilacs in spring. Other slaves cut the rubber that held its legs fused as one. Water, both perspiration mingled with piss, dripped to the floor as it set into fits of shivering; suddenly the room was too cold. Sheets were wrapped around it while others washed its lower body. Six arms lifted this slave onto a gurney, blankets were tucked around its body and it was taken from the uncrating room, down a hallway that was not hewn from rock and into a room with a painted white ceiling.

A doctor took vitals, gave it a shot and spoke quietly to a dark skinned man at his side. "We are lucky it arrived early. We can allow it to rest a day and recover from the effects of its journey. Make certain while it's sleeping to have it shaved again and remove the plug seated in its ass. For that matter, wait till its asleep to remove that, then flush it out. I gave it enough in that shot to keep it out cold for at least twelve hours, use that time wisely to prepare if for their first meeting."

It awoke early, reached up to feel its head and found it totally devoid of hair, as this slave prefers. It felt great and told the attending doctor as much when he entered carrying a tray covered with linen. Whatever was under that linen smelled wonderful and it thought the doctor was pulling a cruel joke. He would eat an incredible breakfast while it sucked on their concept of slave gruel. Luckily, as usual, this slave was wrong. The doctor made it look at him as he unbuttoned his collar to reveal his steel slave collar, which was his way of explaining that slaves eat a better fare here within his hospital so they recover faster. The tray of food was put before me and it was permitted to eat what it wanted on the tray, for today would be rather hectic once this slave departed the hospital.

It was amazed how good simple basic food could taste. How long had it been since it started its transformation from freeman to slave? Two maybe three years had passed without tasting orange juice, a thick slice of ham, four eggs and grits, much less to have the pleasure of eating toast with strawberry jelly. It was astonished that it ate the whole platter of food and even mopped up any residue with its fingers. No wonder it was like a lazy kitten resting in the sun when two very distinct men entered the room with the doctor following in their wake.

The shorter, nevertheless more powerful looking of the two spoke quickly to the doctor, "Spoiling it already, aren't you doc?"

The doctor replied in curt chopped words, "That is my job as I see it. Get them sewn up, healed and ready for duty ASAP. Good food makes them heal faster!"

The taller of the two handlers spoke as he took a position on the opposite side of the bed, away from the door in which they entered. "Is it ready for detailing? Our Lord is getting anxious to see the gift sent to him from Buena Vista."

"Let me give it one more shot, just to help it through any problems that might arise. Then it will be ready for your kind to get your hands on it."

It was the way the doctor said, 'your kind' that peaked my interest and made me think this doctor was a rather interesting fellow slave. Once the shot was driven into my hip and a leash attached to my collar, this slave was led out of its room and into a busy corridor. By the looks of the people in this area, almost all wore white and were medical staff, treating a great quantity of slaves and handlers within the hospital's wards.

The two handlers took it before an elevator. The short one inserted a key into the keypad, turned the key and waited while the elevator door opened before he withdrew the key and stepped in with us. We descended and it observed the panel to the left of the door. Many buttons but no markings to define to what they connected. Nor were there any markings over the door. The door opened and we stepped into a very quiet, less traveled, corridor. Its escorts guided it down the passage and through a glass front doorway to stand before a receptionist. A female receptionist, mind you, and I was naked. She did not even blink an eye; it gives her credit for being not upset easily. She picked up the phone, spoke quietly into the receiver, "Sir, the gift has arrived, Sir. Sir, yes Sir!" She looked up and motioned us back towards a heavy wooden door. "He will see it now. Go right on in gentlemen, my Lord is waiting."

They removed the leash as we left her company and with a hand under each elbow it was moved forward towards the big wooden door. For some reason this slave grew nervous, worried and began clearing its throat as it drew closer to the door. The door swung open as if opened by invisible hands and we moved forward together as one.

The office was nothing to write home about. True, it was a grand room; books lined two thirds of the walls and one third was a floor to ceiling window looking out towards a big city but which this slave could not say. The doors closed as silently as they opened and my handlers turned it facing a huge wooden desk with a chair back facing this slave. With a push on its shoulders its knees hit the floor and its head fell forward. Its handlers backed away, leaving it to occupy the space before the desk. The chair squeaked as boots hit the floor, making steps ring out loudly as he approached. It got nervous and dropped to all fours, placing its head to the floor, waiting patiently for him to acknowledge this slave.

Peeking from the corners of its eyes it watched his boots move around this slave as it knelt before him. Brown ostrich skin western boots by what it could see and he was wearing a business suit. His steps were strong, weighed before he moved as if it was being studied. He snapped his fingers. The handlers moved forward and lifted it to kneeling position; it continued to stare at the floor, not wishing to be too anxious to see who its owner would be. He snapped his fingers twice, then paused and snapped again. One handler kicked its legs open as the other bent its head down and spread its butt cheeks. His - or one of the handler's - fingers were inserted into this slave's ass, shifted in and out. A final snap was given and it was dropped once again to the floor.

Boots stepped before me; he sat on the edge of the desk. He snapped his fingers under my nose and crooked his finger, calling me to crawl to him. His hand lifted my chin so it could see who my new owner was. My heart dropped. It was only Captain Hicks. It prayed at the moment that it was not his gift.

He spoke to the handlers, "It looks good. Looks like Buena Vista has taken the unnecessary edges off this creature and made it into what it was born to be, a slave. It would seem Masters Dan and Schmidt did make the best choice after all. This slave, I believe, will suit him better than any other selection."

They replied in unison, "Sir Yes Sir!"

Captain Hicks raised my chin, forcing this slave to look up at him. "Now it is where it rightfully belongs. Kiss my boots, slave!" Without so much as an ounce of hesitation this slave leaned forward and kissed Captain Hicks' boots. He gave it the order to tongue polish his boots. While this slave's mind and body were serving a superior's needs, he was issuing orders for where it was to be taken and how it was to be prepared to meet its owner.

Captain Hicks walked out from under this slave's servicing tongue and it was literally picked up and put on its feet. We departed his office and found ourselves back in the elevator, still descending when it realized whose boots it had serviced without so much as an ounce of regret or holding itself back. Captain Hicks was none other than Cappy, Master Hunter's right hand man. Could it be that this slave had made full circle and was owned by Master Hunter?

Stepping off the elevator it found itself in the middle of a leather guild. Shields of all the major houses were hung on the entrance wall. To my amazement there was another receptionist sitting behind a desk. He was dressed in black and blue leather uniform. The short handler mentioned that they were here to pick up the gift. We were led back into a private fitting room and asked to wait.

A door opened. In stepped a handsome muscular man, shaved head, and beard with tattoos covering his arms. He carried a suit box. It was directed to stand on a raised platform. It was as if everyone knew of its coming and had prepared things for its arrival. This slave was fitted with a very tight and very secure hood that was doubly padded. The man took his time pulling it in place, checking nose fitting, chin placement and ears before the hood was laced, zipped and secured. The hood was almost identical to the one Master Dan had shipped it out with, however there were exceptions. A small ball was inserted within my mouth; the straps were snapped on either side after which a faceplate of stiffer leather was snapped over its lips. The chin cup was buckled in place, locking its closed mouth tight, sealing the ball within its mouth. The hood had tiny holes under its nose through which this slave could breath. Double padded eye cups were placed over its eyes, that strap was buckled tightly locking out all sight. That is when it realized its ears were locked into silence; it heard nothing that was going on within the room.

Its hand was pushed into long ill fitting sleeves that seemed to hit its knees. While it was bitching within its head about the poor fit, they began lacing up its back panels then buckling them up as well, drawing the jacket tighter around its torso. Straps were pulled between its legs, its cock and balls were lifted before they were fitted into a tight cup. Once complete, the straps were pulled tight and buckled in place at the rear of its jacket. Leather straps were cinched around its wrists before the arms were pulled in back and buckled in place. Another strap that was located over its breastbone was cinched tight, locking its wrists squarely in the front of its body. It would seem it was locked into a leather straightjacket. No manner of squirming or jerking its arms would release this slave - only its new owner.

One leg at a time was lifted, slipped into leather pants that felt too baggy but this slave knew - like the jacket - they too had to be cinched tight to fit its body. They lifted this slave, as they made certain it was inside these pants. The waist was cinched closed and they began lacing up the outsides of each leg. They drew the leather tight from the ankle to the knee and from the knee to the thigh, allowing some movement abilities only at the knees. These pants felt as if they were painted onto its body, that's how tight they felt.

My left foot was lifted from the floor. It was inserted into a boot, which was laced tightly up to my knee before they fitted the right foot, repeating the lacing procedure. It felt hot to be inside the bondage outfit and it would have loved to see it, but that was denied to this slave. It was, in itself, the gift and the package that would be given to its new owner. One pair of hands rotated it slowly, looking for missing details. An adjustment was made here and there. Its chin was lifted and a thick posture collar was snapped in place fusing its head in one position. The hands helped it off the raised platform and others held it in place while restraints were placed around the boots just above its ankles.

It left the leather guild encased from its head to its toes in full leather. They took it into the elevator this time ascending and helped it slowly climb a dozen steps. They halted it and it had the feeling we were outside, but where? They pushed it down into a squat and it was led forward. One handler helped it place its boot onto a step while the other held its head down as it entered a vehicle. Hands helped it adjust its position by bodily lifting and placing it into a seat. Straps were pulled down from above its shoulders and locked between its legs in a crisscross fashion. As if to insure that this slave was not going to flee, the restraints on my ankles were locked together. It felt a door slam and we ascended and banked. It was wowed by the possibility that it was in a helicopter in route to its owner in full leather. Never in its wildest dreams would it have ever imagined this possibility.

Who was its new owner? Could it possibly be Master Hunter or Captain Hicks, or even the Vice President for some other company? Thousands of questions ripped through this slave's mind, but no answers were forthcoming. It allowed itself to nap, not knowing what demands would be requested of it upon arrival. It lost track of time while resting until it felt a sudden change in direction.

The 'copter began its descent and landed, but it felt like wherever we had landed rolled and pitched. Someone released the straps at my crotch, grabbed a handful of leather at each shoulder while someone else grabbed my feet and it was lifted. In this fashion this slave was carried down two short flights of steps and down a short corridor. This slave's legs were lowered, the restraints at its feet modified and it was forced upright and led a few feet. Hands pushed downwards on its shoulders, indicating it should settle. It failed to move quickly enough and its knees got pushed out from under it. Once down they allowed this slave to settle into a comfortable position. The place where it found itself continued to move ever so slightly which made this slave concerned for a moment as to where its Master may be located. That's when it began to worry, fearing that Master Hunter did not own it as he rarely left the comforts of his beloved Buena Vista and the mountains of the Shenandoah Valley.

So who was this Master of Masters? Well, I thought, let's see who the clues point to. Master Dan said he, too, had served him and the way he said it meant he had served him in another way than just a handler. Was it possible that Master Dan was a switch? Ok, how did he mean he served this Master? By breaking this slave? Is it possible that Master Dan and he are alike in some ways? That was yet an unknown. Why is it bound this way? Could it be just because it's a gift or is the leather and it something of a series of gifts? How did Cappy figure in on this? Wasn't he or didn't he only serve Master Hunter? Its head went in a long spiral trying to figure out to whom it belonged. Lost in deep thought, it almost failed to feel his presence. It was as if a warmth surrounded this slave. If it would have had hair they would have stood on end. Some sort of a slave sense kicked into gear. It was as if it knew it was being admired, someone was standing close by watching it breathe. It was as if the volume of air in the room shifted, colored and became richer as it waited, holding its breath, hoping, commanding whoever to touch it and break the isolation.

He stood at its back, hands wrapped around its leather encased head, holding it and exploring the face as if he could see within the wrappings of the leather while the slave could not see without. He walked around to face the kneeling slave, placing his hands under its leather bound arms and lifting it high to set it on its booted feet. This Master was strong, very strong! He held it till it got its legs beneath its feet and one hand withdrew. The other slowly walked, as did he around my body, drawing a line from the center of its chest across and down. He seemed to like what he felt beneath the leathers. His hand withdrew and this slave's body felt empty. The hand settled over my gagged lips, taking purchase and with a rip removed the panel to reveal its lips. His finger teased its thin skin and this slave's response was what he had not expected, as it sought out those fingers seeking to draw them within its mouth. Hadn't Master Dan toyed with its own lips like this for hours till it craved that touch? Was this Master pleased? His hands wrapped around this slave's chin, pulling its face towards this Master. The Master's lips pressed hard against this slave's, his tongue raped this slave's mouth. Slave all but melted and would have been a puddle on the floor when it tasted Sir's tobacco flavored kiss. Released, it had to stand alone, remembering all kinds of emotions that had been stolen from it within the cathedral of pain as they flooded back and its body demanded to know, who was this owner?

He grabbed ahold of my jacket and pulled it where he wanted it, kicked its legs out spread, leaning against something hard. He walked behind it, gave it a push and it fell forward. A zipper located on the back of its leather pants was opened. His hands sought what he knew was within, released the straps and the plug was pushed out. The plug gone, his cock entered this slave. The girth was larger than Master Dan's and the length felt more to this slave's liking. At that moment, this slave knew who was occupying its body and it rose up on its toes to give its owner better purchase. We both knew!

If rape is possible of a willing body, he raped this slave's body, mind and soul as he plunged his hard cock deep within this one's bowels and worked to bring this one into unison with his needs. Never in all this one's life did it so greatly want to cum than when Sir came as one that day. It did not matter that it would be beaten for losing profit, all it wanted to give this owner was all that this slave had to offer. Our minds fused as one as his cock forced this one's body into higher states of ecstasy. He found panels within the leather jacket, opened them and began working this one's nipples, giving this one the much needed pain/pleasure that it has grown to need. Sir was drawing close to his climax when his lovely cock was withdrawn, leaving it empty; it mewled, feeling the emptiness more than any time before.

Sir returned, having made some interesting additions to his hard cock. Speed bumps! Sir had slipped a few of them down his cock by the way they felt in this one's ass; rubber cock rings. Now the Sir grabbed this slave's attention as his piston reground the surfaces within this one's hole. Damn! Master Dan had never put this slave through this before, but this could be why Master Hunter is known as the Master of Masters. He always has a trick or two up his sleeve. He came rapidly once Sir knew this slave was with him in his desire to crack this slave's asshole open wide and make it his. As Sir shouted he was cumming, this slave joined him by tightening its ass muscles and milking his cock, it too came. Slowly Sir's cock softened and he pulled it out, pulling the zipper up the rear of its pants. It was lifted, walked a short distance and pushed back on to its knees. Master was not overly eager to unwrap his new gift, it seemed.

Master was playing an evil game with this slave. Sir would remove something like the ball gag, pull the slave up and put it to cleaning his boots, sucking on Sir's fingers or serving as his ashtray. Sir was helping the slave understand the level of devotion his owner wished of this slave by these simple observances.

It had no idea of the time of its arrival. It was happiest when it served its Sir. After his initial possession of his slave, it was lowered to the floor, boots were put under its lips and it worshiped its unseen owner and prayed that this was Master Hunter. There was nothing that told it for certain to whom it belonged. It was left to wonder, perhaps as a test, to see if this one's training and changes were genuine; it was ignored and treated as just another slave on the floor before its owner. It gave to those boots its total devotion, crawling when it could grab purchase with its boots, working its away around his boots until it found spurs. An alarm went off; only elders wore spurs within Castle Enterprise or trusted superiors of the Master's rank, it was what set them apart from those self-proclaimed masters on the outside. When this slave had reached as far as it could, it was lifted, pulled by strong arms into the 'v' of Sir's legs. Sir closed them strongly around this slave, a boot heel settled upon its trapped cock and balls. The Sir was busy at something that did not concern this slave. It was happy just being with Sir. It was happier when the Sir played the slave's lips with his finger or rolled slave tits, making this one squirm and purr within its hood. That pleased its Sir. This slave melted into him and took comfort in giving this new owner pleasure.

He rose, it was lifted, the posture collar was stripped from its neck and his hands worked under the leathers till he found its iron collar. Using the iron collar as his leash, he pulled the slave forward, guiding it slowly. It bumped the wall as it was exiting the room, tripped over a high threshold and was caught by the Sir. Together, Master drew the slave forward, slowly walking it over new turf as one who had only been blind a few minutes and forced to trust a stranger. He turned, it followed and it was led to a place that chains could be attached to its collar from two sides.

Fingers opened the laces on its boots. The right foot was pulled out followed a short time later by the left. The laces on its pants were released; the pants were pulled without ceremony off this creature's legs. He took a towel to wipe the sweat from its legs. Its boots were fitted back on its feet and laced back into position. He paused, as if thinking, trying to decide if to keep this one in the straight jacket or to remove it. He opted for remove, and the straps and buckles were snapped open. In rapid time, the jacket was lying on the floor as its feet. Its arms dropped casually at its side, then it thought better of that position and relocated them to the small of its back. Cold steel locked them in place.

He stood behind me and stepped forward, placing his body to this slave's. It could not help it; it leaned back into him, my hands connected with his material covered cock, which was rising in appreciation of having this slave before him. His arm rose up on the other side and its head was pinned with the muscles of his arm. He could have broken this slave's neck right then if he had so desired; instead, he tilted its head, leaned down and bit its shoulder hard, grinding his teeth into the flesh of this slave. It howled like a wounded animal and it felt him laugh. His right hand coasted over this slave's chest; touching, tweaking, tasting via torture the strengths of the slave within his arms and he seemed to like what he found. His hand dropped lower; there he found its hard cock snared by a ring through its cockhead, padlocked to a ring beneath its balls. Sir's hand seemed to linger there, rolling the meat between his thumb and forefinger, making this slave twitch and jump with his administrations. The Sir moved from the back to the front, pulling its head down while his hand rolled over the slave's scarred back. True markings of a slave are the markings on its back that tells of its training, the cuts into its soul

Sir unclipped the chains on its collar, pushed it to its knees, reconnected chains and began unlacing the hood. It was so excited and so nervous; what if this owner was not Master Hunter but another? It knew the answer before the questions fully formed; it would serve giving of itself fully to please its owner. It no longer had any choices or options open before it save obey completely without thought. The chinstrap slipped off first, then came the eye patches, its head was lowered so it could not see anything save the Sir's big black knee high boots and his spurs, which were gold in color, the mark of an elder. It was willing to risk it all just to raise its head and see, but its training held.

The heavy hood slipped and was worked over its head. A dry towel was used to wipe its head free of all the sweat and, before it could get up the courage to raise its head, a thin double spandex hood was pulled over and down. It cursed itself for not taking the chance to see. He must have anticipated some move as his deep bass chuckle told this slave that he knew it would try to see before it was his time. Straps were placed over its head and face, one on either side of its nostrils, other surrounding its head and a thick muzzle cupped its chin, blocked its ability to speak and all were cinched tight, locking it back into darkness.

Sir released the chains on its collar, grabbed a hold and pulled me behind him. We ascended a flight of steps, the air changed from the colder climate of the compound or the city to a far warmer climate. We stumbled and he laughed as he guided it up yet another flight of steps. He led slowly across a fifteen foot space before he stopped, he sat and pulled it down between his legs. He kicked its legs open, settled one boot in between, released the cuffs at his back and placed the other boot as a back support. No longer just concentrating on his lead did it realize others were present. Male and female voices spoke to the Sir; did it hear that voice say Master Hunter?

They were talking about it as if it was not present, asking if he liked his presents. Yes, he did find them to his liking he graciously answered.. Another voice asked if the gift fitted properly, he chuckled and said it will eventually, like they all do. Someone tried to talk business, and it seemed that someone got taken away. After all, this was the Master's birthday and a time of celebration for his friends and him.

Food came, it could smell it nearby and Sir picked up on the aspect that his slave was hungry. Would it have mattered? None. The Master ate while his slave sat comfortably between his legs, arms wrapped around large strong booted legs as the Master stroked the slave's body in an unconscious fashion, the same way, and Master Hunter would do when we were together. The same way, damn it that Master Dan did. What was the connection between those two?

The muzzle part of the strapped head harness was removed and, using a knife, he pulled a section of the hood forward and sawed it off. With the hood pulled back in place a hole existed where there was once none. His fingers, greasy with meat drippings, found their way into its mouth and it loved sucking them clean. After that first encounter with his fingers more food was fed to this slave. Bits of a banana, an orange section, a small chunk of meat, a small square of cheese and a small ball of some non-descript paste; all of which reminded me of home. Oh, God, it realized it was slave slop! Sir made certain it was aware that he had options to feed his slave. It was fed chunks of slave slop rolled into balls and followed with chunks of fresh fruit or tiny bites of meat until Sir was quite certain that his new property had its fill.

Sir placed his hand over this slave's mouth, as if waiting for something. It almost lost its chance. It doesn't know why it did it even now, but it leaned into his hand and kissed it lovingly to show him this slave appreciated his care. The fingers of his hand closed around this slave's chin, lifting its head and body, drawing it up onto its knees. He leaned forward, pulled off the straps from around its head, took its face between two hands and pressed his lips to the slave's. Sir's tongue pressed inwards, invading this slave's mouth and it opened to him. As he drew his lips away the hood was withdrawn and it was allowed to see who owned it.

It almost shit! It sucked in a chest full of air and breathed out in one fast rush that made its head spin. I was kneeling before this slave's owner, Master Hunter! It began to cry; unashamedly tears ran down its face and its head dropped into his lap. His cock stirred within his pants as his hands ran over its bare head, and he spoke, ordering, "Slave 9-745, take my cock and balls out of my pants. Do it, slave."

It did not hesitate it did has it was told. He leaned back, thrusting his hips forward and the party that was in his honor forgotten as he played with his gift. "Kiss my cock."

It complied.

"Suck it all the way down, 9-745, I want to feel it resting on its heart."

This slave did as instructed, relaxing its throat and taking it all the way to his balls. There it stopped and waited till an order was given that this slave may lift its head and complete the job that was before it, making its owner feel the prowess of this slave. The order was given and this slave went to work. It wanted to drive this owner, my Master crazy with the techniques it had learned while in the caverns. He was babbling and gasping within the first few minutes, this slave knew it was in control - at least for the moment - and loving the control it had over its owner.

Master Hunter could have cum at least twice, but about that time it had a coughing fit and would have to withdraw its mouth from his cock before it resumed sucking on its owner's cock. The third time Master Hunter was aware of what the slave was doing and held its head in place, forcing the slave to complete his assignment. It was such a pleasure to finally drink the cum, knowing that it was serving the man that it had craved to serve for the past three years. Master Hunter's cum was the sweetest it had ever tasted and the most pleasurable it had taken in a long time.

Having completed its task, Master Hunter gave it chilled water to drink and it returned to its place of honor between its owner's legs. Those who attended the party had to see two radiant smiles on our faces. Master Hunter's face smiling having just blown his second load into his slave's body and this slave realizing that he, finally, was worthy of serving his Master. The one man who occupied his dreams from the onset of this slave's entrance into slavery. My Master Hunter.

He stayed with the party for a good time after it had completed its assigned task, but this slave noticed Sir was getting antsy. He rose, taking this slave with him, chatted with a few attendees for his party. That is when this slave realized it was onboard a huge yacht and, by the feel of the air, in the southern climate as it was nude and extremely comfortable being and being seen in mixed company in this fashion. Till told otherwise, this slave stayed near Master's side. When Sir would stop to converse with someone, this slave would drop to its knees or squat between his boots. That way it was out of harm's way and in sight of the Master.

Other slaves were on hand, caring for the needs of the ten or more guests. Some it knew from the caverns, others it did not. Perhaps they belonged to those within the company. It hoped it would see J.D. or mike but this one assumed that they would be wherever their Master, Cappy would be.

Sir made his move, nearly dragging this slave in his wake. He turned and bade everyone a good night. We disappeared down the steps and he led it into his stateroom. Once the door closed, he stopped in the middle of the room, turned to this slave, and demanded, "Undress me, slave!"

The phone rang, he went to answer it and this one followed. It began by unbuttoning his shirt, removing one arm, waiting till he took the hint and moved the phone receiver till this slave could finish removing his shirt. The belt in his pants was easy and it had gotten off one boot before someone knocked at the stateroom and it was sent to open the door. A man pushed this slave aside and halted when Hunter grabbed him none too politely around his shirt collar, and escorting him out. He was told - as he was being shown the door - that whatever it was would have to wait till morning.

This slave had the second boot off when the knocking returned, Sir answered it this time and he damn near ripped the door from its hinges as he opened the door. The same little man was standing outside in the corridor, Sir looked in towards this slave and barked an order. "Pick up the phone, punch 666 and ask for security to come to Master Hunter's stateroom, stat!"

Before this slave could hang up the phone it could hear boots running down the ladders and some even jumping past the ladders to arrive at Sir's quarters in record time. Hunter had gone from a handsome tan to red-faced as he tried to explain to the drunken man that this was not the time to discuss business. He turned to the guards, "Put him to bed and see that he stays there at least until dawn. Oh, and make certain there is no alcohol within his room or belongings. If we are to talk business I want him cold sober not pickled. Thank you, gentlemen, dismissed."

He was about to close the door when he thought different of something, leaned out into the hall and called out to one the guards. "Post someone at this door till the party is over. I could use a good night's sleep, if that's at all possible with this crew of prima donnas on board." He bid someone good night, closed the door and turned back to his slave.

This slave walked to him, unbuttoned his jeans, and dropped to its knees while pulling his pants down. He used its head to steady him as he stepped from the pant legs. With a deep sigh he was free of clothes for a little while. He decided to show this slave where things were stored within his stateroom since, from now on, it would be its job to find things he needed as he desired.

The walls were covered in rich reddish brown wood, behind the wood panels were hidden compartments where his clothes were hung, drawers for folded clothes and racks for his boots, shoes and sandals. One compartment was designed so a slave could be neatly bound and tucked away, out of mind and sight, till needed. Another compartment held a Ham radio for outside communications as well as a computer terminal and Mars phone system. He could have been talking Greek by what he was trying to explain to this one, it remembered as it was taught to do for his needs.

We stepped beyond a small door into his bath. He took his time showing this slave where he stored his razors and were its safety razors were stored. It was, after all, this slave's responsibility to keep its body clean-shaven as well as my owner shaved as he desired. He made certain it was aware of its hidden surroundings throughout the stateroom, even showing this slave where he kept his personal toys, whips and things that he enjoyed using on his personal slaves. Having been given his fifty-cent tour of the stateroom he ordered it to prepare him a tub.

Once the water was to his liking he stepped into the tub and pulled this slave in with him. It was required to scrub its Sir's back, feet and give extra attention to cleaning Sir's cock and ass. Master took pleasure in scrubbing his new property, even to plunging his thumb into its asshole. This slave enjoyed its bath extremely and, when the Sir permitted, slipped to his back and massaged his shoulders while he lay resting his head on this slave's chest. This slave could actually feel the tension flow from his body as its hands massage knots out of his muscled back and shoulders. He would have fallen asleep in the water if this slave had not risen and pulled him from the tub, patting him dry before helping him into his bed. It returned to the bath to open the drain, clean the tub and dry off before turning off the lights and returning to him.

This slave was lost not knowing where it was to sleep. It had pulled out a sheet and was preparing to lie on the floor next to his bed when his hand patted the bed beside him, sleepily he yawned, "Get in bed with me, 9-745."

It complied with his desires.

He rolled on his side facing this slave, looked down on it, "I have dreamed about this night for a long time. No one can take it away from me again. Isn't that right, 9-745?"

It became bold, lifted its head and kissed the lips of its Master.

A Boner Book

About the Author

I was born where "good ole boy," applied to both men and women. Where "honey" and "darling" are applied to all women and they did not think it to be a sexist statement. Where being politically correct was something city folks did because they failed to respect, honor and take pride in all those with whom one associated. Where a man's word and handshake was more binding than any piece of paper. Where honor, pride and respect were a state of mind, the 'human' in humanity. Experience, they say, is the key to being a great artist. If that's the case, well, I am a frigging Picasso or one hell of a writer because I done my share of hell raisin' and placating while here on this good ol' Earth of ours. One thing I have learned to be an outstanding truth (and one that we tend to forget) is, "Everything is connected to everything." Poison our Earth Mother, and we ourselves are poisoned, heal her and we are healed.

Graduated high school in '69, went to Morehead University for a start on my degrees. I've been a retail merchant, badge carrier, training and education officer within a branch of the Old F.E.M.A. I'm a healer and medicine man within the Hiawatha Shawnee Hidden Society out of Kentucky. Came to Florida to cross-reference Woodland tribal magic with that of Tropical tribal magic and found an expanded universe that's absolutely awesome. Moved to Miami, Florida in the early 1990's to undertake the fire vision and survived. People either love or fear me; it's just that simple. Moved from Miami to Ft. Lauderdale - also known as Ft. Leatherdale - due to the amount of leathermen and women who have moved into our beautiful city. Once in Ft. Lauderdale, I immersed myself within the leather community became a public figure. Became a leather tailor and later ran a leather business with Amy O. In '99, I was the president of Leather University, an educational faculty, teaching safe, sane and consensual S&M, B&D arts and sciences.

In 2000 I was involved in a major car accident that broke more parts than I thought was possible. The accident awoke a sleeping childhood disease, polio, bringing it back as post polio syndrome. I was told I would live the balance of my life in a wheelchair but a Sensei taught me water karate and I regained my limbs. In 2003 I found the love letters that my slave had returned to me while he was on a road tour. These love letters are the premise for the story *Hand and Glove*.